# CALIFORNIA STATE UNIVERSITY, SACRA  P9-BHU-104

This book is due on the last date stamped below.
Failure to return books on the date due will result in assessment of overdue fees.

# STEERAGE

**and**

**ten other stories**

José Rodrigues Miguéis

# STEERAGE

### and

### ten other stories

with an Afterword by

Gerald M. Moser

*Edited with a Foreword by*

**George Monteiro**

**Gávea-Brown**

**Providence, Rhode Island**

Cover and Design
*Teófilo Ramos*
Cover drawing by José Rodrigues Miguéis
for the first edition of *Gente da Terceira Classe*

Illustration
*The Steerage* (1907) by Alfred Stieglitz
Collection of Whitney Museum of American Art, New York

Published and distributed by
*Gávea-Brown Publications*
*Center for Portuguese and Brazilian Studies*
*Box O, Brown University*
*Providence, RI 02912*

Library of Congress Catalogue Number: 82-084530

ISBN: 0-943722-06-3

to

Camila Campanella Miguéis

# CONTENTS

# FOREWORD

In the naked bed, in Plato's cave,
Reflected headlights slowly slid the wall,
Carpenters hammered under the shaded window,
Wind troubled the window curtains all night long,
A fleet of trucks strained uphill, grinding,
Their freights covered, as usual.
The ceiling lightened again, the slanting diagram
Slid slowly forth.
Hearing the milkman's chop,
His striving up the stair, the bottle's chink,
I rose from bed, lit a cigarette,
And walked to the window. The stony street
Displayed the stillness in which buildings stand,
The street-lamp's vigil and the horse's patience.
The winter sky's pure capital
Turned me back to bed with exhausted eyes.

*Delmore Schwartz*

*Among José Rodrigues Miguéis' unpublished papers, I am told, exists a statement to the effect that critics have failed to perceive the most important thing about his writing: that it is all autobiographical. Publication of such an admission (claim?) by this Portuguese writer, self-exiled in the United States, would not have stood him in good stead in Portugal during his lifetime nor, one suspects, would it serve to enhance his reputation in Portugal even today, where no one would bother to see what might be behind Miguéis' statement. Surely, he could have meant by the statement (and probably did) that he wrote only about what actually happened to him. The key though is in*

13

*discerning what he might have meant by "what happened." The answer to this question, if there is one, is in the fiction itself. What I have in mind, specifically, are those individuals in Miguéis' work, usually the narrators themselves, who spend countless hours in their rooms, in their beds at night, listening to the sounds of the* pension, *the apartment, the hotel, perceiving by limited cues—old, new—the drama that unfolds and folds. Perception for Miguéis' people in this case works hand-in-glove with the imagination to piece out the narrative of "happenings" outside of the "walls" of his bed. So we see in Miguéis' work, early and late, the figure of the recumbent, restless narrator, mixing memory and desire with the fears of the tender imagination. In this respect, the man who longs for Léah is of the same blood type as the old man in "Tendresse" who waits in quiet anguish for the younger woman who will share his apartment but not his bed. Like Delmore Schwartz, Miguéis in these stories is a New Yorker; and these stories, wherever they are set in time or place, are, again like Schwartz's most typical stories and poems, imagined by a dweller in a Manhattan apartment. Imagination we take for granted in a writer, but memory we give short shrift to. Miguéis' stories tell us many things, but that memory suffuses all he shows us over and over again. And it is not just the past and primarily the past that feeds memory; it is rather the present that takes us over. "The Inauguration," narrated in the present tense, is a story of memory, of the presence of memory not only in the events of the past, but of those in the present—and, remarkably, of those in the future when the club so auspiciously inaugurated will live out its life.*

*José Rodrigues Miguéis' work has been compared to that of the French realists and the late nineteenth-century Russian naturalists. And there is large merit in such comparisons. But I should like to sketch out another possible comparison, one that has nothing to do, I supect, either with the literary sources of Miguéis' work or any notion that his work shows the influence of his reading. John Steinbeck was, give or take a few years, a contemporary of Miguéis'. Even as Steinbeck, in the 1930s particularly, allied himself with the human crowd of marginalized and social and political immigrants, in such works as* Tortilla Flat, In Dubious Battle, The Grapes of Wrath, *and* Cannery

Row, so, too, did Miguéis, in O Pão Não Cai do Céu *(written largely in the 1940s and '50s but not published until 1975-76) and in many stories such as, to name only stories appearing in* Steerage, *"Cosme," "The Stowaway's Christmas," and "Steerage." But unlike Steinbeck, who in* Tortilla Flat *suffused his band of social misfits with touches of Arthurian magic-sparkle, Miguéis saw his "third-class" humanity, when he found it to be such, raw and half-cooked, that is to say that he was more tough-minded about, less programmatically pro-letarian in his judgments of the humanity under his focused eye. In short, Miguéis did a better job, of keeping his politics of humanity out of his fiction in the 1930s and his politics of state in the 1960s, largely saving his political—social pronouncements for his journalism and in-proper-person commentary.*

*To a greater extent than John Steinbeck, José Rodrigues Miguéis was a man of letters in the large European manner, but, like Steinbeck, he will be best remembered, as he would have ex-pected and desired, for his fiction. And as a writer of novels and stories, he will be remembered for his closely observed, ac-curately detailed memorializations of twentieth-century life in Europe and the United States. An intellectual by temperament and a democrat in spirit and politics, Miguéis rewarded his readers over a long career spanning six decades and ending only with his death in 1980 with a series of richly felt narratives whose core of sentiment was uniquely enhanced by the writer's talent for quick caricature and his propensity for trenchant social criticism. And this is as it should be, for Miguéis was above all a story-teller. It was narrative that counted first and foremost, not narrative experimentation, in an age so betaken and bemused and beleagured by modernist devices and ploys, but stories in themselves told in direct and clear style. Miguéis made no bones about this. "As for style, I am totally indifferent to it," he explained the year before his death; "I tell a story because I like to tell it. For me the style is the subject itself. It is the subject which sets the style, as the substance of a given mineral predetermines the shape into which it must crystallize" (see "Last Word: Miguéis on Miguéis"). Nowhere in the corpus of Miguéis' fiction are there any examples of what in the same*

15

*commentary he called, with scarcely withheld derision, "the continued obscurity and structural complexity of certan authors who thirst for novelty and have little to say." The complexity of Miguéis' narratives lies elsewhere: in the psychological realism of his narrators, named and unnamed, and of their observations about the human beings who fall within their ken. Miguéis had at his command full knowledge of the grand traditions of Western literature as well as the metastatic experiments of the Modernists (including those of their forebears and heirs) and he chose to follow the example of the masters of narrative. Mixing memory with desire in the alembic of his imagination, he saw himself in a line stretching back to Balzac.*

# TEXTUAL NOTE AND ACKNOWLEDGMENTS

The title "Steerage" is the editor's rendering of "Gente da Terceira Classe," which might have been translated more literally as either "People in Third Class" or "Third Class People." As such, it can be argued that "Steerage" as a title has no authority in the work of José Rodrigues Miguéis. Yet the editor (who is also the co-translator of "Gente da Terceira Classe") would suggest that "Steerage" fulfills the true spirit of Miguéis' poignant story about emigration and enough of its letter (as well as the spirit and letter of so much of Miguéis' work) to persist in using it not only as the title of Miguéis' famous story but as the title for this volume, the first selection of Rodrigues Miguéis' stories in English translation.

*Steerage* presents eleven stories by José Rodrigues Miguéis. Ranging in date of publication from 1940 to 1977, they are presented here in the order of their publication by their titles in the original Portuguese: *Léah* (1940), *Beleza Orgulhosa* (1940), *O Cosme de Riba-Douro* (1944), *Simbólico, na Cúpula da Pena* (1947), *O Natal do Dr. Crosby* (1947-48), *Saudades para a Dona Genciana* (1956), *O Natal do Clandestino* (1957), *Gente da*

*Terceira Classe* (1962), *Uma Casa Portuguesa* (1968), *A Inauguração* (1969), and *Tendresse* (1977). The translations, the work of various hands, are, in each case, the responsibility of the translator(s): *Léah* (Raymond Sayers), *Proud Beauty* (Camila Campanella Miguéis), *Cosme* (Maria Angelina Duarte), *Return to the Cupola* (Alexis Levitin), *Dr. Crosby's Christmas* (Alexis Levitin), *Yearning for Dona Genciana* (Carol Dow), *The Stowaway's Christmas* (Nelson H. Vieira), *Steerage* (George Monteiro and Carolina Matos), *A Portuguese Home* (Gregory McNab), *The Inauguration* (Gregory McNab), and *Tendresse* (Nelson H. Vieira).

Miguéis' commentary on himself, which appears here as "Last Word: Miguéis on Miguéis," has been excerpted from the *Journal of the American Portuguese Society* (1979).

The editor wishes to thank his colleagues, Onésimo T. Almeida and Nelson H. Vieira, for their counsel and aid in this project from its inception to its completion. At an early stage he also benefitted from advice given kindly by John Kerr, Raymond Sayers and Maria Angelina Duarte, and wishes to record his appreciation here. He also owes a special debt to Carolina Matos, who first suggested that they translate Miguéis and who generously assisted him in the early stages of the venture, and to Camila Miguéis for her unfailing cooperation in this venture and her generosity in permitting the publication of these stories in English-language translation.

Finally he wishes to acknowledge gratefully the generous support of the Instituto Português do Livro and the Fundação Calouste Gulbenkian of Lisbon, Portugal.

# LÉAH

How well I remember the quiet afternoon I arrived at the door of the *pension* to move into the furnished room that I had taken without board: *Chambre à louer.* I pulled the big brass bell and waited a few seconds. The door opened and I saw a strong, blonde, pink-cheeked woman with untidy hair, wearing a soiled, striped apron. She smiled and welcomed me cordially. She was the owner—Annette Marie, Madame Lambertin, "Pleased to meet you." Then she took me up to the fourth floor, which I took to be the top, jangling her keys and talking continually in a hoarse voice that at the end of the climb was coming in gasps. She was almost unable to speak. I wondered whether she might be an alcoholic or had heart trouble. On the way up I learned about all the other guests, who were "very quiet people, causing no trouble." A mongrel, small, black and tailless, ran happily ahead of us—she was Bouboule, "a little love." On the landings she jumped up my legs and licked my fingers like an old acquaintance.

The room had two large windows that looked out on old slate roofs and chimneys crowded together under a milky sky.

There was faded wallpaper on the walls, and on the floor there was worn linoleum that was patched in places. There were a wide, soft bed and an old-fashioned iron stove. It was a modest room and the rent was reasonable. I decided to stay.

Right from the start I noticed an atmosphere of deterioration, neglect and unconventionality in the *pension*. It was not dirty, but it was less hostilely spotless than many of those I had visited up till then. There was a rank, horrible smell of potatoes fried in mutton fat all through the place. But what else could one expect? It was the same thing everywhere. Actually, I came to the conclusion that fried potatoes are delicious when, like partridges, they are eaten holding one's nose.

Madame Lambertin was obviously Flemish and kindly and free and easy in manner. She must have been well past thirty. Her smile, when she smiled, filled her whole face. Her eyes were green and lively. From my window I could see her crossing the street every day on the way to the *brasserie* on the opposite corner, where she would go to pay tribute to a relentless god. She always returned with a basketful of bottles of *gueuze*. As I learned later, she had reached the point of drinking eighteen to twenty a day, enough to spoil the freshness of her skin, which was still attractive beneath its embroidery of red veins. Her husband, of whom I only caught a glimpse, would return at nightfall from his work, whatever it was, put on his slippers and install himself beside the stove in the basement kitchen to read the *Dernière Heure* and suck on his pipe. It was a typical middle-class existence, I suppose. A young, insignificant *Wallon*, he seemed to be oblivious to everything around him.

Darkness came early and I choked with nostalgia and sadness. I had not yet had time to form any friendships, my work in the laboratory was vague, and I found it impossible to take any interest in the people with whom I occasionally had some contact. I would leave home in the morning before dawn and return in the early darkness. For years I had been dreaming of independence, which I had never really been able to enjoy, and now that I was my own master, I suddenly felt unable to take advantage of it. On first contact with what was foreign I felt disappointed and I would draw back. The truth was, as I soon learned, that the price of personal freedom and peace is solitude. Contradictory though it may seem, only the presence of other human beings can awaken in us the reactions that force us to think, mobilize our knowledge and our acts. That is why I never succeeded in living alone or in far-off places though those were two things that I had always deeply longed for. And that is why I was never happy when I was alone and why the only ones I ever could make happy were those I knew only superficially. Perhaps this misanthropic dialectic (or was it timidity?) is too specious for you, Léah.

At any rate, that was the life I had dreamed about. I had to endure it. I shunned the cafés and wandered along the boulevards, eating haphazardly and at irregular hours, bewildered by everything, especially myself. Everything I had craved disgusted me, and everything was an excuse for hesitating, drawing back, and abstaining. I fell into a hardened, negative attitude. I would return home discontented and worn out, not knowing what I wanted or even what I lacked. I was held there only by my mice, my guinea pigs, and my first, fruitless experiments. For a while I fought against the temptation to sail for Brazil, where a relative in the perfume business had given me a vague promise of a job in a laboratory.

I would close myself up in my room, sit down on the green velvet sofa, which, you may recall, was lopsided and losing its stuffing; and I would stare sadly first at the embers in the stove as the wind whistled down into it, next at the enormous, empty bed, and then at the low curtains of clouds covering the sky above the roofs darkened by smoke and age. I could not bear to read; it was impossible to organize my notes and my backlog of correspondence, and my cigarettes seemed to taste awful, like straw or dry earth. The room was poorly lighted and poorly heated, and the washbasin was wretched. Autumn filtered in through every chink in the windows. I don't know what kept me from clearing out in my second week; perhaps I was afraid of getting into something worse, what with my scanty means and my ignorance of the milieu and the customs. (I've always been like that. Wherever I am I hang on until I am desperate; then I take a leap into the unknown.)

But it was a spacious room, and I could walk all around my bed in the silence of the twilight as I gnawed away at myself from within. The light-colored wallpaper made the room seem larger. Through the windows entered the sadness of that sky, which was painted with colors never found on an artist's palette. It was the middle of November and by three o'clock in the afternoon it was practically night. I was suffocating with impatience and I had the habit of running out into the drizzle to look at the cafés filled with people and light; then I would have my dinner in some restaurant or other where everything repelled me. One day I dropped into a Russian restaurant where in a corner some of my compatriots were reviling the food in unison. I did not return. I did all I could to be late in getting back home, where there was nothing waiting for me. I finally settled down in a café where I could read books and magazines and write my letters while I drained my cup of bitter black coffee and listened to the electric phonograph. No matter how much it rained or the wind blew, I always walked home by the longest route. I kept away from the women of the *trottoir* who would accost me in their furtive way. *"Bonjour, mon petit, comment ça va?"* Or, smiling familiarly, they might invite me to have a beer with them. Sometimes from the darkness of a doorway or a side street they would whisper, *"Un peu d'amour. Un tout petit peu d'amour."*

It was fear of myself—not of them—that held me back. Yet I cannot say that the Belgians lacked hospitality. It was just the contrary. But I did feel ill at ease in the relative luxury of their lives, which contrasted so sharply with my poverty. One night (I never got to tell you about it) I woke up choking in a dream about being in hell. Gasping for breath, I opened my eyes and saw a strange form. Incandescent red, it might have been the moon about to break through the clouds or, just as probably, Beelzebub himself burning in a slow fire. Terrified, I leaped out of bed, and then it dawned on me that I was in the Lambertin *pension* and that the red glare was my glowing stove. On top of it the enameled pitcher of hot water (which the landlady refused to let me have at six a.m.) was also blood-red. It was filling the room with suffocating steam, which, fortunately, had awakened me. I threw the windows open; and wrapping myself in a quilt, I sat down sadly on the sofa. I laughed and sneezed in the coldest, most desolate dawn I have ever seen, and I cursed my luck. Léah, if I did not die then, it was only because other, greater punishments were in store for me. At any rate, it is only now, so many years later, that I am able to savor the charm of those bitter hours.

The landlady drank, chatted, walked her Bouboule or sat in the kitchen with its saturating smell of *frites*. There were many boarders who took their meals in the living room on the ground floor. One afternoon I returned early and *Mme* Lambertin invited me to come into the room, where I met an Indian whose life in Brussels was as shiftless, dreamy and lacking in content as he himself was in flesh. There were two or three tipsy girls, against whom my shyness left me defenseless. We told risqué jokes, played the piano and sang, smoked incessantly, drank cognac surreptitiously, and at one point (since I was so thin) I found myself sitting majestically on *Mme* Lambertin's lap, kissing her smiling, still-soft cheeks. "Sowing his wild oats," you are probably saying. It was just a debauch, harmless and a bit sad; *Mme* Lambertin held me tight, laughing strangely, even a bit frighteningly. The girls danced and whispered and the Indian observed it all with a fleshless, impassive smile, his legs crossed and his full glass in his unusual hands. I wondered whether the landlord was downstairs in the kitchen. I paid for my brandy, the girls went off with their companion, and I felt remorseful and disgusted with myself. The biting acidity that I tasted at those moments and the subsequent black vomit of remorse must have been due to my loneliness.

Meanwhile, my room seemed tidy and tolerably clean; I had no problems in that respect. In a vague way I knew that there was a maid. Sometimes, from the depths of the house, *Mme* Lambertin would shout, "Léaaaaaah," and from one floor or another a voice would answer, "*Ouiiii.*" Or else, "I'm coming." It was you. In my loneliness, the words seemed almost poetic. None of this, Léah, has any bearing on our brief relationship, and yet it is ominous that, as I recall it, I experience a strange, painful pleasure. My lyricism was coagulated, as it were; I felt disoriented, discontented and inferior. How can I express it? And I was becoming morbidly sensitive.

A tiny room next to mine—it was little more than a closet—harbored a youth who said that he was an engineer. He was of Russian origin, but because of the war and its ensuing complications, his nationality was problematic. His name was Perlman. We seldom saw each other. He would leave early, before me, and he would return at seven when it was dark to change his clothes and go out again immediately. When I got back home in the wee hours, he would be asleep. Saturday afternoons there would be a great racket in his cubicle, along with the sound of a woman's voice and laughter. I envied him for his conviviality. I would sit for hours with a book in my hands, always open to the same page, listening for the sound in my hands, always open to the same page, listening for the sound of movements and footsteps from his room. Yet nothing suspicious went on behind the sealed door. One day we happened to chat on the landing of the staircase. And when I complained about something or other—perhaps the lack of heat or my tiny wash basin—Perlman, pink and white-cheeked, opened the door of his room and invited me to step in. One had to leap sideways to get on the bed; the enamel of the washbasin was cracked and black with dirt (it was hardly bigger than a soup-plate), and the room was unheated.

"You're the one that complains," he said with a smile of superiority. "And I always sleep with the window open."

"Of course, but you only wash once a week." I snapped back and walked out.

Little did I know the risk I had run climbing over that bed that blocked the door.

More than once I heard your voice through the door to Perlman's room, where there was space only on the bed or above it. I was quite morbid with resentment, while he was merry and whistled melodiously like a bird. He would call you—everyone but me called you in that house. I didn't even know you—and you would come upstairs and linger. Then I would hear laughter, conversation in an undertone, arguments, and the door opening and closing. I would kneel on the sofa with my ear to the door, struggling to eavesdrop. This went on especially on Saturdays, when the youth would call for hot water to bathe in the enameled dish as he whistled away like a bird. That was the day water would flow out onto the landing.

At other times the guest in the back room was the one who called. You would rush up to the fourth floor, stay there for an eternity, and you would go back again and again.

"Léah," the guest would shout, harshly and abruptly. And you would fly up there from the lower depths, with an attentiveness that would have blessed had it been for me. You entered, closed the door, and then I would hear conversation, arguments, periods of silence, or all of this in succession. And eaten up with rage, I went more than once to listen at the door that separated me from that neighbor. I did not perceive anything abnormal in the other room. There was a wardrobe pushed up against the door.

I could not read. I was homesick, nervous and queasy. Sometimes I heard the clinking of glasses and the jingling of coins, and then my head filled up with all sorts of conjectures. I felt left out and frustrated, and like all who think that they are being deprived of something, I experienced spurts of morality and protest. I had gotten into a house of "ill-repute," and so on. I didn't know you, and yet I came to hate you, Léah. Offended dignity forced me to keep my door closed, in addition to my pride, my timidity, my rigidity, my inability to pursue anything that fled from me, or to fight for anything at all. But you can't really trust shy people.

Then one afternoon between three and four o'clock I returned home a bit earlier than usual (by then I was working busily all day long in the laboratory), and I walked into my room to find everything just as I had left it in the morning—the bed unmade, the stove cold and the ashes scattered around, the basin full of dirty water and the room freezing. What a sight. It was not the first time this had happened, but I had never complained, for I could imagine the work it must take to keep things in order with so many people under one roof. But this time I did become furious, for I had been planning to spend the rest of the afternoon reviving my wretchedness in long letters. Feeling that

I had to leave the *pension* (I would really have done so then and there if I had not paid half a month in advance), I ran to the landing and shouted downstairs with all the lung power of a Portuguese mountaineer, "Léah."

An alarmed voice answered, *"Oui, Monsieur,* I'm coming."

In an instant, to my great astonishment, you came flying up the stairs. Oh, you looked so active, so diligent and so delightful.

My grateful heart, even now, still skips a beat.

*"Monsieur,"* you said. You were pale, you were breathless, and your eyes were open wide.

"What is the meaning of this?" I exclaimed, and without looking at you I turned in the rudest way one could imagine and pointed to the room. "This mess, the dirty clothes, the bed unmade, the bucket overflowing and the fire out."

At that moment I turned to you, Léah, and I saw you for the first time. The light from the windows fell full on your face and I noticed how pretty, young, and serious you were. Your white, delicately spaced teeth showed through your partly opened mouth; your round, gray eyes stared with genuine horror at the untidy room; your strong, bulging breasts were still rising and falling after the race up the stairs. In your white, firm neck I could see a delicate crease and a throbbing artery. Your wavy hair was a ruddy blonde; you were almost my height and you glowed pink and fresh like a large fruit. Your waist was narrow and your hips widened in a strong, fecund curve.

As I looked at you, my voice dropped and became gentler and softer: *"Mademoiselle,"* (and my heart beat hard) "what is the reason that my room has not been done? I came home to work and now I have to go out again. Don't I pay my rent? You only pay attention to the others while I..."

You fixed your eyes on me; your face filled up with a smile of kind, ironic understanding: *"Pauv' M'sieu Carlôss."*

We went in.

"Léah," I said as I closed the door, "why don't you ever come to my room?"

"But you never call me. If you called, I would come; and

26

anyway the landlady says you want your room to be cleaned by her, not me."

"Oh."

"She has a lot of regard for you because you're a college graduate. She says that you're the best lodger in the house and the most respectable. And I think so, too. You're such a neat man, with such good manners. But you're very proud. You don't speak to anyone."

Your alarm was so adorable and sincere that I burst out laughing in relief. You laughed along with me. I grasped your hands, and then you explained to me in a gentle, confinding voice, that *Monsieur* Albert paid a fortune for his back room, a thousand francs, and so he had to be treated well, and he was weak-minded and was always calling you, and he spent all day long stuck in his room, and he wanted candy all the time, and you were always running upstairs and downstairs because of *Monsieur* Albert. He was a fool, but he had money to spend that he got from his family, for they had come to an agreement with *Mme* Lambertin to keep him there, and she drank beer and cognac to *Monsieur* Albert's health, and he paid everything in advance every week and even more. You told me, your eyes wide open, your nostrils quivering as you came closer and closer to me, pushing out your wide lips, which I could not stop looking at.

"Yes," I said cautiously as I drew back. "But you spend so much time amusing him."

What a thing to say. Perhaps, Léah, you don't realize the worth, the charm, the power of frankness. At that moment you were the living picture of astonishment. (It was I whose soul was full of venom.) And as if that had not been the first time that we spoke to each other (in fact it was the first time that we *saw* each other), as if between us there existed an old, moss-grown friendship or a love already fossilized into habit, an unconscious intimacy that an unexpected fact, a hitherto unrevealed trait of character, had caught unawares, you exclaimed, sad and amazed, regretful at having hurt me without knowing it:

"Then you were jealous. And I didn't know. My goodness, if I had known... Excuse me."

You unfolded like a sweet-scented flower. You appeared to be almost falling over, and I had a pretext for grasping your waist, Léah. It was from that moment, I swear, that I loved you. From that moment the ice broke up within me, and I wanted to embrace you and kiss you and fall asleep on your good Flemish bosom. But I restrained myself.

"Oh, I'm not jealous, only proud, perhaps, as you said. I just don't like to get involved with other people, that's what it is."

I've told you already that the poor fellow is a bit soft in the head. The landlady has given me orders to amuse him. He doesn't know how to do anything for himself, not even tie his own necktie. It's awful. I spend hours and hours straightening the drawers in his dresser."

"All right, but what about Perlman? He's a nice-looking fellow."

"Oh, yes, Monsieur Perlman," and you drew your lips down in disdain, "that one, poor fellow..."

"What? Who'd have guessed it."

He himself says so. And I believe him. My sister—you haven't met her yet—goes out with him on Sunday, sometimes on Saturdays. But he... You understand?"

"Oh, he goes out with your sister, but she doesn't complain about him, right?"

"Just the opposite. He takes her to the movies, but he never kisses her or anything. You see what I mean?"

"I see. I'm in favor of morality. I don't like some of the things that go on."

I breathed more calmly. How I had envied you two when I heard you laughing in his room, and when you went out together, and how I had tortured myself in my loneliness. I sat down and lit a cigarette.

"So it's the landlady who cleans up for me? When she cleans, that is. But why does she do it? I never asked her to. In that case she really does do some work?"

"She drinks more than she works. This month she hasn't even paid me my salary. She still owes the rent. One fine day she'll be put out."

"Of couse," I said disconsolately, "and I am the one left holding the bag. How much do you make a month, Léah?"

"Five hundred francs, with room and board." And you sat down beside me on the threadbare sofa. "It's not bad, is it? If she would only pay me. The good thing is that every week I have a day and a night off."

"A *night*? But why a night off? Can't you sleep in your own room?"

You were going to say something when *Mme* Lambertin shouted from down below, "Léah."

You leaped up with amazing agility considering your robust build. You had the figure of one of Rubens's women. You ran to the landing. *"Ouiiii."*

"Why are you staying so long up there?"

"I'm doing *Monsieur* Albert's room."

"Oh, all right."

You came back laughing (*M*. Albert was out, by some chance), and I greeted you with outstretched arms and hugged you to my heart, every fiber of my body filled with the ether of desire. You were kind, Léah, and you understood at once that I was thirsty for love, even though the thirst may have been only superficial, that I was suffering from loneliness, exile, neglect and pride, for you had a maternal intuition of my suffering. I felt in that first kiss that your flesh was responsive, tender and sympathetic, and it was free of problems. What blessed simplicity. But then you said, as you freed yourself from my embrace:

"The room has to be cleaned. She may decide to come up here."

And so we cleaned the room. You learned that I was working in biology, and I learned, among other things, that you were French, from Calais, not Belgian. You may recall that as we were straightening the sheets, I asked you what you were doing the following Sunday and you said with charming naturalness while you beat a pillow between your vigorous arms:

"Going out, but I can't go out with you."

"Oh, you're going alone?"

"Oh, no, I'm going with Ferdinand."

"Ferdinand? Who's Ferdinand? One of the lodgers?"

29

"Oh, no, I'm engaged to Ferdinand."

"Engaged?"

Heartbroken, I stood holding the pillow to my breast. My expression must have been comical. Once more I felt that I had been robbed of something that was not mine. How could you possibly be engaged? My house of cards came tumbling down. You stepped over to me, tenderly, sympathetically, and very seriously.

"Does that seem wrong to you? I am nineteen years old, and he insists he wants to marry me, *pauv' Fe'dinand.*"

"Poor Ferdinand," I exclaimed indignantly, pummeling the pillow. "A man who has the luck to... But if you don't care for him—I can read that in your face—then why are you leading him on?"

"Oh, but I do care for him, *pauv' Fe'dinand.* We are good friends. He has a heart of pure gold. He's good looking and decent. And he's got a good job."

I felt ill-humored, and I stopped talking. Then, when the room was tidy and the stove had been lit and was comforting me with its heat, we sat down again on the lopsided sofa in the early afternoon twilight and you told me, as if I were an old comrade, the story in its entirety. I listened to it, you may remember, with my head resting familiarly in the warmth of your lap, my eyes watching through the window the dark death throes of the day. As you spoke you stroked my forehead and my hair with those fingers that were soft in spite of your hard work. But didn't I hear a note of complaint in your voice? As I listened to you, Léah, it was as if a floodgate of selfishness and coldness deep down inside of me were being pulled open, and I felt that all my discontent was tying itself into a knot and escaping up through my throat to dissolve into tears. Could it have been because you were the humble daughter of a fisherman-farmer from Calais and you hadn't had much schooling and everything about you seemed so simple and honest and you were recounting some love affairs—which were all very recent—with the candor and melancholy of someone who is drifting along aimlessly in no particular direction? Or was it because you were able to touch my own innocence and disguised humility? Léah, I was suffering with the grateful pain a man feels when he has a wen that is being squeezed. I suffered because of all that useless earlier suffering—the waiting, the loneliness, the ambition, the peevishness. I don't know what I was suffering or perhaps the suffering was coming to an end—because, after all, it was so easy and so good to be there with my head on your sweet, robust, Flemish lap, listening to your velvety French as you told the story of your love affair with Ferdinand (whom you complained you couldn't love), and being caressed by your almost maternal fingers, which touched the depths of my being with their gentle perfume. And I suffered, Léah, because you had lost your virginity a few months before, one night in the Bois de la Cambre, and it was as if I had come there or had passed my youth waiting for your fresh sweetness to be happy and suddenly that happiness was slipping away between my fingers, dissolving like a mirage in the desert. Your distressed, confiding voice entreated my tears in the darkness. Poor and lonely as I was, I believe I had never experienced to such an extent the presence of Woman in her perfect nudity and intimacy. And when you bent toward me and kissed my lips murmuring, "Oh, if I had only known. If you had arrived a little sooner," I realized that in your honest simplicity you, too, had waited for me without knowing it. Your sadness, like mine, possessed the sweet bitterness of the irremediable. Happy in my despair, I got up, clasped you in my arms, pressed my face against yours, which was burning, and kissed you fervently, relieving my old, useless pain.

"But you're weeping. You're weeping," you said; and you embraced me and wept with me.

Then a door slammed and *Mme* Lambertin's voice called you from below. As you ran out, you kissed me briefly and said, "I'll knock at your door when I go up to my room at ten."

In my heart from then on, Léah, there was a different pace, another kind of restlessness. You would come into my room and linger, and I had your hands, your sincere mouth, your warm, strong flesh and your voice to quiet and console me in hours of exasperation and depression. How many times while my head rested on your hospitable lap, I watched the twilight coming into the city. And as you came in, so would you leave, happily, fleeing as one would who has committed an innocent crime. You brought me peace and the fullness of your joy, exuberance and stability. This simple, healthful nourishment fed me till the next day. Your presence rejuvenated my room, where you would spend an hour or two. *M.* Albert would call in vain, and Perlman was away all day long. And down in the basement, *Mme* Lambertin entertained her visitors, carousing and drinking. They were wonderful hours, such as I had never before known. I had but one regret (it was pride no longer): that of being a competitor with Ferdinand for the savor and the freshness of your sweet-scented, ample youth.

But you would never let me go up to your attic room, even though I only wanted to go out of curiosity. Why? Modesty, embarrassment about your own humbleness, and the wretchedness of your lodging? I was the one who should have been embarrassed about my poor man's vanity.

Influenced by the change, perhaps, I began to work more regularly and persistently on my problems. Full of enthusiasm, I would leave the house earlier, and I would spend long hours in the laboratory bent over my little animals, torturing and scrutinizing them implacably. (Cruelty is, at times, so humanitarian.) When my task was over, I would run to the library or the bookstores, where I spent all the money that I did not need for my more than frugal existence, and I would return home as early as I could. A rather sudden change had occurred in my life, but I wasted no time meditating about it, for psychology has never been my strong point; and there was no room for it among the problems of my heart and my passion for experiments.

With all the lodgers gone, and *Mme* Lambertin out also, the *pension* was ours. *M.* Albert sulked alone in his *quartier*, or stalked down the stairs, swearing furiously. We would go from bedroom to bedroom and from floor to floor. I helped you a bit, we chatted, laughed, and you showed me something of the wretched lives of the boarders, who were refugees from all over the globe, refugees who had been harassed by hostile winds. In love as in tenderness you were impulsive; you took the initiative. You threw yourself at me with all the weight of your exuberant, realistic, spontaneous nature, putting me on the defensive more than once. Then you would laugh victoriously. But my heart was grateful to you, for it does a man good to know that he is loved by someone with as much life and vitality as you had.

The weeks flew by. One afternoon, when we were gently tired, you announced that your sister was coming.

"You'll see how pretty she is," you said, your eyes damp with tenderness and pride.

You had an ingenuous, a pagan enthusiasm for beauty, as if you, good, delicious fruit that you were, were not beautiful, too. Your sister arrived. She was going to go out again with the little man in the next room. You brought her to me to admire, possibly—who knows—for me to fall a bit in love with, too. She was really lovely: indeed, she was beautiful. She had her unusual, refined beauty, but you also possessed charm, a charm that was both rustic and nourishing. Yet, you did not appear jealous of her beauty; your attitude was fair and sporting, that of someone who does not dispute but rather admires superiority in another. In it there was no feeling of cheap rivalry, and so I was able to admire her at will, unreservedly, unabashedly, as one admires a work of art, happy that between us there was no inhibition, prejudice or irritation, but only an honest love of beauty, which purifies and uplifts. Is there any other woman, Léah, who would be capable of your altruism and your generosity, who would be capable of facing such a risk?

"Seventeen years old," you murmured with an almost maternal pride, grasping my arm, as if she were your own creation.

Seventeen well-spent years. She was taller than you. Her features were radiant, aristocratic, and free of the scars of misery that hard work generally leaves on the faces of the poor. She was cheerful, healthy, and as clean as an upper-class Parisian woman, as blooming as an American girl. She had all the freshness and ready wit of youth, coupled with the graceful fullness of a woman. She was dressed in the uniform of a baby's *nurse* in a wealthy home, which she was.

"Isn't it true that she is lovely?" you insisted, emotionally, as if the contemplation of beauty were purifying you. And then, with an all but imperceptible note of sadness, perhaps of repentance, you added with intimate intensity, "And she's still a virgin."

My heart burning, I clasped your hands in silent understanding that your sadness was directed at me as a reflection of my own wounded prejudices. She was sitting opposite us, glowing with pride and youth, like Helen in a beauty contest, her two little breasts rising beneath her white blouse—smiling and happy at being admired and desired—and then, as if yielding to a sudden irrestible impulse, you stood up, pulled her skirt slowly above her smooth knees, which were pressed together tightly, and you exclaimed in astonishment with a flame of love in your gray pupils:

"Look at these legs."

They were long, thin, wonderfully rounded, truly the most graceful legs I had ever contemplated. My head reeled and we all became embarrassed and red. Then, carrying your sacrifice to an unbelievable extreme, you said to me with an expression of suffering and renunciation that made you sublime: "Give her a kiss."

That image and that kiss remain clear in my memory. I wonder whether I am being indiscreet if I say that I still recall the crimson velvet rose that she wore coquettishly in the collar of her coat. Could it have been pride in her or in me that made you force us to exchange that kiss that caused you to suffer? The mystery remains, but your eyes were brimming with tears.

Then I sensed how many aspects love has.

It rained almost all the time, and you would come to nestle in my arms. You liked making love and you did it with a naturalness and seriousness that bewildered even me, and I come from a land of repressed, violent people. In your hands everything that up till then had seemed sacred and mysterious became clear, simple and pleasant, like transcendent subjects when they are painted by artists of your race. How natural, exuberant and healthy.

On one of those dark, rainy afternoons you had been with me a good three-quarters of an hour when *Mme* Lambertin shouted up the stairs to tell you that Ferdinand was still waiting for you in the street. "Waiting for you?" I jumped to the floor. Right at the door? And you were there with me? I got annoyed and I could not hide my feelings from you. Once more my ancestral sense of morality had been shocked. Then, whispering innocently in the half-darkness of the room, you led me by the hand to the window and, kneeling on the linoleum, you lifted a corner of the curtain, peered at the street and murmured pityingly:

"There he is, on the corner where the *brasserie* is. See? Waiting almost an hour for me."

For a few moments I gazed at him as he stood there in his soaked raincoat with a package under his arm. By the light from the cross street I sensed rather than saw the pale, serious face and the light-colored eyes staring up at the windows on the front of our building in the hope of seeing you. I pulled back, disgusted, and (that's how men are) I could not keep from criticizing your conduct. You told me that you had had a lovers' quarrel and that he wanted to make peace. Well? Even so, that was no way to treat a man who waited for you an hour in the rain, and you there with me, all the time knowing that he was waiting for you. You could at least have spared me that sorry spectacle. Instead of laughing proudly, I rejected your sacrifice. But then in your kind eyes I saw pity and remorse; you *are* kind, Léah, and you always will be.

"He wants me to go out with him tonight. He came to complain to the landlady about me. But she's not my mother. I don't want to go, I told him so yesterday. Why does he keep on? I'm irritated. Listen, wait here for me and I'll go downstairs to talk to him. I'll be right back."

Off you went, and I didn't even have time to finish a cigarette before you were back. You came in with a package in your hand. It was from him.

"He went away happy. After all, we are going to go out together tonight. *Pauv' Fe'dinand.* Look, look what he brought me."

With childlike joy, with a candor that hurt me, you opened your fiancé's present, a silk *écharpe*, on top of the bed. But it was not without some protest from me. That day, Léah, if you

35

relished the kisses I gave you, it was because life had already taught me to lie. Inwardly, they tasted bitter and cold.

Meanwhile, things were not going well at the *pension*. *Mme* Lambertin was drinking more and more, she shouted at the guests, she didn't pay you your wages, and the house was a mess. *M.* Albert stamped about, drooling, stuttering and imbecilic. One afternoon you came into my room and said,

"I would like you to come with me to the *Prud'hommes* Court, to help me claim the wages she owes me."

It seemed a natural and amusing thing to do. I went, made a deposition, and said I would be a witness. When *Mme* Lambertin learned about it, she was furious. She had never expected I would do such a thing. The place became a madhouse. You went on strike to upset the guests and get them to force her to pay you. The angry arguments of the two of you would disturb the house and bring everyone out into the landings to listen. Some days later, when you couldn't stand it any longer, you decided to go away; but you insisted that I must testify for you if the case went to trial. I promised I would. There was nothing I would not have done then for you.

I knew it would break my heart to see you leave, and the prospect of my loneliness began to torment me. What would become of us when we were living under different roofs? What could we expect from my lack of initiative? We kissed sadly and slowly. It is true that my work was not going well and some of my guinea pigs had died, the victims of my carelessness or faulty observations. Everything had to be done over.

The next day after supper, I was reviewing my notes when I heard shouting on the ground floor. I opened the door a little to listen, thinking it might involve me. I heard my name shouted once amidst a volley of insults and unintelligible words, and then I heard it again. "Hell," I said to myself, "I hope it's not a fight." I was going to withdraw prudently when I heard your voice calling to me from downstairs:

"*Monsieur Carlôss. Monsieur Carlôss.*"

I snatched up something or other to use to defend myself—I believe it was a cast-iron ashtray—and I rushed down the stairs to help you, prepared for heroic deeds. On the bottom flight I stopped in embarrassment. Whom did I see but Ferdinand in his neat raincoat and with the eternal package under his left arm, you, *Mme* Lambertin, and two other women I did not know. "This is nice."

You wanted me to "explain," to defend you, to tell the "truth." But the landlady broke in.

"Come on," she screamed, beside herself, perhaps after her tenth bottle of *gueuze*. "Come on, I'll show you up in your true colors, right here, in front of her family. I'm going to bring everything out in the open. Ferdinand, Léah is lying to you, she's not faithful to you. Every day she spends hours in *Monsieur Carlôss*'s room. Such behavior in my house. She's shameless; I don't want her to darken my doorstep again. And still she wants to be paid. She has not been doing anything. Look at those stairs. Let *Monsieur Carlôss* pay her, he's the one she's been working for these last two months. This is a respectable house. If I am forced to talk, I will tell everything in the *Prud'hommes*. And you," she said, turning to me. "can pack your bags and clear out. I don't want you here another day."

I was calm, though a bit shaken with surprise; and turning to Ferdinand, who was watching the scene serenely, I said, *"Monsieur*, this woman is an inveterate alcoholic, an irresponsible person who doesn't know what she's talking about. But anyway I'm ready to offer you any kind of explanation. If you wish, I will step outside with you."

"It's not worth the trouble, *Monsieur*," he said politely, smiling vaguely. "I understand perfectly."

I wondered what he understood. Could you have told him? I turned to *Mme* Lambertin and with some epithets that I prefer not to repeat now, I added:

"As for this respectable house, do you recall the afternoon we were drinking cognac in the living room with the Indian prince and the three tipsy girls? And I was sitting on your lap, and how we kissed so much, that I'm even ashamed to tell. Don't talk too much. If you're so scrupulous about morality, why didn't you watch out for this young girl? How many times did you go upstairs when *Monsieur* Albert, Perlman, the Finn and the others called Léah and kept her with them? This is a pretty late date for you to begin to feel the itch for respectability.''

*Mme* Lambertin was going to open her mouth to reply, probably with some obscenities, but she grasped me and began to weep noisily. Just then from downstairs we heard the owner clearing his throat and a chair scraping on the floor tiles. *Mme* Lambertin released me, and I took advantage of the confusion to flee up the stairs and lock myself in my room in a rage.

Everything returned to the *status quo*; that is, you were absolved, though without a penny of your salary, and for two or three days more I remained in that house, where everything had become odious to me, from the smell of the *frites* to the wallpaper, and where my *poêle* was never again lit or my bed made. I won't bother telling how I got even and the condition I left the room in.

Léah, we believe that men are distinguished from the beasts by a sensitive callus that animals do not possess. Men have a conscience. From that day on I thought more about Ferdinand, who was so calm and so dependable, so honorable in the midst of such vulgarity, and so full of honest intentions toward you. I felt guilty beside him, but it is possible that the change of atmosphere and the period of rest that followed may have had some influence on my state of mind. I have never suffered from any actual religious anxiety, but people inevitably reflect the moral climate in which they have been reared. Instead of following your example and enjoying our love, our youth, and our freedom, untroubled by problems, I began to brood that I had been guilty of treachery and disloyalty.

I moved into another house some distance away, where there were responsible people. Against the wishes of your older sister, a farmer's wife, who was conniving with Ferdinand to snatch you away from the city, you began to look for work. I was more relaxed and completely absorbed in my experiments, which were bearing fruit, and I had less time to spare. Occasionally we would meet haphazardly and furtively at indefinite hours and places. There were no more of those slow, gentle rainy afternoons when, with my head on your consoling lap, I watched the coming of night. The *whens, wheres,* and *hows* that are the bane of all lovers began to persecute us and I caught myself frowning with impatience. I was never one who could solve certain practical problems, for I always found it hard to make a decision, and if I did make one, it had to be noble and decisive... until it fell apart. It never occurred to me to live with you, to steal you from Ferdinand, to marry you—where would we get the money? Furthermore, I was completely absorbed by my work and I did not feel that I could live a life divided between love and duty.

Sometimes we had a brief evening at a movie or a café, but yet many nights, in spite of my missing you as though you were a part of me, as I watched the time go by and thought about the following day and my work, I would finally say to you, "Let's leave it for tomorrow." I was intimidated by the chance encounters, the habitual lies, the restaurants with rooms upstairs, the curiosity of strangers, even by our own escapades. Today? Tomorrow? Since we had separated physically, I had been losing my limited capacity for initiative. Was it the astute strength of conscience that impelled me to hesitate? Léah, I don't know. Realizing that I couldn't make up my mind, you became anxious and tried to get me to move to the house where you were working, but there were different people, a different atmosphere and different standards there, and the price, which was much too high for my thin wallet, frightened me away. I could not accept the help you offered me. You wept. For the first time I lost my temper and I felt homesick for the Lambertin *pension*. I don't know what it was, but I was afraid of a disappointment. I remained where I was, where I could work in peace, and where no visitors were allowed.

From time to time, on your day off, you slipped away from Ferdinand, who was in a hurry to get married, and you came over to meet me. And once we spent the whole night in that little out-of-the-way hotel to compensate for all our difficulties. What a night that was, Léah. How comfortable the atmosphere was, how sweet our love, and how sweet the stars sparkling at dawn before the eyes of the satisfied lovers. In the morning we were a little pale when we went down to the café for breakfast. We sat at a window, remote from the world and our problems, watching the sun come up over the proper, neat building while the workers from the neighborhood walked with firm strides along the echoing sidewalk. Everything seemed to be settled. Nothing was.

At the *tram* stop, under a still hesitant sun, you looked at me with a kind of serious, decided expression in your large, gray, honest eyes. You were pulling your modest fur collar up around your cheeks, which the morning chill had reddened. Your eyes looked damp. What were you thinking about? And then you overcame your hesitation, and with great emotion, you proposed that we should "run away."

"Let's go to Paris," you said entreatingly and tenderly. "I'm French, I'm strong, I can work. There no one knows us. We could be so happy."

There you were, so close to me and so entreating that the passersby smiled tenderly at us.

"Let's go... the two of us. You can live there for your animals, for your books." What kind of cowardice, what expectations, ambitions, what vanity, perhaps, held me back? To what hopes, duties or ideas of duties was I being faithful? Could I have been tired out after that sleepless night? Your eyes, soft and gentle, had all the melancholy of the sea at Calais. I shrank away from your entreaty. I laughed at the heroic garret that you proposed and that was, really, the same one I was dreaming about. But inside of me it was not virtue but cowardice that won. Cowardice has power, cowardice is heroic when it is masked by lofty purposes. I did not know exactly what I wanted or expected from life and from my still confused ambitions. To live for others. And you, what did you want? To escape from a monotonous existence? From Ferdinand? To travel, to fight life's battles, to experience sacrifice and the lasting union of two humans who labor and enjoy themselves, who create and suffer together? Your dream was too exalted for my cowardice or too simple for my ambitions. That was the reason. Today I see clearly that though I longed for love and its satisfactions, I selfishly desired that it would fit into my life without altering my routes or goals.

Together we got into the *tram* that took us back to the city and to the orbits of our respective existences. Our separation was melancholy, but I felt some relief. Love was threatening to overturn the scenery of my dream; but also, other people's suffering has always disquieted and stifled me. It was not for myself that I suffered, for I was beginning to walk on solid ground, or so I thought; it was for you, through knowing that you, too, were suffering. And at such moments I do not know what I would have given not to be with you so as not to have had to pity you.

Bad luck, missed encounters, and our obligations came between us; and we spent long days and weeks without seeing or communicating with each other. Perhaps it was because I was trying to forget you. Other plans began to take shape in my restless spirit, which was in rebellion against everything that was "personal," and that would appear to disturb the lofty purposes of existence. You seemed to live for love, exclusively. In your confusion you left one job after another, and at one point I did not even have your address. Then I met you on a winding, lonely street in the Ixelles district, and you were so pale, so lethargic, so unkempt, that you seemed to have come from another world. You wanted to go to my room or some café to chat. I explained, and it was true, that I could not take you into the house with me and that I had an appointment with the head of my laboratory. Your eyes entreated, but I was pressed for time, confused, lukewarm and, above all, afraid. How much I suffered during that brief encounter. How horrible it is to pity a human being whom we have thought we have loved. So I glanced away and promised to meet you that afternoon in a suitable place. Could I have been lying consciously, or was I sincere in my promise? I cannot recall. You persevered.

"You're definitely coming?"

"What a question," and I laughed. "Did I ever stand you up?"

But I did not go, Léah. I wonder whether you have forgiven me.

And how am I helped now by repentance? Repentance is always useless.

The days, the weeks, the months, a year, perhaps more,

slipped past. I worked, traveled, struggled, suffered, developed other interests and worries, took on other responsibilities. I experienced the bitterness of disappointment with myself and with others. Then I returned to Brussels, and one afternoon curiosity, the desire to revive the past, remorse, God knows what, took me to the Lambertin's *pension*. On the door I saw a sign—*A louer*—torn and blackened by time. Peering through the dim ground floor windows, I could see the empty, dusty rooms. Instead of the old familiar odor of *frites*, I smelled a sad dampness and neglect, the sadness of an abandoned grave. In front of the door, on the steps, and along the sidewalk there were bits of rubble, sand and lime. The building was being remodeled, and the Lambertin *pension* was just a memory. In the *brasserie* on the corner I was told that it had failed and had been closed months before. I hurried away sadly as if part of my past had been stolen or obliterated.

One tumultuously sunny afternoon I was walking slowly along the Chaussée de *W*____, enjoying the sight of the throng of strangers—I have a deep love for the anonymous—when from behind me a familiar, surprised voice exclaimed,

"*Monsieur Carlôss.*"

I turned around. It was you. You looked blooming, pink-cheeked, a bit plumper, well-dressed, in short, a fully developed woman. When I saw that you were not alone, I tipped my hat and prepared to escape again. But you had halted and were looking at me in your frank, kind way, and the persons with you were smiling, too. I walked over to you, feeling confused, and shook your hand, which grasped mine energetically. And I saw Ferdinand, who appeared strong and healthy, handsome and happy, and who was holding a baby in his arms. He greeted me familiarly and introduced me to his family, which was now yours, too.

"We have been married for more than a year," you said. "Look, this is my child."

Your child. I looked at him, Léah. Plump, with your large gray eyes: he smiled at me as if I were an old acquaintance.

"It's a boy."

I turned to you. Your eyes were moist and you were

laughing. All those around you were smiling. And in a tone of
tender reproach, which I am sure I alone could understand, you
repeated these sweet words,

"He's *my* child."

After many failures and much fatigue I got a better job in a
laboratory in a free clinic where before my eyes, I saw the spectacle of all human misery passing, enveloped in a smell of car-
bolic acid and formaldehyde. My only concern was to live, just
to live, and I gave myself to it with my usual fervor as if I were
not being gnawed from within by persecution, loneliness and
bitterness. I had been forced to give up all my research and all
my dreams, everything that had separated us that pleasant
morning in Ixelles, and only my garret remained to me, the
heroic, brave garret of a laboratory technician in a free clinic,
that and the acrid, nauseating smell of misery. And, I must add,
the memory of my mistake. And by then you were probably fat,
perhaps a farmer's wife in the flat land of Flanders. As for me
all that remained of me in your memory was surely no more
than a faded image and a mispronounced name. Even for you I
must have been ceasing to exist.

One day, as I left the Clinic in that remote, rain-drenched
place, I went into a café to buy cigarettes. As I was leaving, a
woman sitting in a dark corner got up, walked over to me,
seized me by the arm and stared at me. I did not recognize her at
first glance, but the puffy face, the reddish nose, the wavy, gray
blonde hair and the gray eyes reminded me of something. For a
few minutes we looked at each other, and then in a hoarse,
cheerful voice she said,

"Why, it is *Monsieur Carlôss*."

It was *Mme* Lambertin. She had fallen almost to the lowest
rung of the ladder. How she had aged. Her disheveled, dirty
hair hung about her flabby, swollen, almost expressionless face.
She was wearing a filthy, sopping dress. She turned to the insignificant men seated at the table behind her and said,

"Don't you remember? It is *Monsieur Carlôss*, the college
graduate, the Portuguese."

The man, who was wearing a cap, stood up to greet me. I
sat down with them and ordered a round of *gueuze*. "What
wrecks,"I said bitterly to myself.

Then they told me about their life. Everything had gone wrong. They had been evicted from that house, an excellent business. And there were debts, bankruptcy; it was hell, including six months up in Saint-Gilles, behind bars. A dog's life, one could say. But, I heard in a whisper, couldn't I do something for them?

I gave them a few francs that I had left for the rest of the week, and we sat silently listening to the unbearably monotonous rain on the square. I couldn't wait to leave the place and those biting memories. Suddenly, as she drank her second *gueuze*, the woman pointed at me and said,

"Look. *Monsieur Carlôss* has got so much white hair."

And covering her face with her hands, she began to weep like a child. The husband gestured to me discreetly, put his arm around her shoulders, and spoke some comforting words in an unintelligible jargon. And then she murmured, smiling through her tears, "How Léah loved you."

And that was the last time I heard your name.

*Translated* by Raymond S. Sayers

# PROUD BEAUTY

Along the coast the storm rages. Livid, furious, the Atlantic sweeps deserted beaches, swallows fishing boats, picks up battered ships to fling them inland. The tornado uproots trees which saw the landing of the Pilgrims, rolls before it—like so many matchboxes—houses, barns, cottages, human lives too many to count. Steel bridges vibrate, bend and snap like reeds. Trains topple over. Pulled up rails are contorted into the forms of tetanized snakes, and telegraph wires rip, whistle and tangle in the wind like locks of copper hair. Lifted weightless from the roads, automobiles lie as strange scarecrows in devastated fields, or upturned in ditches. Industrious rivers, now turbid and choleric, leap over their banks, drag dead cattle, houses, stray boats, children's cradles. Cries of distress.

Feverish and raucous, the radio talks on without letup, swelling the anxiety of the people. It is America, giant of contracts, struggling. Six o'clock, and it is dark. The bars full, the lights dim, the music languorous. Right here, as if suspended from the skyscrapers and impelled by the wind, the immense, compact curtain of rain rounds the corner of the hospital, racking and howling, and breaks on the street below with an angry foam, which the wind picks up and dissipates. The asphalt of the pavement is like a dark, oily river running unbridled. No one in the streets. The tall buildings hum musically in the wind, and the frames of the windows chatter like horror-stricken jaws. The city seems hallucinated.

Suddenly, mingled with the cracking whip of the rain and the wind, a scream. Instinctively, I look across to the windows of the hospital—closed, serene, incandescent. Enormous, the hospital stands up against the storm. No, it didn't come from there. I listen closer. It's from below, it's from down below. Jesus, what's happened? People are yelling and yelling. Always some trouble brewing—will we never have peace?

I run to the stairs and cock my ear. It's down there, in the depths of the building. I rush back to phone the janitor: "What's happening? I hear screaming." And his quiet, slow voice contrasts with the fury of the weather: "Yes, it's here— we're having trouble down here." I drop the phone and shrug my shoulders. But already, from the street, comes the screeching of the police car, weird in the storm. I run to the window. Five men, guns in hand, jump out of a dark, lustrous limousine, and race under the rain toward the door. The homicide squad. My God, what can it be?

In slippers, as I am, I race down the stairs. The screaming has stopped, and a mortal silence rises from the bottom of the building. They won't let me through to the cellar so I push my way along the hall to the street. The rain pours on me and I have my feet in the water. Never mind. Down the street an ambulance waits, doors wide open. Near the iron railing, in front of the house, a small crowd peers and whispers. Through the large window, a little below street level, I see the body of a woman lying on a blue rug, her legs exposed and glowing in the dazzling light of the room. What's going on in there? Now the ambulance doctor and two agents come up the short stair, carrying a man on a stretcher. They take him to the ambulance and leave him there alone, the door open. I come close. He's a young guy, thin and pale, his head soaked in blood, his broken shoes pointing outward. But aren't they going to do anything for him? Just leave him there like that? Is he dead, then? An arm hangs out, the hand livid and skinny. Of a sudden—he frightened me, I thought he was dead—he lifts his hand and moves it limply as if talking to someone, explaining something. And again the hand falls inanimate. But for Heaven's sake, what happened? Who is he? Nobody answers. The rain beats down. Someone drew the shade and all I see now are the feet of the woman. But the crowd continues to peer, crouching, almost kneeling in the rain, gloating over her body.

Soaked to the skin, I make my way back to the hall and down the rear stairs to the cellar. After all, I live here. "Excuse me, sir, I'm a neighboor, a friend. I heard everything." And I walk in through the kitchen door.

The apartment, flooded with light, is invaded by people. It looks unreal. Like a rehearsal in a moving picture studio. All these men standing around. Such a silence. That bald, quiet man walking around slowly in shirtsleeves. Oh, so he's the father. Yes, the janitor of the building—why, didn't you know him? And to think it had to happen on a night like this. A storm as no living man remembers.

Such an education they gave that daughter. She was proud and beautiful, and now, lying on that blue rug, she has a coin of blood right on her forehead. Her perfect, well-joined, professional legs have a strange glow in the crude light of the projectors. Just as in a show. (Hell, it's stifling in this place.) Exposed in death, without modesty. Her pride. Miami, Bermuda, Broadway. Dead. This time she will make the first page of the *Mirror*, the *New York American*. Publicity. Too late. Burnished and cold, those legs will only cause horror. The night clubs will soon forget her, business must go on, there are so many pretty legs, such a thirst for *manhattans* and *cuba-libres*, for swing and oblivion. No more garlands of lubricous gazes climbing up her pure legs (pure, except of ambition and pride). Only worms in procession, creeping silently, without benefit of tips to waiters. (What are you thinking about, mister?)

The detectives look annoyed, their hats on, smoking five-cent cigars, thinking maybe it's getting late for supper, waiting around for God knows what. Such an education her parents gave her. No sacrifice was too great for that daughter. And to

47

have her go like that. Doesn't make sense. And on such a night, too. A storm to knock you silly. Look, they're taking more pictures. Someone carried the youngster to a neighbor's house. Poor child, he saw everything. Oh, so it was he, screaming. The voice sounded like him. It was him. Frightened, hysterical. The one over there is the older son. A very nice boy he is. And the nice little lady near him, that's his wife. Such nice people they are, all of them. I saw the husband carried out to the ambulance. Was he still alive? Of course. They threw him in, and left him there alone, with the door open. His head was covered with blood. (A little quiet, please.) Sh! The detectives are getting the mother's story. Poor soul, her eyes are dry from so much crying. She's so dazed, she can't make head or tail of it.

Oh, so she was not living with her husband. No, they'd been separated for months. His parents died when he was only a kid, and left him big money. He spent everything. When she met him, he had no money, no job, no home, nothing. I don't see how any woman would fall for him, such a poor devil. Looked like a bum in those broken shoes. Wouldn't work, said he was sick. Such an up-bringing. Wanted his wife to go live with him again. But what a jealous bugger he was. Wouldn't let her work and she had to support him. Her one passion in life was to dance. Since she was a little bit of a thing. They did everything to give her an education. Never let her soil her hands.

So he'd come to see her, beg her to return. No, I've got my life to lead, my career, my future. Poor girl, only twenty-two years old. They had an apartment and everything. She paid the rent. Sorry for him, you know. But that jealousy. A couple of months ago they offered her a contract and she went to Bermuda. It was the beginning of her career, everything. She returned another woman, gay, beaming with health. Look what a beautiful shape she had. When did she come back? Only yesterday, if you please. Her agent wouldn't give her any rest. "Study, work." What for? She came back full of hope; seems she was in line for another contract. And now look at her, stretched out under the eyes of all these people. Her wardrobe trunks are still in that corner, see? More than a hundred dresses, not to speak of the rest. A pretty penny they cost. Maybe they can sell them.

But how did it happen? Her agent had invited her to dinner this evening, some place uptown. And the mother insisting with her to go, you need to have a little fun, he's such a nice man, so much interested in you. They argued for hours. She goes, she doesn't go. And she didn't. Just think, waiting around here for her death. But why didn't she? Didn't want to be seen with a Jew. Said it was bad for her reputation. But I thought *they* were *Jews*. Oh no, they're Lithuanians. Poor old souls, what they didn't do for that daughter. The agent came to get her (Mr. Goldstein, I think they called him), and she: "The weather is so bad, I hope you won't mind." He went away in his car. "Some other day, maybe. Don't worry, kid. Take care of yourself." She changed into a gown, put on her dancing sandals. Golden sandals, look at them.

Well, in such bad weather who should show up but the husband. He wanted to see her. They'd see each other now and then, though she avoided him when she could. He'd come down, they'd give him dinner, felt sorry for him. He wasn't a bad sort. They were just sitting down to eat, wouldn't he join them? And he accepted. Very quiet he was. They had sandwiches and coffee, there in the kitchen. (Look at the dog. Her puppies are just a week old. She howled like anything but never budged from their side.) Well, he started the old story. Please come back to live with him. He'd already found a job (a lie), why didn't she quit dancing, and those night clubs, and the bad company? Whoever would have thought? Such a natural conversation. They went to the front room and suddenly he says to her: "So you won't come back to me?" Just as natural as that. She smiled. "Please, Bob. Let's remain friends. Let's talk about something else." He pulled out his gun. "If that's how you feel about it, I'll kill you." They thought he was fooling. The girl opened her mouth, and he fired the shot right between her eyes. One shot, to kill. Now you can't see it, they've covered her face with a burlap. (But why don't they cover her legs, the poor thing. It's cruel to make a show of her like that.) She lifted her hands to her face, as if refusing to see death, and dropped without so much as a cry. Nobody could believe it. He began to walk around the house like a loony, the gun in his hand, talking away to himself. He seemed puzzled, as if he couldn't make up his mind. The mother and the youngster began to yell. It was over in a minute. He aimed the gun at his head. Look up there, do you see where the bullet lodged? It went through his brain and landed up there, in the frame of the door. He was crazy, had even been under the doctor's care. Always carrying a gun, that was his mania. And didn't the doctor warn the family? Of course, but who ever listens to such things? They could have saved her, reported him to the police, that would have fixed him. Once, when they were living together, he shut himself up in the bedroom. She heard a shot and ran to him. He was laughing, revolver in hand. "I knew you'd come running. You expected it." He'd fired the shot into the pillow. Crazy as a bat, that's what he was. Always talking of killing himself. But he didn't want to go alone. Ever see such selfishness?

Listen, that's the telephone. It's from the hospital. Dead? That's that. Just a minute ago. Never talked again. The detective who went to his apartment found two guns, both loaded. He left a note for his sister. "It had to be." And another to the police. "Sorry to bother you, gentlemen." So he had it all figured out, the b——

• • •

Proud beauty, blonde beauty, one hundred dresses, a future, a career. Stretched out on the rug where she danced silently, looking at the heels of her golden sandals. And the sacrifices of her parents; all their lives spent in the cellars of cheap apartment houses, stoking in coal, lighting fires, emptying garbage, carrying around the bunch of keys for showing the empty apartment, listening to complaints, fixing leaky faucets. And in their hearts, the old country, a hopeless hope. And that daughter with her hard, closed face, beautiful, proud, who never spoke, forever gazing at her golden heels. Professional beauty dreaming of a future. Dead. The mother never let her soil her hands. "Watch your nails." And there she is now. America, the future, pictures in the papers, a career, her incomparable legs, and such an education as they gave her.

That wind, will it never let up? They say the damage is something awful; and the deaths, and the floods. The rain falls as in the movies. A real American rain.

The neighbors are still waiting. What for? The detectives seem relieved now. The reporters finish their notes. The father went out, quiet, cowed, in shirtsleeves. It's time to shake down the ashes, collect the garbage from the dumbwaiter, which lets off a gust of putrid wind. "O.K. Let'er go." The janitor goes about his business. Who's dead is dead, life must go on.

Look, I forgot to shut off the radio.

The rain is letting up now and the air is turning warm. The evening seems tired of the storm.

Gee, we've gotta go to the movies tonight—have a little fun. This place reeks of the crime.

*Translated by* Camila Campanella Miguéis

# COSME

"Look," said one of my friends as we entered the club bar. "Didn't you want to meet him? There he is." And he pointed to a man over six feet tall, who stood against the bar, a glass of beer beside him, talking with a group of friends around him. I recognized him immediately. I had seen him some time ago, leading a parade; he had been proudly carrying a huge banner that the wind was whipping about and cracking as if trying to yank it from his tight grip. After that I had heard a lot of talk about him. So that was him. I looked at him closely before approaching—ruddy complexion, slender body and broad shoulders like an athlete's, a head that was almost delicate, solidly set on a long thin neck. His curly light-brown hair accented the candor of his small lively grey eyes, of his smile, and of his slightly sibilant voice. He spoke loudly, with the exuberance of our mountainmen from the North, using large expressive gestures; the men around him listened attentively and laughed along with him. He was dressed in a well-tailored suit that showed off the muscular elasticity of a laborer's physique. Cosme radiated strength and contentment.

When we were introduced, he shook my hand vigorously, and rested his left hand on my shoulder fraternally. We both said at the same time: "It's a great pleasure to meet you."

He immediately offered me a glass of beer, which I refused, risking offending him.

"Thank you, but I've just had dinner with these friends of mine, and have already reached my limit."

Cosme smiled with a touch of irony and said,

"Never say no to what is freely offered to you. And what the hell kind of man are you anyhow? Come on, have a drink. I already have ten of these under my belt, not counting the ones I had at dinner, and look at how steady my hand is."

And it *was* steady. Cosme could hold his liquor, like the majority of these pick-and-shovel journeymen, used to irrigating with their sweat the highways, bridges and railroads of America under the merciless summer sun or in the freezing cold of winter. I felt small, and drank to his health. All present joined me. Then we had another round for the "cause." Cosme added grandly:

"Here we only drink for the 'good cause.' We have to help this club, to keep it from going under."

I liked him at first sight, and I think he felt the same about me. It's a pleasure (and I feel proud) to meet a Portuguese like this one out here, smiling and healthy. When the party was in full swing, he came up to me and suggested that we step outside together, to get some fresh air. Our people are used to fresh air and hate jobs and recreation behind closed doors, in stuffy atmospheres.

"We've already done our part. Let them have a good time now. Tony will see to it that they do."

We left them to amuse themselves with traditional folk dances, *fados*, and raffles, while we wandered about Greenwich Village. Then we went up to 6th Avenue. A light, warm, autumn rain was falling. Cosme was hatless. He told me about his life and experiences with gusto. I delighted in listening to him. He had been born in Barqueiros in the province of Douro, and told me that he had been in America for nearly twelve years. "Since I was 21," he added with reflective preciseness. Therefore he must have been thirty-three, but he looked older.

"Do you like it here?" I asked, and immediately regretted the question. Cosme gave me a quick glance and laughed.

"Do I like it here? That's a good one." We walked a few steps in silence, and he added slowly, "Of course I like it. If I didn't I wouldn't have stayed here. But don't ask me if I like it better *there*. It's not a question of taste. When I ran away from home, I didn't know how to read or write. My mother was poor, and couldn't send me to school. In my little village there wasn't even a school. The closest one was six miles away, over steep paths. School was for the rich. I had no shoes and no money to buy them. Young as I was, my mother needed my help. Over there they say, 'A child's work isn't much, but he who wastes it is crazy.' The first thing I did, when I arrived here, was to learn to read and write on my own."

He stopped and pulled out a book he carried in his pocket— it was a poem by Junqueiro.

"I always carry it with me. I know almost all of it by heart." He put the worn booklet back in his pocket and continued: "Yes sir, I like books, I've always liked them even before I learned to read. At home, we had a very old book, bound, in which my grandfather had learned all he knew—the *Encyclopedic Manual*. I brought it with me to America in the hope of someday learning it by heart also. An old book, falling apart. I have it put away."

He could now read Portuguese fluently, could take a stab at Spanish, and spoke enough English to get by with his companions of other nationalities and with the bosses.

"I was about fifteen when that saintly woman bought me a pair of yellow shoes, too big for my feet—they were the first and only pair I had back there—to go to church or to some fair. I grew up, became a man quickly, and the darned shoes stayed the same size and they pinched. In order to walk in them, I had to use a staff. May God forgive me, but not even Christ, perspiring sweat and blood under the weight of His cross, suffered more than I did to go to church on Sundays, to see the young women. I had only one suit, made of coarse wool, that she bought me at the Marco fair with the fruits of my labor. But it was only for special occasions."

55

He smiled to himself and ran his hand over his face to wipe away the raindrops.

"Poor thing, she gave me many a whipping to make a dedicated worker out of me. But I have to give her credit, she never forced me to go to confession or to catechism. And please understand, she was not the sort of woman to miss a mass, no sir."

"What was your occupation back there?"

Cosme looked at me with genuine surprise, as if I were ignorant of something fundamental. Then he stretched his long robust arms out in front of him, and closed his knotty fists.

"I was a boatman, what else could I have been? A Douro boatman. Except for doing some tree-pruning work, or grape-harvesting, when there was nothing else—but I never liked that; it's women's work—I was always a boatman. Like my father and my grandfather and all the men in my family. That's the life, sir. We used to go up there to Peso da Régua, to load up the wine barrels to carry them down the river to Vila Nova de Gaia. We worked at that day and night, hardly eating or sleeping, fighting the river current (do you know it?) with the strength of our arms to keep the boat from being shattered against the edge of the rocks, which are as sharp as razor blades. We walked around in tatters, barefooted, with our feet burned and cracked to the point of bleeding from the sharp rocks, when it was necessary to pull the boat by hand upstream, against the current. That was men's work, yes sir, for strong men, because it's not every man who can do it.

"Our food was stale, sometimes moldy, cornbread with a hunk of cheese or a handful of olives, when God provided them, or a rancid sardine. In the summer, the sun's heat was smothering, and what a thirst we had! Then, do you know what we'd do? We'd open a small hole in the casks, with a drill-bit, and the wine would squirt out like a golden thread in the sun."

He stopped in the middle of the sidewalk, wiped his lips with his hand and turned his face toward the rain that was falling softly.

"Then we would stand there, our mouths open, taking turns, to catch the sun-warmed stream from the winecask. With the swaying of the boat, the wine would run down our chests and would soak our rags. We'd become sticky with that honey. And happy! How we laughed. That blessed wine the field laborers squeeze from the hills with their sweat and suffering was as good as the blood of Our Lord Jesus Christ. For us, it was our water and bread and the strength of our arms. It helped us to forget the poverty and the hunger. When we'd had enough, we'd plug the hole with bread crumbs. One of the men would then begin to play the harmonica or the accordion and the rest of us would work like lions. (Cosme laughed softly.) Can there still be people who would call that stealing? Hard work, poverty, a bed made of boards, starvation wages—could it then be stealing? It seemed to us to be the most natural thing in the world."

After a brief silence, Cosme began again, seriously: "Yes, I suffered a lot of hunger and did without a lot of things. A pack mule would not endure as much as I did. With a flock of younger brothers and sisters crying for bread... And not even the hope of escaping from all that. To buy a new pair of shoes, or some new sack-cloth clothes, one had to work at least three years. And shouldn't a man marry? Who could even think about that? Oh those Douro mountains, with the river raging down below, the blue sky hanging above, they were beautiful, but they weighed on my heart like a coffin-lid.

"One day I heard someone talking about America. Gold was so plentiful one could trip over it, food was abundant, the work easy, and the workers rode everywhere in automobiles. It was enough to make a saint's mouth water. I couldn't sleep a wink that night. I couldn't get that image out of my head. I didn't have a moment's rest from then on until I left home. But I waited years. Gold is something I've never seen here. It's well guarded. Work, certainly, on the highways and bridges. Now I'm a gardener. I've got an easy life. Got no cause to complain, thank God, because even when there were millions out-of-work I never lacked for employment. What else does a man have two arms for? Work has never been a burden to me, thanks to the way that saintly woman, my mother, taught me.

"Now, in our country, you can slave your life away and

never get anywhere. When a man dies, shrivelled up like some critter, he goes to his grave with the same clothing, the same pair of shoes, he wore to lead his bride down the aisle. One's stomach is never really full. Nor do we ever get ahead because the bigwigs and the 'doctors' drink our sweat and eat the marrow of our bones. While here... Just consider this. With what I earn in a week, I can dress myself from head to toe, including underclothing. And I can always read a book, and I can afford to have a friend over or go to a show. I live as I please, and don't have to account to anyone, nor do I have to go, hat-in-hand, begging for favors from the bosses or the bigwigs. I do the work of any two men, it's true, but I'm in control of my own life. I owe no one, and no one owes me. I'm free. And you still ask me whether I like it here.''

It was after three when I got to bed that night. I had difficulty falling asleep. Without realizing it, Cosme had made me see things that up until then I had not understood. It's not enouth to have principles and convictions; it's necessary to experience first-hand the reality of men in order to understand how they work.

We met many times after that. One day he told me:

''Don't think that abundance is the only thing I like about this land: That's important, but it's not everything. I don't close my eyes to what's going on around me. I know there are lines of unemployed persons waiting for a cup of soup or coffee, rackets, dirty politics, and all the rest. There's all that and more. That's America. You have to take the good with the bad, take it or leave it. You either fight for what you want, or give up, and be crushed. But you *can* fight, and that's very important for a man like me. You can't fix everything at once. But you *can* accomplish some things, do you understand? The things we enjoy are worth a lot. Hunger taught us that. But the right to protest, to improve our situation, is worth even more. True freedom is this, a struggle, a daily conquest.''

He stopped in the middle of the small rented room where I had come to visit him, as if he were searching for the proper words to express his thoughts.

''What I see here is the promise, the seed of the future. Of a society organized for man and not *against* him. And believe me, there is nothing I wouldn't do to stay and help.''

His eyes sparkled. He caressed with his hand some multicolored brochures that he had on a small pine bookcase, smiled and turned to me with an expression of vague resentment.

''If our people could at least open their eyes and see. America for them is money: dollars! They think of nothing else. Some live well, it's true, but it's as though they lived only for the things money can buy. And many don't even know they're in the land of comfort and hygiene. They live like animals, in filthy boarding houses, with no bath and no heat; they don't spend a cent on anything but the barest necessities; they don't go to a meeting, they don't read a newspaper. They hate the unions, and they think it's all the same racket. They work like beasts of burden, eat poorly, save for years, and for what? Their ambition is to return rich to buy properties, and then spend the rest of their lives living off the sweat of others. They want to be bigwigs like the ones they left behind. They want to go from exploited to exploiters. And they subject themselves to everything, reject solidarity and struggle, just to save a few bucks. Just try to talk to them about politics. Or about freedom. They'll start calling you... Ah.''

He gestured and made a face of displeasure, and then began pacing anew:

''They don't even know how to be grateful to those who've given, and continue to give, their freedom and their lives for the rights of all of us. They came as slaves, and return as slaves. But some who considered themselves rich have come back here quickly enough. The bigwigs and the 'doctors' take the shirts off their backs. And their poor relatives with their envy and 'gimme-gimme'... No one forgives them their wealth. And they may be right. In the final analysis, living here is a privilege and the ones who stayed behind, doing without, can't help but be envious. It's a big world, and there would be enough for all of us if we only knew how to share the fruits of our labors. Money and the things it buys should only be used to elevate us and to give us dignity. Beyond that, money is the poison of humanity.''

Cosme looked me in the eye.

"You don't know Frank Sousa, from the docks, do you? He was crippled for life because he told the truth. Imagine, in order to work on the docks, one has to pay the dock master, who is always in collusion with the Union racketeers. Our Portuguese, very humble, accustomed to begging, hat-in-hand, would offer a box of cigars to the Italian, and would put a ten or twenty-spot in the box, as a bribe. They pay the initiation fee and the Union dues, and on top of that, they buy the right to work. And they think this is o.k., taking their friends' turn, for money—they think this is right. Bunch of spineless weaklings. Sometimes the bosses hire them for a week or two and then fire them. What they earn during those two weeks hardly covers what they had to spend to buy the job. Do you understand? Others are in line waiting for their turn with the box of cigars and the twenty-spot. Frank used to see this and was revolted. On top of everything else, it's illegal. He went alone to speak to the Assistant District Attorney, told him everything, and was told: 'Frank, if you can bring me two witnesses who can confirm all this and repeat it to the grand jury, you're worth your weight in gold. We'll rid the waterfront of gangsters and racketeers.' Frank is not a snitch, he's an organization man— he's an organizer. He went and tried to get some fellow-workers to go and make declarations to the District Attorney. They all slipped away; he couldn't find a single one. Fear. It's not just fear; they think it's easier to subject themselves to this feudalism than to fight. That's what the rackets thrive on. And there's always the possibility of getting shot. I tell you this: they want only the advantages, but not the risks—that's not for them. Give us this day your daily dollars.

"Frank didn't give up, and went around the docks distributing pamphlets and gathering men for a meeting. Sullivan is the one who gives all the orders down on the docks; Frank was threatened by his bodyguards several times: 'Do you want to take a trip down the river?' Many have vanished down the river. One morning, he was alone at the entrance to the dock of the Clyde Mallory Line (there are over one hundred Portuguese workers there), distributing pamphlets to the men as they entered, when he saw a group heading straight for him; he spotted them right away. All alone, he had nowhere to run: he clung to a lamppost—they'll never drag me out of here alive. They fell upon him. What can I tell you? Not a single companion came to his aid. There was a policeman on the corner. As soon as he saw them, he turned and disappeared. They don't want to have anything to do with gangsters. They're all well greased. Sousa was laid out. He was in the hospital for three months mending his broken bones, and then he got arthritis; he was crippled for life. He now earns his living making toys, sitting down, an invalid. It's even said that his wife left him and went to pot; she frequents the bars at night.

"That's how life is, the struggle. But nothing ventured, nothing gained."

These and similar opinions had earned Cosme, with his utopian views, a reputation as a "radical" among his countrymen for whom the buck was the supreme goal, the only salvation for the oppressed of this world. Humiliation seemed to them a small price to pay to put food on their tables.

Far be it from me to say that Cosme was perfect, a saint; he was simply a man, a human being, genuine, sincere, an excited idealist, sometimes crude. One could say about him what he'd say about America. He had some good and some bad, and to appreciate the good side of people, one has to accept them provisionally as they are, with their flaws and virtues, in the hope of improving them, isn't that so? Little by little, through casual encounters and conversations with him, and by hearing about him, I completed the picture of this fighter.

He was impulsive and hot tempered. His love of Justice would sometimes blind him. But even in his most outrageous gestures, he revealed his inner generosity. One day, where he was working, he caught a truck driver stealing another worker's tools. He grabbed his arm and twisted it in such a way that he left it limp and hanging. "Drop it. You slob, stealing a comrade's tools, his living." This impulsive act cost him dearly in medical and hospital bills, compensation, a lawyer, and lord knows what. But he paid it gladly, first, because "the thief deserved to be taught a lesson he'd remember"; and second, because "the poor fool, with his broken arm, couldn't even earn a living for weeks."

That's how Cosme was. But he had a good sense of humor; he could take a joke. At one point he got it into his head to ride around on a motorcycle. He got into various accidents that left their mark on his scalp. One day he went off the road, in Yonkers, hit a lamppost and broke it off at the base. He was taken to court, where the judge, who already knew him from previous misadventures, but empathized with him, told him, upon pronouncing his sentence, "Look, Cosme, if I sentence you to two years in prison, you're going to cost the state a fortune, and it won't do any good because you are hopeless. There is only one thing for me to do: to sentence you to ride only a motorcycle. Sooner or later, you'll spill your brains out on some wall and we'll have peace once again."

Cosme laughed, paid the fine and damages, and never again rode the motorcycle.

About the time we met, the spectre of oppression was beginning to grow over Europe and the world. The structure of democracy was cracking and shaking perilously. World War II was looming on the horizon. Cosme, aware of the tragedy that was beginning to take shape overseas, and feeling personally threatened by it, was burning with impatience. Fascism had meant something quite clear to him; it was the triumph of those who had kept him in a state of hunger, ignorance and poverty, and not just him, but countless millions around the world. It was the perpetuation of the evils of humanity, the death of hope and of the struggle. And the threat involved his adopted country, too, the country of his hero, Lincoln. He could read the warning of History, and decided to awaken his people from the apathy in which they were vegetating. For this reason, he made many moral and material sacrifices to enlighten those who had eyes but could not see and had ears but would not listen. He became an energetic and pleasant organizer. He joined organizations and helped to found clubs, spoke at meetings and assemblies, walked for miles to visit Portuguese communities, marched down streets, took up collections, discussed ideas, copied and memorized pages from books, and exhorted his fellow workers to fight against the aggressors and aid the underdogs. Although he lived far from New York, he never hesitated to go there to collaborate in some festivity, where he encouraged and stimulated others with his presence and vitality. If he couldn't sell a pamphlet, he would give it away and pay for it out of his own pocket. In this he was a champion; even the most intransigent adversaries accepted his "literature." Scrupulous and straight in his accounts, he never paid attention to the expense. Countless times he spent a hard-earned dollar to collect a twenty-cent donation. But he returned with a triumphant smile, and would say with childlike obstinacy, "they've already begun to understand, see? What is necessary is to educate them, teach them to see and think, to organize themselves."

But ideas do not penetrate human minds as easily as the pneumatic drill penetrates concrete on the highway. The human beast is not always easy to convince. Portuguese and, as such, thirsting for perfection, Cosme was desolate upon discovering that logical evidence, facts, reading, preaching left so many men unmoved before their most basic interests. He believed words should suffice to convince them of that which, to him, was implicitly obvious.

He began to get angry. More than once, he called men whose biggest fault was lack of consciousness or fear, "rats," "cowards," "renegades" and "traitors." He was losing his composure. He, who was cordiality personified, started conflicts and made enemies. One night we left a tumultuous assembly where the cause he served had lost an important vote. He felt abandoned, worse than that—repudiated and defeated. He was conscious of his ideological error, of his abstract sectarianism, and judged himself severely.

"I'm too pig-headed, stubborn as a mule. I get angry over the slightest thing, and in society one can't be that way. Why did I speak the way I did, won't you tell me? I wanted to convince them and ended up turning them against me. I'm destroying something we've all worked so hard to achieve. And it's a pity because there's so much to be done. Me and my dammed mountain temper."

"Tony is from the mountain region also, and he doesn't lose his temper."

"That's true, but it's no longer in my hands. I can't put up with the stupidity and hypocrisy."

"People only learn through experience, and not even then. Patience, Cosme, is the weapon of the spiritually strong, of those who have vision."

He remained quiet for a while and then continued more calmly: "You know what? From now on I'm going to do my job and keep my mouth shut. I won't speak out at meetings any more. Lopes is right: the best man is the one who keeps quiet. And I have a serious personal problem, you can't possibly imagine."

He did have a problem, and it was serious. Without rejecting his native land, he'd made up his mind to become a naturalized American citizen. He did so either because he had been advised to do it, or because he disliked the precarious condition of a mere resident without political rights; I don't know which. Maybe he wanted to feel "equal"; to feel he was a part of something greater than himself. I know of no one else who fought as hard to realize a dream. But only someone who has lived and worked among immigrants can understand. We were at a Portuguese club in New Jersey one night, speaking with a large group about illegal immigrants, and Cosme said at one point: "If we were to count, we'd find that over half of us here are illegals." The others laughed and did not deny it; it was the truth. At that time the number of men who entered the United States illegally was great. Cosme was one of them, but he never told me when, where, or how he had entered. One day he was denounced by some enemy or rival—among these men without women, denouncement is almost always motivated by jealousy—and was arrested.

The Immigration authorities invited him to show cause why he should not be deported. But, either because the case required a lengthy investigation or because the bureaucrats empathized with this uneducated man who was passionately in love with "free America," the fact is they let him go in peace, and advised him to return to his country of origin of his own free will. Which he, needless to say, did not do. He stayed on while others, perhaps older ones, were expelled.

He'd resolved to file his "first papers," that is, his declaration of intention to be naturalized. If, among other things, he could prove that he had entered the U.S. before June, 1924, and had done his military service in Portugal, American law allowed him to leave the country to reenter with an immigrant visa, obtained from an American consul outside the country. Only then would he be able to begin the long bureaucratic process of naturalization.

Well, it seems that he could prove none of those things. He filed petitions and filled out forms, which were never approved. Tired of putting up with him, Immigration officials gave him this friendly advice: "If you come here again with requests, you run the risk of being arrested once again; if you force us to get into your case, no one will be able to keep you from having to go visit your mother."

Blushing and smiling, Cosme replied boldly in his broken English "Well, I won't give you a moment's peace until you make me a citizen. I entered this country of my own free will, I like it, I earn my living here and want to stay. I owe no one anything, have committed no crime, and have not even spent a single day in the hospital without paying for it. If you have me deported, I'll enter again through the Canadian or Mexican border, or I'll jump ship and will come back in even if I have to swim in. Look, I learned to swim in the Douro River."

They laughed and sent him away.

I was busy and preoccupied and did not see him for a long time. In the meantime, many things happened. Along came the Munich Pact and the invasion of Poland, Paris fell and the Germans turned to the East. America, inert, was on the edge of catastrophe. The outlook was bleak, and many times, seeing uniformed men marching in parades with unfurled swastikas, I thought, "What would Cosme say about all this?" Then one day he came to see me. He was concerned. We discussed the situation and found we were in agreement about everything.

Cosme concluded, "Now that it won't be long until America is attacked also, I want to be naturalized more than ever. What if they make me stay here in prison, or deport me without giving me a chance to fight those pirates? Huh? No sir.

I want you to take me to a good lawyer right away. It hasn't been easy getting it all together, but now I have all the papers I need.''

I took him to an attorney I knew, an honest man who specialized in Immigration matters, and left him there. I did not want to know the details of the case. Cosme provided him with all the documents and witnesses he required. About a month and a half later, I heard he had returned; he had gone to Cuba to legalize his situation. He was triumphant, smiling broadly; with his immigrant visa, he was now ready to file his "first papers.''

And suddenly he disappeared. A few months later, the attorney called me to his office. He was furious. What kind of man had I brought to see him? Cosme had lied. The police were looking for him. Where was he hiding? "I don't deal with people like that.'' I was shocked to hear the following account.

Upon seeing him return from Cuba—an immigrant with everything in order—the authorities became curious about how he had been able to prove the unprovable. They had his birthdate and other details checked in Portugal, and came to the conclusion that he had obtained—long distance, by sheer insistence and money—a birth certificate that made him three or four years older than he really was; he'd bribed witnesses and forged documents to prove that he'd lived and worked in the U.S. since 1923. Neither he nor the "witnesses" could be found to account to the authorities, who were convinced he had entered only in 1925 while still a minor. It meant a few years in prison for all of them, deportation, and maybe worse.

How did I know where Cosme was? I tried to explain to the attorney that these men, accustomed to hereditary oppression, always try to slip through the cracks in the inequitable laws, because they have no other recourse. The law for them represents exploitation. Dissimulation, secrecy and contraband are their only defenses. How can we judge them in the light of an evolved ethic? We have to see them through a different prism. But the attorney, feeling his reputation and good faith violated, did not want to hear any excuses. The law is the law.

I left there concerned and wondering. Was Cosme disillusioned? The America he loved refused to accept him and repudiated his strange sacrifice, in the name of judicial technicalities. Now that I knew him well, I was sure that he wasn't capable of committing a crime for money. Had he arrived around 1776, he would have been a Revolutionary War hero, another Peter Francisco. His case transcended current norms and the understanding of people accustomed to seeing the law respected (when it is). But could Justice recognize that he had behaved with the best of intentions, to serve his adopted country? These fervent believers are nearly always supect to the rational.

I tried to track him down for about a month, until one day I caught up with him around Mineola, where he had gone to hide.

"Well, Cosme, what did I do to you that you never came to see me again?"

I saw him blush and try in vain to draw from his throat a confused explanation, and I laughed.

"What did you do? Why are you hiding?"

I walked in and closed the door.

That's when he exploded.

"And what did you want me to do? Did you want me to let them arrest me and deport me? I had no one to turn to; who cares about Cosme, the Portagee? Look at what's happened to the others. Not even the organization wanted to hear me out. We're a weak minority, we have no influence, no prestige, no votes. We're *alone*. Ah! if I'd only gone to see Vito Marcantonio right away, instead of listening to unscrupulous people. Yes sir, I came here at 19, clandestinely, what of it? I arrived here in 1925, so what? What's it to them? I've spent fifteen years working here. Isn't that enough to make a man feel like an American? I was not born here by chance, like them. I came of my own free will, can you understand the difference? I like it here and want to stay. Have I stolen? Have I killed? I have spilled more sweat and blood on the highways, bridges and ports of New York State than have millions of those who were born here. I've slaved and suffered and been happy—yes sir, *happy*— and these are roots every bit as strong as those of birth.

I perjured myself, what of it? It was not to harm anyone. It was to have the right to live and work—and die, if need be—like any citizen. You're staring at me? I know what you're thinking. I, too, want to return, yes sir. Not to hunger and humiliation, but to fight with a weapon in my hand. Why do you think I've worked all these years? You know very well that money means nothing to me. I spent my last dollar to keep those in Portugal who helped me to get the certificates from going to prison. If I ever cross the sea again, it'll be to fight for my rights as a man—to help to overthrow those who want to reduce and subject us to hunger, ignorance and dependency. When this is possible, I will go. But not before, and not alone."

Thus spoke Cosme, flushed with indignation and eloquence, with a spark in his grey eyes that was no longer one of childlike candor. And upon hearing him, my blood boiled in my veins with pride. In his sibilant voice there was an echo of thundering prophecy. He was a fighter ready for anything, ready to bleed and die for what he believed was just and good. And the "land of liberty" was repudiating him. I was the one who had to judge him; that small, humble room was the courtroom—and he would be absolved right then and there, for although it may seem romantic and sentimental, sentiment is still one of the great forces in life.

Cosme knew perfectly well that in his attempt to stay in America, to love her and serve her in what he perceived she had that was good, he had caused more harm to himself than to the Law; and, knowing it, he suffered both for himself and for her ingratitude. Once again I felt we could not judge men and their actions according to the strict letter of the law. An act can, technically, be a crime and the intentions that dictated it be pure. We have already seen intentional, premeditated murderers absolved amid applause, because theirs were "mercy killings" or "crimes of passion." And how many people are walking around this world free and prospering, having committed crimes infinitely greater than Cosme's?

I advised him, nonetheless, to go see the attorney and face the consequences of his actions squarely.

"You believe in Justice, do you not? Well then, if you present your case frankly and with conviction, I'm certain justice will be done.''

I shook his hand and left. But, deep down, I feared for him. His language was not that of a conformist; it was the language of those who place the truth of their principles above all considerations of personal conveniences or of prejudices. He was what we call a "sectarian."

Pearl Harbor was necessary for America to enter the war at last. After some time had passed, a mutual friend informed me that Cosme had enlisted and that his deportation process had been temporarily set aside. He was now a soldier, and he was going to go overseas. A group of friends was giving him a going-away dinner, and would I like to attend? How could I not?

I went to the dinner, in the same club where we had met a few years earlier. When I entered the room, Cosme came to meet me immediately, his hands outstretched, with an open and joyful smile. He seemed more robust, taller and healthier than ever in his well-tailored khaki uniform. The military training had been good for him. We hugged each other.

"Didn't I tell you? I'm going back there, but I'm not going alone, or empty-handed.''

Now that he was a soldier, they would make him a citizen. It would surely happen when he got back. The America of freedom would finally accept this believer, this loyal friend, and Cosme was happy beyond words.

After dinner there were speeches. Cosme rose to speak. I remember his words clearly. He said, ''I'm happy because I'm going to fight for what I've always believed is just. In some way, one has to be able to prove one loves democracy and freedom. If I'm going to war against Fascism, it's because I want to help put an end to the misery and the evil that exists in the world. Before we used to fight with words and with the few bucks we had. But words are not enough. This battle requires our blood as well. I'll give it gladly. And believe what Cosme, the pig-headed, is telling you today because it is quite possible you will never hear him again—and you haven't always wanted to listen. If I die over there, I'll die happily because I'll have done my duty and will have been faithful to what I've always preached. I ask all of you to forgive my offenses. Thank you very much.''

A few days ago, upon opening a little Portuguese-community newspaper, I noticed a column entitled *Luso-Americans killed in Combat*. And, below the title, I read these laconic words that brought a lump to my throat and clouded my vision: "António Cosme, age 37, resident of the Bronx, born in Barqueiros (Douro), in action in North Africa.''

*Translated by* Maria Angelina Duarte

# RETURN TO THE CUPOLA

For more than an hour I had been seated there, in front of the Cafe Martinho, watching the world go by and suffering acutely from a sense of alienation, almost of rejection. I had dreamt of my return as a triumph over Time and over myself and loneliness; as a bridge that might traverse the gulf between past and present, a blissful re-encounter, a glorious and renewed sense of possession—and after a few days I felt confused, distanced, without any connection (other than an imaginary one) to this world which formerly had been mine. Like a depersonalized patient, I began to doubt my own existence. A touch of anxiety warned me that the time for resolution had come.

I had left twenty years before, retaining an ecstatic, crystallized image of all this, an image that was alive and present just inside me, for preserving it meant saving my own skin and retaining a sense of myself as myself. And now I saw with a shock that what I had carried with me was nothing but a bouquet of withered flowers, a well-preserved corpse, from which I had to free myself. My life had been stopped short at a given moment in the past; it was like a still from the movies, old-fashioned and laughable. How could I bring it up to date, make it once again be here, present, moving, taking place? I suffered, then, like someone who, looking at himself in the mirror, cannot recognize his own image. I realized (too late?) that quite insensibly I had been drifting through the world; that in order to live, to survive it all, I had had to undergo a metamorphosis. And no one can match step, all of a sudden, just like that, with the irreversible course of things and of Time. On top of all that, I had gotten older as well, which was just as serious a matter.

I had borne with smiling face the loneliness of the world and the struggle, for I had carried within me, like a talisman, that crystallized image, but I wouldn't be able to bear this new loneliness, so unexpected, surrounded by people and things that had once been familiar to me, that had once been mine. More than twenty years of toil and trouble in the fixed hope of coming home, of reestablishing myself, of being—and suddenly it all seemed a lost effort, a useless task, a dead weight, life lived in vain. Worse: as if, in order to go on living, in order not to sink, I would now have to free myself from something that had, without my knowing it, become an inescapable part of me, and that no longer fit in with the present.

To disengage myself from a dead weight—it was easy to say! And then what? Then, I would be like a man who has missed his train. This life had continued on its course, while I had followed my deflected destiny, with a mummified vision hidden in my breast. How could I take my place again among those who had passed me and gone off in another direction? Only now did I understand certain ominous dreams that, out there, had so often attacked me: seeing myself lost in a crowd of strangers, surrounded by ruins, running after something, after someone fleeing from me, meeting friends and acquaintances who wouldn't recognize me or who would turn away from me.

I looked around—someone to talk to, if you would only talk to me. My conversations now were like those of all emigrants without family. I would talk to the doorman at the hotel, the waiter in the cafe, the barber, a chance woman. Someone. Someone who would recognize and restore me, link me once again to the continuity in me and in things. (Not like yesterday's newsboy, from whom I had bought a paper with a silver coin; the kid looked at the money in astonishment, lifted two fingers to his beret, did a somersault, and gave me a wink. "O.K., American!" — More than twenty years of faithful love, and a smart-alec comes along, a little genius of observation, and labels me foreigner in bold face.

The sun, meanwhile, had been smearing the surrounding houses with honey, and now it came to sprawl at the cafe tables with the laziness of an old cat in a boarding house for widows. On the Pombaline rooftops the moss of yesteryear was turning green again. In the warm breeze there floated the heavy smoke of cigarettes, the thick murmur of voices, an almost nauseating sweetness, a warm suggestion of sensuality, a troubled drowsiness. The gentle breeze was the same as always—as were the shouts, the cries, the rattling of the streetcars, the blaring of horns, snatches of songs, exclamations, arpeggios of a guitar weeping from the cornices like garlands at a festival that has come to an end. Dolled-up demoiselles, more Parisian than those in Paris, passed by, treading with provincial firmness the asphalt of imaginary Europes. The same old yearning for Something-Else leaping over inner barriers—ideas, new books, *chapeaux*, beautiful refugees, eagles, flags, films, *Ici-Radio-Paris...* everything that no longer existed. Just a little less fervor, a touch of forgetfulness. But underneath it all, I suddenly sensed that the drama was really still the same, the hope and the despair of former times still the same—simply more evident and, at the same time, more masked.

I looked around again and sighed. Yes, it was always in the drama of people's lives that I had known how to find myself again. Over there, just as here. And with that comforting thought, I felt that I was beginning to re-enter the general flow of things. I didn't see any familiar faces, it's true, and no one recognized me. (On the other hand, I always went unnoticed wherever I was.) Ah, but I knew them in another, impersonal and subtle, way—as people, as drama. I had an advantage over them. I was one of them and yet I watched them as if I were not. The same and different, alien and a part of them. They thought they had changed, but they were really the same, for their drama in essence hadn't changed. My heart beat more quickly. I myself, a stranger now—might it not be the same with me? The same hot blood of love, the same gelatinous and unifying lymph, the same indefinable feeling that annoints us all?

Until that moment I had been watching them as a solitary, compassionate conscience observes a drop of life through a microscope. And I felt with a start that I was bursting through a barrier and penetrating into that drop of sparkling life; that I was becoming absorbed and integrated into it, and that I would finally dissolve, flow into, become one with it, in a word *be*. And that reintegration, that surrender to the flow of passing people, that mutual impregnation of subject and object, gave me a liquid impulse of love so vehement and profound; that double vision was such a rich source of comfort, pleasure, and joy to me, that I had to cover my eyes with my hands so that no one would see my tears.

At that moment, a group of hurried travelers, loaded down with suitcases and bags, ran across the square in the direction of the Station. I looked up at the clock and checked it against my watch. "The express for Sintra leaves at 1:50," I murmured. And I leaped to my feet. The gentleman at the table next to mine, who had been struggling for the truth between the lines in the newspaper, jumped with fright, suspecting perhaps that I was about to attack him. I paid my bill and began to run across the square, filled with its sunlight and confusion, following the travelers, who had already climbed the steps of the entrance.

I went straight to the ticket window.

"Sintra, round-trip. Can I still catch the express?"

The ticket agent looked at the clock and calmly replied, "You have five minutes."

So, I'd made it for sure. Surprised and happy, impatient as a twenty-year-old with the slowness of the escalator, I mounted the stairs two at a time. It was as if I had picked the winning number in a lottery, this strange jubilation, this certainty that something was still going on, a secret just between me and the world of my return. A few moments later, miraculously ensconced in the second-class carriage, with that pleasant taste of smoke on my tongue, I heard once again the nostalgia-laden whistle of the locomotive, the same as when... "But what a bore," I thought. "Leave it all alone. Today is *today*."

Those excursions to Sintra had always been my great joy. Of course, I loved cultivated fields, beaches, bullfights, soccer; but whenever I felt the need to flee this simulacrum of Hell open to the Heavens—it was Sintra for me. There I would walk all the blessed day, my hat in my hand, a whistle on my lips, ah, the good shade, Seteais, the fountains, luncheon at the *Lawrence* (or at the *Pomblnhu*, depending on my finances), then the Capuchine monastery, the ruins, the Pena. Once, I even fell asleep, alone, on the battlements of the Moorish Castle. It was in the summer; I can't remember another August that hot. The most extraordinary thing—I'll never forget it—was that the sun set just at the very moment that the moon, in its full glory, burst forth. A spectacle like no other I had ever seen, no, not the midnight sun nor the aurora borealis. There were two suns, one of them larger, the other redder, hanging on the horizon, on opposite sides of the world. It was like an hallucination or a case of natural reflection. For a few moments I had the illusion of confronting a "phenomenon" or a cataclysm. The universe stopped and hung motionless between those two enormous eyeballs of copper and red. Then the sun went down, and the moon rose, turned pale and cold, and became a moon out of the ballad to Soares de Passos. Well, in the end, I stayed there all night and, as a matter of fact, wore myself out chattering with cold, up there without an overcoat, in an August hotter than any spoken of in tales of enchantment.

"And here I am, headed for Sintra, no more no less, just because a noisy bunch thought to cross the square just at the hour when there used to be an express, with me seated there gnawing over my problems on the terrace of the Martinho." Looking out at the harsh countryside of Cacém, a silly question came to me: "Do they still have black swans in the lake?"

Having arrived in Sintra, I shook the torpor from my legs by walking to town. What had always attracted me there, above all, was the vegetation, the shade, the fountains, the scenery, the heights. Standing now in the Gothic archway of the Royal Palace, I looked up at the Pena heights and wished I had wings to fly above the rocky crags, graze the tops of the trees, and land on those towers and battlements worthy of Walt Disney. But, to be frank, I had neither the wings nor the legs. Seen from down here in the town, the Pena seemed to me a most forbidding affair, an eagle's nest, a mythic rock, a mound of infuriated monsters, claws set, tearing at the sky. How could I have climbed up there once on foot, after having hiked all the way from Lisbon? And what was it that was now drawing me up there again, what memory, what beloved thought, what secret desire, what yearning to leap over the gulf of Time, what heart-rending nostalgia, or breadth of vision? For it was there that some need was calling me.

I ran to take a carriage that was quietly ageing in the plaza, tied to some worn-out nags, and asked to be driven post-haste to the Pena. No, not to Seteais, not to Capuchinos, not even up to the Cruz Alta—but to the Pena. In a short time, legs crossed, hat in my lap, a whistle on my lips, my soul set free, a fresh breeze on my sweaty pate—amidst the creaking of the springs and the panting of the exhausted beasts, I was ascending the Mount of mounts. I asked to stop at the fountain, and there I drank, repeating the well-known gestures of one who re-establishes an old friendship or practices a ritual.

I got down in the Park, told the coachman to wait, and walked up with a group of tourists to repeat my visit to the castle. The same as ever. The guide (I could have sworn I recognized him) again showed us the ingenious liquor service of King Dom Luiz the First. In the study of Senhora Dona Amelia, pointing to the writing desk, the guide monotonously chanted the information that tourists always listen to in a religious, historical silence: "And here we still can see the very magazines that her Royal Majesty was reading when they came to bring her the news of the establishment of the Republic. Everything is exactly as she left it when she fled to Ericeira."

I leaned over a blue velvet cordon and noticed an old copy of the *Pall-Mall Gazette*, the color of weathered brick. Well now, the last time I was here, I'm certain, the cover was *blue*. But what difference does it make. The musty smell in that crypt of royalty made me nauseous, there among drapes that a breath would turn to dust. Impatiently, I turned my eyes to the windows and the blue sky, the outline of the mountains, the distant sea, the tattered clouds outside. It was this that had always drawn me there, and not those funereal curiosities.

We finally came out on top, on the cupola, and I took a deep breath and felt renewed. Ah yes, that, that was what was royal and everlasting. Fingers pointing, the tourists punched holes in the canvas of the countryside: Mafra, Cabo da Rocha, barra do Tejo. There were mouths agape with Ohs and Ahs. They could see everything. But I could see more and much further. A panorama that stretched beyond the horizon, back through my soul for a good forty years. I withdrew from the group and stood alone before it. And then I decided to climb to the top of the cupola by the outer stairway, the kind that makes one dizzy. The guide was against it and said that he would not be held responsible. The other tourists offered me sensible advice, saying that it was dangerous, that one false step and zap... I climbed up nonetheless, almost on tip-toes. One had to have nails. And yet it wasn't the first time.

Having almost reached the top, I sat down on the stairs and rested, all alone. To be alone up there was not to be lonely; it was to be withdrawn, on retreat, plunging my roots into something other than the panorama that actually surrounded me; absorbed in watching a picture with a second vision that gave me an inestimable advantage over the others who lacked it. Seated there, I remembered how often in this world, hearing the wind sigh in the windows of a sad Chicago skyscraper or in the rigging of a lonely ship, I had suddenly felt myself transported by nostalgia back many years and many leagues to the heights of this mountain range and of this cupola. I would then shut my eyes, and the world around me would cease to exist—there would remain only that sweet, grave, and gentle hum of the musical wind, and I would see myself again, with head bare, bathed in sun and freshness, at the top of the cupola, listening to the murmur of the Atlantic breeze, filled with distances, Indias, and illusions, with calls, chimeras, sirens, and worlds. I would be lying were I to say that those moments did not make up for much hardness and difficulty in my life; for even the most practical and realistic of men (and I am one of them), those who most value diving in and losing themselves, taking part, entering the struggle, feel, at times, that impulse of absence, of asceticism, of flight and withdrawal. This time, the moment towered inside me higher than the mountains themselves.

I closed my eyes. The wind blew, with its grave and gentle murmur, and caressed my face with fresh hands of invisible love. I breathed deeply, breathing in all the lost years that were returning, but now with a strong and deep tranquility. Now the breeze no longer brought me that other time's mysterious call from beyond. Those worlds (should I regret it?) had lost for me the attraction of things unknown. I had learned what only useless experience teaches us: that the call is in us, and not in things. It was a breeze of restitution, which gave me back to myself, and to my things, and to my people. Seated there alone—that is to say, seeing the countryside as time and action, separated from the group of tourists with no secret intimacy with the surroundings—I let myself be enveloped, bathed, penetrated by the blue, the sun, the freshness and the horizons. I floated like a body without weight; I was filled, I was dissolved, I was in communion. Beneath the caress of the breeze singing in my ears, come from so far and deep within, so much my familiar and confidant, I let all that, the blue sky, the bitter sea (if you only knew), the green of crops, dark patches of brush, outlines of mountains, fallow fields, naked and brown, sand and glistening foam, the sheer slopes of icy peaks, the flight of birds, all of it melt together with me in a mighty harmony. The breath of the ocean's immense curve called forth in me a great élan, a gush of life-spirit that had always been there. Upon how many others had it not exercised its magical attraction, its illusory song, drawing them far away, race that we are of hearts broken by the Earth? But as for me, that breeze from the blue carried me now only to the Indies-right-here-at-home. I let myself be possessed by the joy of an endless resurgence that could only be compared to the spreading of wings in a dream, to a floating into space, from there on the Pena itself. A joy that came neither from the scenery nor the breeze, but just from me myself, from the certainty of being alive and well, of having survived it all, of having climbed up here, returned unto myself, from my dissipation among alien things and beings, of feeling finally that I was going on, that things no longer would repel me like a stranger, that perhaps I would belong to myself once again.

Clinging to the fragile railing so as not to fall—my hat pressed tight between my knees—I surrendered totally to the voluptuous dizziness of being there. The sun streamed over my face, sweetly; it warmed my eyelids like a prolonged kiss, in a purple brightness that didn't burn. I soared in the light, and with it I reached the peak of euphoria.

Just then, down below, a sudden tumult arose among the tourists, a confused scuffling with muffled cries. I leaned over, and what I saw made my blood curdle. At the foot of the staircase, a fat man, bareheaded and in shirt-sleeves (his shirt, by the way, a bright blue), was straining to free himself from the arms of other men, struggling to climb up after me. His gestures, movements, tone, all were suggestive of a disconcerting intention. Perhaps he wants to kill himself, I thought in horror. Looking down from above, I saw the powerful red nape of his neck glistening with sweat, his curly locks shaking in the struggle. My heart pounded painfully. The man leaped from the arms that were holding him back, quickly ran up a few steps, stopped, and turned toward me his torn and troubled face: and I, without knowing him, recognized him. In a mixture of fear and confusion, I called forth the memory of a strange hatred, of a rival. A *rival?* And what did he want now, with so many years gone by and everything forgotten? And suddenly it all became clear to me. He had come here for revenge. And I felt the imminence of great danger.

I was practically at the top, just a few feet from the cupola's spire. Beyond this highest point, true end of the earth, which one could only reach by crawling along a dangerously steep slope, was space, the abyss, nothingness, certain death. There was nowhere to flee. Unless, by a prodigious feat only possible in dreams, I could float away in the ether, there was only one course of action, and even that of dubious value: to defend myself tooth and nail. And for this I prepared myself. If I didn't flee, it wasn't for lack of wanting to. The demoniac mounted slowly, approaching with feline care, to tear me from the stairs. I don't know if my blood was boiling or freezing; I had ceased to feel it at all. He paused, and I could now see his huge, bestial face contorted with hatred and contempt, glistening with sweat, demented. He bared his strong white teeth and snarled: "This time you won't escape me."

The dizziness of danger blocked all else from my consciousness. I only knew that that man had lured me there for his revenge. I grasped the rusted handrail with determination and vowed to sell myself dearly. My body tensed, I waited for him to reach the point where I could kick him one in the jaw. And that's what happened. A moment later, with a leap, he tried to grab my feet. Solidly positioned, and from above, I aimed a double kick at his head that made him sway. Blood spurted from his nose. But he quickly returned to his task. Then, sure of myself, I unleashed an array of blind kicks at his face, his head, his formidable huge paws stretched out like tentacles trying to grab hold of my shins. Never would I have thought myself capable of such vigor and agility. Again and again I hammered his skull with the heels of my shoes: at first, with a natural impulse of legitimate defense, in a panting rage—but then, as I warmed up, with a positive pleasure, an incarnation of troglodite blood-thirstiness. For the first time in my life I had lost my head and had gratified myself thus upon an adversary. And it shocked me to note that it felt almost voluptuous.

Both of us gasping for breath—he below, powerful, roaring, foaming at the mouth, hideous with rage, only his teeth white in the sticky dark mask of blood, I above, clinging to the railing, teeth clenched, throwing myself in violent plunges against the aggressor's skull, with all the weight of my 175 pounds. But that head was made of steel, of reinforced concrete; anyone else in his position would have already passed out, his brains splattered about, would have crashed down to the ground or have died right there on the spot. My feet were aching from so much kicking, and he was still trying to grab my legs, as if I were hitting him with a flower. His strength had not abandoned him, nor did pain cause him to hesitate. On the contrary, it seemed as if his rage and his energy redoubled as we fought on.

I understood that nothing would make that indestructible enemy give up, that my strength, even though multiplied by the threat of danger, would fail me before he would give out. In a moment of clarity, all the time kicking and twisting to keep my legs out of his implacable clutches, I saw the scene as if I were below, among the spectators, At the peak of that steep cupola, from which there was no escape but in death, two men were fighting to mutual annihilation for obscure motives; if exhaustion were to overcome them, if the railing were to give way, or if they were to end up grappling hand to hand—they would roll across the metal-covered cupola like a couple of cats locked in battle, only to be torn to pieces on the battlements of the Castle or on the rocky cliffs below. Or, if I were to weaken, it was almost certain that the other would drag me from my vantage point by my feet, and perhaps hurl me, by brute force, out into... It was absolutely imperative to continue to batter his huge head until he gave up—or till his brains came pouring out.

But that moment of lucidity weakened me. I wanted to cry for help, maybe even beg abjectly for a truce, for pardon, who knows. Taking advantage of the opening, the aggressor grabbed me by the shin with a hand of steel, and I felt myself being pulled violently down. I saw that my strength was about to fail me, that it was trickling off into space. Would this be the end of everything? Silently, I cried farewell to life. Just then, a great exclamation of horror rose from the spectators. Sensing their support, I came back to life. Calling on all my reserves of strength, clinging to the handrail as if to the last hope, I gave a tremendous jerk and flung out at the attacker. Taken perhaps by surprise, the devil lost his balance, let go of my leg, slid down the stairs, fell backwards, rolled off with a hideous bellow, and went tumbling into space with a convulsive leap, like a wounded leopard.

Dripping with sweat, terrified, in agony, I drew back, almost rising in a posture of involuntary defense against the fall, and I saw him fly through the air, flailing first his arms, then his

81

legs, like a windmill—or as if he wished to swim, a futile hope—as he described the astonishing curve of an acrobat on the flying trapeze, his mouth wide in a scream of rage and death, his glaring round eyes growing smaller and smaller, his body spinning in the end like a rag doll, until he hit the ramparts down below and, bouncing off, disappeared in the vegetation and the rocks.

The confused uproar of the crowd continued, then degenerated into peals of laughter, and I felt a weight like lead in my frozen legs. Limp and weak, I saw that I was losing consciousness, sobbing...

In fact, I woke from the nightmare. I opened my eyes. The guard, in a rage, was shaking my foot, bellowing: "Wake up, damn you. Wake up, for Christ sake."

At the foot of the stairway, in a cluster, the tourists were laughing themselves sick. I understood it all. I had let myself fall asleep, rocked by the breeze, under the open sky, with my hat squeezed between my knees, at almost two thousand feet of altitude and nostalgia. I had climbed up there to take my afternoon nap. And the people down below, watching the painful mimicry of my nightmare, had filled themselves with pleasure at my expense. I must have been quite a sight, kicking right and left, jerking about, probably growling—until the guard, fearing that I might lose my grip or else stay there all afternoon and cause a scandal, had decided to climb cautiously up the stairway and jerk me awake. And all this had lasted perhaps no more than a moment.

I went down embarrassed and confused, my face burning, disturbed quite beyond any reason. The guard muttered, while shaking the dust from his uniform: "He almost knocked me off with all his kicking! Look at these two smacks he gave me, right here." And there were the prints of my shoes, quite clear, right across the chest of his modest uniform. "What an idea, to go up there to take a snooze. Didn't I tell you? If I wanted to, I could have you arrested."

I put a tip in his hand and, with lowered head, not daring to face the amused tourists, who opened an aisle for me to pass through, much abashed, I left. What bothered me most of all was something that, luckily, they couldn't have seen: that exhibition of valor *in a dream*.

When I found myself in the Park again, safe and alone, I sat down on a bench beside the pond to watch the swans, some of which, by the way, were still black. I was slowly calming down and beginning to think things over. But where did that image come from? "Where the devil did I dig up that face, that *rival* whom I had never set eyes on before, if in my whole life I couldn't remember having had a single conflict, hatred, or fight?" Calmer, I dried my forehead with my handkerchief. "And how could I have recognized him? My rival. Rival in what?"

Frankly, now that the shock of the dream was over, what I felt was neither fright nor shame: it was relief, it was almost a sense of satisfaction. As if through that imaginary person I had satisfied buried desires to attack, beat, and kill. It was as if I had been freed from a weight. I had a confused feeling that something had induced me to come to the top of the cupola of Pena, to free myself from a hypothetical persecutor and leave the place with this sensation of relief. In truth, I did not understand so quickly what it was all about.

As I was reflecting thus, rather bewildered, I lifted my eyes to the cupola, on whose parapet other tourists appeared, black figures looking out, exclaiming, piercing the horizon with pointing fingers. And for the first time in many years, I was surprised by the sudden memory, so live and so real, of cousin Henriqueta. It must have been about twenty years ago. She was about sixteen and I must have been twenty-four. There had been a hazy romance between us, oh, far less than a courtship. She had been timid and pure then, and I, a young wastrel, a vagabond, given to revelry, carousing, gambling, bullfights, women, and wine. I had never had that kind of a sweetheart before. Love, for me at that time—only the kind that quickly bore fruit and as quickly withered away. As for her, no one had ever known her to have a suitor.

The memory grew clearer. I had taken them one day to Sintra. Her mother, the widow of a distant cousin of mine, didn't dare climb up to the cupola, and so remained in one of the rooms below, seated in a leather chair, gasping from asthma, and counseling us: "Well now, watch out children. Take care and don't lean out too far. It could make you dizzy."

We got dizzy alright, but in a way that was different and a lot sweeter. We were alone up there in the warm breeze, framed by this very same sun and blue sky. And there, on the parapet of that cupola in execrable taste, looking out at the countryside and breathing in the smells carried by the breeze, both of us penetrated by an ineffable desire, I had taken her in my unfeeling bohemian arms, and for the first time we had kissed. We remained locked together in fervor and tenderness, feeling that the desire and love we shared had been there for a long time, ever since her childhood. I gave her long, slow kisses on her eyes, on her cheeks burning with emotion, on her succulent and ingenuous mouth, half-open in wonder. Then we came down from the Mount and from our dream.

Some time having passed, resolved to behave with prudence, I left Portugal as a sailor on a freighter, to learn the ropes in this Godforsaken world of ours. I did not think of my cousin again, at least not consciously. I sailed the seven seas and was well on my way to being a bachelor. We never wrote and I never heard anything about her.

And now, seated on that bench in the Park, looking up at the tower, I remembered her image as I had seen it for the last time, white and modest, in a somber little dress, on the veranda of the house, with her ringlets of hair falling free, lifting her handkerchief to her eyes as if waving me good-bye forever. So vivid and real was my memory that my heart beat with tenderness, as on the afternoon of kisses at the Pena. I smiled—that *rival* of my dream, pure fantasy. Yet he was connected with the idea, the memory of her. It all seemed so ridiculous that I burst out laughing. But I quickly stopped. I, who in a dream had so brutally beaten him, with blood-thirsty delight, now felt a pious gratitude for this strange character, creation and victim of my fantasy, the fruit perhaps of a sweet memory that was just reawakening. I almost felt remorse for having mistreated him, and wanted to go to lay flowers on the spot where, in my imagination, he had been smashed to bits.

I looked up again at the tower where twenty years before I had sworn a false love, and, my eyes brimming with tears, I murmured: "Thank you, noble and stupid tower, with your vapid bourgeois-king's cupola. They served some purpose back then, those castle towers where one could furtively kiss one's cousin, a shy, protected creature and a virgin."

I lowered my eyes to my watch without thinking. Three twenty-five. I got to my feet. The carriage was still awaiting me at the Park entrance. If the schedule of some twenty years ago held true, there would be an express for Lisbon at 3:55—and I had to catch it. I would be at the Rossio an hour later; I would take a taxi to Rua dos Navegantes. I had to see her, it was urgent that I talk to her, remember, relive—if only she hadn't, pushing forty, become a fat matron, married, the mother of children, with no memory of me. But what difference—better disillusionment than uncertainty—and I fostered an overwhelming hope that made me light as a feather. The dream that had drawn me there, that had almost thrown me down from the cupola, that had awakened memories binding me again to the past, couldn't fail to continue, to end well, to be a truly happy dream. In smashing to a pulp that rival, in seeing him turn to jelly on the rocky outcroppings of the mountain, who knows if it wasn't my mistaken and forgetful past that I, in a dream, was destroying forever, hurling it down into the abyss? Might it not have been a new life, restored, simple, down-to-earth, that I was, in some obscure way, fantasizing, and that now was bursting forth in my lonely heart like a flower of remembrance of that idyll, that kiss, that sweet and languid cousin who... Hurry!

I ran through the Park, leaped into the worn-out victoria, and ordered the coachman to make all haste for the station. The old nags tore down the mountain, sparks flying. I dashed into the station like the wind. I caught the 3:55 express (the same as twenty years before), arrived at the Rossio shortly before five, grabbed a cab, told him to rush over to Rua dos Navegantes—and at exactly five-fifteen was squeezing my "little cousin" Henriqueta in my arms, Henriqueta, fresh, single, and delicate, a mature woman, now bereft—and still as I had left her more than twenty years back. Just a tiny bit fuller.

Some time after the wedding, thinking about the dream on the cupola, of which I had never managed to speak to my wife, a flood of retrospective jealousy rose in me, with no apparent cause, and I discretely questioned her on the subject of admirers. She swore that she had been faithful to me and that she had kept herself untouched for my sake. But, when she was about twenty-five, not having heard anything from me, tired of waiting and dreaming, seeing her youth pass by, and her mother beginning to fail, she decided to accept the courtship of a very serious man of about forty who had a bit of money. What could a girl do in this world, unmarried, poor, and unprotected? Spend the rest of her life bent over her sewing? And her mother with one foot in the grave.

"I consider it perfectly legitimate. And what became of him? Did you break up? Tell me."

"Well, there came a time when I understood that I could never come to love him. My only love, from childhood, was you, and you were still alive within me. And then I had sworn I would only marry the man I loved. Furthermore, he knew; I told him. Poor fellow, he had a strange character: ill-natured, hot-tempered and jealous. Even Mama, who would have died to see me married, went so far as to say, "That man, may God forgive me, doesn't seem to be all there. Better watch out, he's likely to make trouble some day."

"What kind of a man was he?" I asked, my mouth gone dry. Henriqueta described him with gestures—thus and thus. It was the living portrait of my rival at the Pena. I hadn't the courage to say a word. She went on.

"Until one day," she began again, without, so far, having noticed my impatience, "I decided to call it off. I wrote him a letter sending him away, and I went to Caldas with Mama, since the hot baths there made her feel better. Two days later she came rushing into my room, a newspaper in her hand. The poor man had suddenly gone crazy."

Turning pale with nervousness, I persisted: "He went crazy? And then? What happened? Tell me the rest."

My wife stopped working on the embroidery she had in her hands and looked at me, surprised at the tone of my voice.

"Imagine what got into his head. He went to Sintra, climbed up to the cupola of the Pena, and threw himself down from there. He ended up smashed to bits on the rocks below."

"O.K., O.K., let's not talk about it anymore. Let the dead bury the dead."

I dried the sweat from my forehead and got up to give her a kiss. My eyes were glistening with tears. Only now did I feel that the past was dead, and that I was wholly integrated once again.

*Translated by* Alexis Levitin

## DR. CROSBY'S CHRISTMAS
## (FROM THE DIARY OF AN EXPATRIOT)

(November ____ )

The house pleased us immediately—it was old, with two large rooms, high ceilings, old-fashioned fireplaces, and the whole terrace glassed-in from the backyard, a genuine solarium where it would be good to work. Our street, a short way from the docks, runs into West St. to the left: bars, gloomy shops, shady hotels, dark warehouses, the smell of tar, smoke from ships, sirens, the shifting of freight cars, the creaking of cranes, the incessant flow of men and merchandise. At night, an empty silence of exhaustion, masquerading as pastoral tranquility. In the other direction, to the east, everything changes: middle-class houses, mostly of brick, various businesses, bars, and movie houses with a mixed clientele. Occasionally, passing that way at night, I've been approached by men of foreboding demeanor and firm body who, with a scarcely reassuring arrogance, have asked me for a nickel for a cup of coffee or the subway.

In the middle of this contrast between East and West, the green and red island of the Presbyterian Seminary fills an entire block across the way: velvet lawns, great leafy trees, now naked, the austere grace of imitation English Gothic, in stone and brick with the usual New York patina—a great mass of buildings, harmonious in their studiedly free irregularity, dominated by the tall severe tower of a rural university. In the heart of Manhattan, I have the comforting impression of being back on the other side. (We always want to be back on the "other side"...) The church faces Ninth Avenue to the east. At some remove from faith, I am pleased by these touches of silence and verdure, of refuge and architectural gravity in the tumultuous midst of the cancerous city. Alien lives, absorbed, all turned toward the great emptiness of Eternity. This is a neighborhood of professors, artists, those who read books, peaceful, progressive folk leading a Spartan existence. Far from luxury and glamour. All this attracts me to the place. It was Nathan who gave us the address. As for the rent, a real find. It seems too good to be true. Betsy, clapping her hands with pleasure, dances a few steps of *swing* in the brown park. We decide to take it. The day after tomorrow we move in.

(November ____ )

With our half dozen modest pieces of furniture, the apartment, half-naked, seems enormous. A studio, exactly what I need. As I'll be stuck in here almost all the time, it's good to have room to stretch my legs. A work shirt, sandals, to one side the table, to the other, on the terrace, the amateur's easel. The parquet floor creaks at every joint. In the fireplace in the front room one can make a good fire: the radiator is worthless. Mina, who was here today, said right away: "You could give parties here, even hold meetings!"

Both rooms have doors leading out onto the corridor, with its black and white marble tiles; the main entrance of the building is through a door at the top of some steps. Over here it's called the first floor; the floor below, the ground floor, a foot lower than street level, had two barred windows over the paltry lawn in front and a private iron door hidden beneath the stairs. In front, a fence, also of cast iron, separates the lawn from the sidewalk. Above us, on the second floor, lives a bachelor lawyer; we don't know who lives on the third floor, and on the fourth, its three little windows tucked right up on top, practically a garret, there lives an "artistic couple." That's what the janitor told us. Like so many houses in New York, this one had once been the home of a single well-to-do family: now it's divided into apartments, with five tenants. But it retains an atmosphere of intimacy, accentuated by the hall with its tarnished mirror above the console where the postman each morning leaves the mail for all the occupants.

The cubicle that serves us as a bathroom (without a bathtub) has another little door leading to the end of the hall, where I came upon a narrow stairway leading to the ground floor (our downstairs neighbors, then, have two entrances). Our kitchen is on the terrace, in the corner, facing the door, with a little wooden staircase going down to the yard, nothing but scattered weeds and clotheslines for the wash. Already I am dreaming of turning it into a garden. No great comfort here, but one can live without it. What matters is work.

My papers in order, a half dozen books on the shelves, a few modest paintings on the huge walls, the telephone—I feel that everything will go smoothly. It's about time. I'm anxious to set to work.

(December ____ )

This morning, as soon as I opened my eyes, I heard a piano filling the house with sonority: Chopin, a mazurka, and played by the hand of a master. That's something that has always made me well-disposed for the rest of the day, to wake up to music. I, who spent my childhood and youth surrounded by the harmony of music, had lived so starved of it here (since we couldn't even buy a radio) that, upon hearing those vigorous chords, I felt my eyes filling with tears. The desire to dance, sing, make poetry overwhelmed me. Betsy, a real early bird, came from the kitchen smiling, with an egg in her hand (you could already smell the coffee):

91

"Beautiful, eh? But a bit 'forte.'"

"Is it from here in the building?"

"It must be the girl on the fourth floor. She's a pianist and loves to dance."

I watch the sun, still fresh, cast its light on the backs of the buildings across the yard from us. Betsy slides open the large mahogany door separating the two rooms and pulls up the shades of the front windows: the sun enters with a lively, joyful rush, crossing the house from one side to the other. I make out the dark red mass of the seminary. A great peace fills the street, and its warm and empty amplitude gives joy to my exiled heart. When I think of the dark little room in the Village, where we began! All this is her doing. Darling! I get up and kiss her with love and gratitude.

In the middle of the afternoon, I see a thin, ashen fellow, dragging one of his legs a bit, enter down below through the barred door beneath the stairs. He looks at me with surprise and doesn't respond to my light nod of the head. (Idiot, who am I to be greeting him?) Who could the guy be? A day of intense activity, putting my things in order, arranging my papers. At one, I go out to eat lunch at a coffee shop counter, then return to work. In the afternoon, I go and meet Betsy. We come home to give the house those final little touches necessary for us to have more than a most austere happiness.

Six, six-thirty, again I hear music and I search out the source: this time it's from down below. A warm, grave, suggestive voice, the lament of a woman without tears, accompanied by a piano. "A torchsinger!" says Betsy, widening her eyes and letting out a whistle. And she's the real thing, with her wail and her defiance edged in vice, a real tough, with hairy armpits and a razor in her garter. It's the song of the lower depths coming from down there. Nothing bad about it, we enjoy hearing it. The house fills with a gentle and voiceless vibration. The unpleasant image of the pale man returns to me. I'm annoyed, angry at myself for having greeted him without knowing him.

At night the janitor appears, a man with glasses and few words, a German, with the look of a justice of the peace. We inquire as to our neighbors: he answers vaguely that they are teachers, artists. We immediately imagine that they are people who earn their living playing and singing in night clubs. What we were hearing was a rehearsal for the floor-show later that night. What luck, eh? We will have, for free, live, something that still retains for me the irresistible charm of the new, although it's a bit *louche*. New York excites me with its tragic and convulsive movement. Ah, that it may last. We go to bed early. Betsy, level-headed: "Don't get too carried away, these night-club performers sometimes have habits that are just a bit..." She doesn't finish the sentence.

(December _____ )

At two in the morning I awake with a start: what is this, am I hearing an orchestra? I sit up in bed and listen, mouth agape. Betsy sleeps on: the little dear could sleep through an earthquake; it comes from having a good conscience. The sound rises from below, firm, grave, muffled, yet loud enough to have awakened me. The house vibrates silently. Damn, it seems a bit early (or rather late) for that kind of a rehearsal. Could they have come back from... But wait a second, that's Wagner! What in hell... night club performers playing Wagner? Hmm, maybe for the sake of variety... Performers with other aspirations. But Lord, how many of them would be needed to produce the sound of an orchestra? The house is large, it could easily hold twenty or more people. An orchestra could indeed play, but positively not *live*, in an apartment of that size. I don't know what to think. The concert lasts till after three, then the music ends and I can hear the murmur of voices: perhaps they are discussing the performance. I fall asleep without managing to notice if anyone has left the building. That they played to perfection down there, of that there can be no doubt.

(December _____ )

Christmas is almost upon us. The sky has clouded over, the sun which we enjoyed for almost two solid weeks has disappeared, but in compensation the cold has abated. Rain has come, the days are gloomy but short. In the slow darkening of these gray afternoons, I watch hurried passers-by returning from the docks or from offices, headed for a humble meal, annonymous shadows hunched over in the wind and gusts of rain. From the sky, a blend of pale blue and watery pink, an unreal peace seems to flow down with the rain. The seminary grows, expanding in the twilight; and suddenly the stained-glass windows of the church light up, but faintly, like a kaleidoscope, with gold preponderant. It almost gives the illusion of... In the warm silence of verdure and humidity, along with the distant, threatening murmur of the city, there comes to me the grave resonance of hymns and the muffled voice of the organ. Further up, on Ninth Avenue, the neon signs of the bars and taverns are turned on, filling the mist with the light of a flickering fireplace. Further off are the movie houses, which scatter upon the air their multi-colored tremor. And only now do I understand the attraction of all those opiates for the men who pass along the wet and hostile streets, under the weight of a day of drudgery and with the prospect perhaps of nothing but a solitary and anguished evening ahead. Men seek out their narcotics.

Late at night, putting aside my work, I rise from the table and go to the window to look at the great mass of the seminary: rooftops, towers, spires, stand out in the fog reddened by the bright lights.The peace of God in the incessant tumult. I see a light go on in a distant Tudor garret: someone studying or praying. The great oak trees marking the church grounds stand forth to their outermost branches, stripped bare, with the precision of a Japanese miniature in the lacquer of the flaming sky. The enormous trunks, dripping wet, ominously reflect the lights of a passing car. And the city suddenly gives off a loneliness that stifles me. I feel a great desire to flee before it envelopes me... I can only free myself by writing a poem.

(December ____ )

Today, in the middle of the afternoon, Grieg. Seated at the table putting my notes in order, I gave a start. Grieg! If at least

94

it were the torch-singer! They must find Grieg appropriate to the festive season. The building vibrates and shudders, echoing like a resonating box to the March of the Dwarves, played with great vigor, as if we were at a popular concert in the Hippodrome. Just now when I have begun to immerse myself in Spinoza! It is impossible to concentrate like this, impossible to work. Grieg. There's nothing I adore more than music, but nothing can distract me more, paralyzing whatever mental effort I might make. It's another opium. I begin to grow uneasy at this point. It's been three or four days since I've really gotten anything done. Music, music... Too much of a good thing! And then there's the question of personal taste, or of being in the proper mood for listening to Beethoven or Maria Cachucha. Music, so deeply subjective in its effect, is only heard well collectively. It's one thing to listen to a symphony buried in an armchair or perched high in the gallery of a concert hall, and quite another to persevere in thinking, sleeping, or working (or even listening to music!) while seated atop a gigantic organ, with this prickling at the soles of one's feet and one's whole body in a sort of St. Vitus dance or convulsive paralysis. It's impossible for me to meditate upon this passage from the *Ethics* with the whole house shaking beneath my feet, caught up by the divine sensual fervor of Schubert... Yes, for now it is Schubert! I stop working and stretch out to relax until it's over. Tchaikovsky, Brahms, Vila-Lobos.

The result: I accomplished nothing. I smoked, paced the apartment, went out in a rage for a shot of atrocious whiskey at a bar on Ninth. Such a beautiful afternoon, so well-suited for work, look how the genius of music (the evil genius) can spoil everything. Going out, I crossed paths with our neighbor from the top-floor. We greeted each other effusively, and she went up whistling, with a dancer's step, with the lightness of a bird. (I'm coming up with some really original images!) Beautiful legs. I haven't heard her play the piano. Perhaps she doesn't want to enter into competition with the man down below. What intrigues me most is that I still haven't come face to face with those neighbors. Only, in passing, with the one who drags his leg, Crosley or Crosby, I'm not sure which.

(December _____ )

While I cooked our steak for dinner, Betsy went downstairs to complain politely about the musical escalation that is giving us the lives of bandstand pigeons and to inquire if it might not be possible to play a bit more gently and at less inhuman hours. (In this country it is always the women who are charged with such prickly business; the men, rough with each other, are polite and even gallant with them, and that fact, forestalling conflicts, helps to resolve many problems.) Betsy returns with a look of amused surprise.

"Well then?" I ask.

She closes the door and whispers:

"Surprise!"

In brief: Crosley or Crosby, with the smile of an eel, asked her to come right in, then explained that there was no "orchestra" or "singers" in the place: it was all canned! I might have known. He showed her the two large rooms completely lined with a fabulous record collection two-thirds of the way up the wall. "A hundred years worth of music!" she said. At the back of the apartment there were complicated pieces of equipment, lights, pick-ups, loud-speakers mounted all over the place. One of those installations capable of filling a cathedral or a stadium with sound. It was like a radio studio. Crosby (in fact it is Crosby, like Bing) is a teacher at a nearby high school and lives with a younger man, blond and rosy, named Gaylord, an authentic playboy spawned, like Crosby, by mother Princeton. No one else lives in the apartment, except for two Siamese cats, who watch us from below.

"It's obvious that they're a couple of little turtle doves," says Betsy, making a face and cutting into the steak. "Gaylord seems friendly; but Crosby is nasty and sneering. When he speaks he twists his mouth, I don't know if it's a tic or just contempt. They must have been laughing at us."

"Speak softer, dear. They can hear you."

"What do you care? Aren't we in the land of the free?" Crosby got angry right away, declared that he is in his own house, that he loves good music, and whoever doesn't like it can move. The people who lived here before us left because of him. The other one still wanted to cast oil on troubled waters, but it did no good. Did you hear him slam the door?''

"We're done for. Why the hell didn't the janitor warn us?''

I'm in a bad mood, I feel bitter, and it looks as if even the steak won't calm me down. I begin to think of means of reprisal: stamping, turning the water on, making noise while they're asleep, if they ever sleep. But I hate living in a state of cold war, no matter with whom. It's strange that while I thought they were worthy musicians it was all tolerable, in fact I even liked it; but now, when I think that instead of a torch-singer it was a record, I feel irked, duped, as if I've had a con-man's story foisted on me. What have we gotten ourselves into? In a den of music-fanatics, and faggots to boot! Furious, I grab Pirilau (he's my yellow cat) by the nape of the neck and hurl him out into the yard, yowling in despair.

As it happened, the night turned to rain and he only reappeared after eleven—accompanied by another yellow cat, exactly the same, both plastered by the rain. They both ran for the plate of cat food. At first I couldn't tell the difference between them. Betsy had to point out that Pirilau has green eyes and the other one's are golden. There must be a mysterious solidarity among yellow kittycats, perhaps because they are rejected as "inferior" by those circles consisting of cats of good blood!

(December ____ )

It seems that our complaint, made in terms of neighborly good faith, was counter-productive: now they play music whenever they like, with no set program, and with more *fucco* than ever. It is perfectly clear that they are out to disturb us on purpose. And Betsy still doesn't want me to sock him one. That weird, gray-faced man, dragging his leg, is going to give us a hard time. I feel he will endanger all my plans for work. I don't like silent warfare, I prefer open conflict. Normally I either give in or give him what's coming. "Madness!" exclaims Betsy. "It's because you're so timid, so repressed, that you go off the deep end. You put up with everything, it gnaws away at you inside, you let yourself be humiliated, and when you can't stand it any more, then you want to crack skulls. Be like me, laugh at it all. Stop greeting them, why do you want to live on good terms with your neighbors? Each to his own house. If they persist, then we'll take them to court."

"But I'm a guy who wants nothing to do with the courts, who wants no complications at all. I just want my peace. And the one who has to ponder Spinoza and endure that damned symphony at all hours is me. Late at night, when they play music and I toss in bed unable to fall asleep, you sleep like the angel you are!" and I kiss her. That's what saves us after all: our unity.

Last night, music till past three. Talking, loud shouts, the clinking of glasses, the smell of boiling coffee, cigarette smoke seeping through all the cracks and cranies, and bright lights spilling forth into the backyard. There were even bellows from the neighbors out back, who began to hurl empty bottles into our yard, as in the Village. I'm sleeping badly, Christmas is at the door, my work at a standstill. I wonder if I've already developed a complex (over here everything nowadays is a "complex"). When I hear the teacher's footsteps on the tiles in the hall, an irritating click, the other foot dragging, I feel like going out there and insulting him. I grow pale, I get palpitations, I live, in a word, on the edge of aggression. But what solution other than to suffer and be silent? A foreigner... The guy must be a good psychologist. He knows that I arrived not long ago and that I express myself with difficulty, so he takes advantage, abuses me, tries to intimidate me. He's a chauvinist. I've already seen others like him over here.

He's a strange, pallid, furtive man whose presence alone is enough to cause uneasiness. I have the impression that Gaylord, the friend, lowers the sound when he comes home late in the afternoon. Then I hear a muffled argument, irritated shouts—that's Crosby—an exasperated slamming of doors, rapid steps on the stairs. I run to the window and watch him go out. He throws me a look of hatred. He limps a bit, dragging the lame foot, clicking his leather heels. I have no doubt that the reprisals come from him.

The seminary remains impassive. In all this there is a subtle contradiction... A few days ago (I forgot to note it down) there was some great ceremony, perhaps the end of classes: many cars on the street, guests in fancy dress, religious, choral music, solemn vestments, a procession on the grass with canopy and crosses. It almost seemed a festival at home in my old village. I watched the rain chase them back indoors.

(December ____ )

This afternoon we had a visit from our neighbor from the top floor, Swissabelle or something like that; Betsy met her at the front door and asked her in. Without being beautiful, she's a wonderful girl. Large dark eyes, round and expressive in a white face completely without make-up, her mouth protruding and full of motion. A bit full, not at all the standard American, just bones and sex-appeal, but a waist of an almost implausible fineness between affirmative breasts and robust haunches. Strong legs, admirably rounded, dancer's legs that she doesn't hide, quite the contrary.

Exuberant, impulsive, at first glance almost with a bit of a screw loose: she talks (or acts?) seated, standing, raising herself up onto the toes of her flat shoes, doing pirouettes, and falling down, legs spread out, on the parquet floor. She spreads wide her eyes and her hands. It's as if she were on the stage, and yet I find in her the naturalness and candor of a mature and extroverted child.

We laugh ourselves to death over the Crosby story, which she tells us with numerous edifying details and great mimetic power. It seems that the fellow's habits, "musical and otherwise," date from long ago, from his Princeton days. He even once was thrown out of a school where he was teaching. The people who lived here before us left because they couldn't stand the scandal any more. "Why not call the police then?" I ask. Don't even mention such a thing. Once the police enter a house, it gets a bad name. Only in case of death, crime, or fire. What an idea! But lately things have been getting worse. It looks as if the man wants to live in a state of open warfare with everyone.

Not only is he a misogynist, he's a misanthrope. We're in for it. I look at Betsy. What have we gotten ourselves into? It looks as if there's nothing we can do but appeal to the courts. Won't the Holidays be marvelous! With my habit of transforming into humor all that gives me pain, I tell her in my broken English of our recent experience, and she laughs choreographically, that is to say, with her whole body. We become good friends (here friendships are quickly made and quickly broken). Since Betsy is out all day long, Swissabelle promises to come and keep me company once in a while. Needless to say, I accept with enthusiasm and add: "You could come and dance here when our neighbors play music; there's plenty of space!" Dearest Betsy looks at me with feigned severity. But she well knows that my curiosity is as honest as it is boundless. She's a little angel, nothing jealous about her. So all is arranged. If things continue like this for a few more days, we unite. Either he straightens out, or he's out on the street. The lawyer upstairs will handle our case.

(December ____ )

What really counts is that my English is improving noticeably. Nathan has been most dedicated to me. In order for us to be closer together, he has moved to a room practically next door. Now when he comes back from work around four-thirty, he knocks on my door, I make real ground coffee (he says there's no other like it, not even in the Village), and we settle down to chew the rag. I tell him stories, speak of my projects, we make plans. I feel happy and he is pleased. A few days ago he told me: "Forget that you know another language and throw yourself into writing all this down in English, this very night. Don't change a word, keep the sense of spontaneity. Get going. Later on I'll help you out. I've got plenty of time—unfortunately!" Yes, but one has to earn one's daily bread and then there's Spinoza, and I've been sleeping badly... The excuses of a welsher. Life still exercises over me a fascination too great to allow me to dedicate myself with Benedictine patience to a "work." The fact of the matter is that, thanks to Nathan, these last few days my English has blossomed: it's as if an eggshell here within has broken and the words come out ready-made, like a baby chick.

It snowed all night and the seminary is beautiful. The lawns are a carpet of glistening white, and the trees, laden with this weightless cement gently falling from the sky, seem of blackened bronze. The snow gives an indescribable brilliance, purity, and secretness to everything. The cornices and outcroppings of the buildings, with their burden of snow, gain a new decorative power. The silence deepens. In the air there is a certain, what would you call it, a certain festiveness. The whiteness of the rooftops reflects the blue of the sky, but where the sun shines all is pink and frothy. The snow writes poetry... I light the fire and it is a real joy just to stay here and work. Ah, is it possible that one can be poor and happy?—I haven't heard the downstairs neighbors; maybe they're out enjoying the holiday. If only they'd stay out. Far above, Swissabelle plays her Debussy with care and understanding: *La neige tombe...* It's just right for this unreal atmosphere, almost like a submersion. There are times when all men feel the need for a refuge, a momentary escape: perhaps the better to concentrate on the struggle? If this could go on, it would be too good to be true; no, it would be Paradise. In the meantime, I work mechanically for our daily bread. With my excursions to the library, my walks, seeing people, time passes. Have I ended up resigning myself to all this? There is something higher or deeper that has us in its grip wherever we go....

Six in the evening, not quite, knock-knock: I open the door and turn white. It's the neighbor from below. He has guessed he would catch me alone in the house, and he comes to take me by surprise. So, then, he was always there. So silent, something's up. I look him over from head to toe, in his careless Anglo-Saxon elegance, which doesn't hide from me something or other I find disquieting. And I, who haven't even shaved yet today. He stares at me with ill-concealed scorn and twists his mouth in what Betsy calls the smile of an "eel": a forced smile that pretends to be correct and cordial. He moves as if to enter, but I pretend not to notice and spread myself across the threshold, with my right hand on the doorframe. Speak here, if you like. He turns livid. Then, making a visible effort to maintain his correctness and his smile, both as false as Judas, he reveals the purpose of his visit: Couldn't we come to some sort of an agreement, for my "reprisals" were bothering him. And why couldn't I have the parquet floor covered with carpeting, to muffle the sound of our footsteps.

That business about carpeting makes me blow my top. Since Betsy is out, I avail myself of the opportunity and do exactly what I like: "There's nothing to discuss. Either you control your musical monstrosity and keep it to more normal hours, or we will proceed with a collective complaint. All's fair. We already have a lawyer. The rest is up to you."

He came begging, but he got more than he bargained for. We raised our voices, he retreated a step, green in the face, foam in the corners of his mouth, his hands like claws, and, beside himself, called me "foreigner" and "hypochondriac." I controlled myself in order not to bash him one then and there, and, imagining that the other neighbors must have been up above enjoying the scene, I laughed to myself: "It's me who better not tell you what everyone around here calls you." It was a regular carnival there in the hall. He didn't want to hear any more. He rushed off, dragging his hateful leg along the tiles, and from a distance cursed me, calling me "Jew" and other elegancies. (When they want to offend a foreigner, they immediately call him a Jew.) I shut the door, my pulse beating rapidly, but I had had my fun. It was clear that my conversations with Nathan had loosened up my tongue. *Jew.* Wait till I tell that one to Nathan. It's he who says that over here there's no anti-semitism. If Crosby hadn't taken such a hasty departure, we would have had quite a brawl.

Betsy came home and was quite alarmed at my account of the incident: "Don't you realize that these pansies sometimes have criminal impulses? He might even set the house on fire." "Don't worry yourself, my dear; he loves his record collection too much."

In the evening we went up to visit Swissabelle. An evening well-spent. We talked and laughed till eleven-thirty. She played, then danced for us to the gramophone. Her husband, a dry young man, red-haired, simple-hearted, showed us his drawings: commercial work, of course, what can one do but earn one's living? None of it was bad, however. I went back down feeling happy. How genuine and pleasant it is to get together now and then with those who work hard for their living. They are so lacking in bitterness, without false complications of aesthetics, and with no bad faith. An independence touched with responsibility, and exuberance restrained by the discipline of creation. If only everyone were like that, if only there were none like Crosby and his ilk.

(December _____ )

It's been several days since I've even taken any notes. Music day and night. My nerves are a jumble of barbed wire. I never go to bed peacefully. If the music isn't on, I feel anxious, impatient, like a condemned man in the chair, awaiting the first jolt; if the music is on, I get furious, jump out of bed, and make a demoniacal din. Betsy, poor creature, struggles to remain calm. But under these circumstances it isn't easy; she no longer sleeps so tranquilly. Could I be the cause of this? Sometimes I think of the troubles I have brought her and I am attacked by a kind of remorse.

But we still have some consolations: Mina and Nathan had dinner with us yesterday, then the poet J. came to visit with his wife and a journalist friend. Our little circle is slowly growing, and I feel, in spite of everything, more optimistic and confident. This morning, in the turmoil of an atmosphere laden with anticipations of tragedy, I awoke with a poem on the tip of my tongue and ran to write it down... The source of my inspiration has not yet entirely dried up.

(Christmas Day)

Yes, now, especially now, is it worthwhile to continue this Diary. Yesterday we had dinner with Betsy's family. On the pretext of being tired, we returned home early, resolved, while

103

the Virgin suffered her blessed pains, to sleep the sleep of the just. Of the condemned is what I should have said.

Back at our street, the silence is complete, as if we were out of this world. The seminary, in total darkness, sleeps in its bed of white. Only the church, there ahead, is lit up—probably for Midnight Mass. Nearing the house, I note that light is flowing through the curtains of my neighbor's windows. In the tired silence with which the snow seems to have blanketed the world (it has snowed all day), it is only from this house that a kind of trembling arises, of music, voices, laughter. A real blast. My first impulse is not to enter. Why the hell have we come home so early? What a night of rancorous insomnia awaits us, with that hell beneath our feet to poison our peace. It'll last all night. "How idiotic!" says Betsy. "What is it to you whether they play music and make noise or are quiet? Shut the ears of your consciousness and go to sleep!" I stare at her a bit irritated by the immensity of her optimism.

Once inside, we notice that the focus of the uproar is just below the room in which we sleep. So, with great effort, we move the couch to the front room and install it as near as possible to the windows, or rather as far as possible from the heart of the festivities. We light a pretty fire in the fireplace, the house gets warm and comfortable. Well before midnight we have gone to bed, and I read, or try to read, a book. In truth I do little more than follow mentally, with rage and curses, what's going on below: the beating of drums, a rushing about, hoarse shouts, the clinking of glasses and china. A genuine Greenwich Village nightclub! Swissabelle was quite right when she confided in us a few days ago that the teacher's apartment was generally considered a den of iniquity.

As usual, Betsy soon fell serenely asleep. How I envied her her nervous system, so delicate, yet so tough. But little by little I succeeded in calming myself down. The truth is that one can get used to most things, and only if one rebels and protests and has a conflict of will or of conscience, an inner struggle, does one suffer. That is why we have been taught resignation. (But it is one thing to suffer for a dream, an ideal, something one hopes to attain, and quite another to suffer because others are amus-

104

ing themselves at our cost.) What should I do? I try to imagine myself down there, "enjoying" myself in the company of my neighbors, God forbid. Long after hearing the church bell ring for Midnight Mass, I turn off the light and fall asleep, angelically rocked by the tempest shaking the house to its very foundation.

From this I awaken, alarmed, to a noise coming from outside, from the street, clashing with the frenetic sounds to which I had gone to sleep. In the fireplace the fire has gone out, just red coals in the darkness. I listen with pounding heart. Someone is beating loudly on my neighbor's barred door, below the stairs. The music has stopped, there isn't a sound. A bell rings somewhere at great length, pressed by an impatient finger. Then the door rattles on its hinges like metal jawbones and a man's voice, angry and imperative, cries out:

"Open that door! Open that door!"

Betsy awakes and lifts herself up on one elbow to listen, her eyes wide. I murmur: "Something's up. It's at Crosby's door." We jump out of bed and, wrapped in covers, our knees on the floor, peek out from below the window shade. Nobody can see us. In front of the house, its door wide open, a wheel on the sidewalk, sits a light-colored roadster. I realize now that it was the sudden braking, the squeal of the tires that woke me up. A tight curve marked by deep furrows shows in the snow, four inches deep on the road. Our neighbors turn off their lights. But I can make out, quite clearly, the figure of a man shaking the grill over the door in rage and shouting out: "Open that door! Jimmy, open that door for your father!" From within, a gentle voice answers, trying perhaps to pacify him. "That's Gaylord speaking," says Betsy with an excited breath in my ear. I squeeze her hand without answering. That man, then, is the teacher's father... We're going to have *corpus delicti*! "Open the door!" shouts the older man. "It's shameful, how dare he refuse to let his father in on Christmas Eve? Tell him to come here and talk to me. Jimmy! JIMMY!" Again there is the sound of a muffled conversation, while the older man violently shakes the door, spitting insults at those within. No one responds. I hear an inner door slam, then silence follows.

Now the man withdraws to the railing, swaying a bit, and stands and stares at the façade of the building. By the light of a nearby lamppost and the glow of the snow I can now see him quite clearly: he is a man of about sixty, ruddy and robust, medium height, his hair completely silver. In a light colored overcoat, with a scarf and no hat, he looks as if he has just come from a night club. I notice that he is trying to see if there's someone in the building to whom he can speak, whom he can ask to open the door. Tense, he looks like a mastiff who has just lost his prey. From the shadow of the building emerges someone who until now has been invisible. A young man in a raincoat, tall, thin, pale, bare-headed, goes up to the older man and whispers, "Daddy, Daddy, let's get out of here, please Daddy!" The older man pushes him harshly away and the young man goes to stand beside the open door of the car. What a difference between him and his apoplectic father. I could feel what an autocrat the father must be.

The older man seems suddenly to have an idea. He runs up the stairs, and a moment later a rondo of ringing bells makes the house vibrate from top to bottom. But no one opens the door. Some are out, some are asleep, or, like us, are secretly watching this spoiled Nativity Scene. The older man growls some unintelligible words, then shouts: "Open the door, I'm Dr. Crosby!" No one does a thing. He turns to go down the stairs, furious, crosses the sidewalk, shoves the young man who tries to stop him, runs to the middle of the street, stops, and in the silence that blankets the night, begins to yell:

"Nobody dares to show himself, to open a door or a window. But I know that all of you are listening behind your curtains. Well then, hear this: I am the father of the miserable creature who lives here. It's the night before Christmas, I've come to see my son, I'm a father who wants to see his son on Christmas Eve, and he doesn't even let me in the house. He doesn't open the door for his own father. Since their mother died three years ago, none of my sons has come home to visit me. But that's not all. This son of mine is the shame of my life. He's a pervert. A per—vert! His house is a den of fairies and transvestites. His house is full of them and he doesn't want his father to come in. I want everyone to know. My sons are the scum of the earth.''

Flushed, suffocating with rage, the man sways in the snow, silent for a moment, propped up waiting for an answer. But only clumps of snow falling silently from the eaves seem to respond. Betsy squeezes my arm in horror, shame, or pity. Red, wild, with his silver hair flying in the cold night air, the old man rushes once again toward the house as if to destroy it. His vigor is frightening. As his father rushes past him, the young man, in tears, his head leaning on the car, says in a voice of supplication: ''Daddy, please let's go... Daddy!'' The old man turns round and throws a drunk's vague punch at his son's face, but it doesn't touch him. Then he grabs him as if to force him into the car.

Something, perhaps a noise, interrupts him: three men are approaching, three bums coming from the direction of the docks, hands in their pockets, and now they stop to watch the scene. Dr. Crosby releases his son, approaches them resolutely, and begins to speak to them in low tones, gripping them by the coat; I can't hear what he is saying, but by his violent gestures I can see that he is telling them the story of what's going on in the building. Maybe he's even giving them directions. He puts his hand in his pocket and begins to pass out money to those creatures of the night, who accept it with avidity. Finally, he steps back a couple of paces and I hear him say: ''You stay here! Nobody's getting out of this house!'' The three bums nod and post themselves in front of the railing. The old man pushes his son into the car, runs around it to take the driver's seat, and, with a roar and a grinding of gears, skidding and sliding in the snow, he drives away. The white carpet in the street is churned up and creased with furrows. Silence closes in. Betsy whispers: ''He's gone to call the police...'' And I answer: ''What right do those wretches have to block my door?'' I feel like marching forth, I even feel now that I could take up arms in defense of my neighbor. Betsy squeezes my arm again.

The three nocturnal creatures look at the house and talk among themselves in the silence of the street. One of them walks toward the gate in the railing, hesitates, then enters. I hear a lock creaking open, the grated door squeaks on its hinges, and Gaylord, bare-headed and without a coat, comes out and begins to talk to them. They all nod energetic agreement to the explanations he gives them; and once again they hold out their hands for the exchange of bills. Gaylord disappears, and they go to stand some distance off, separated, like sentinels. I understand it all. Within the house, where a moment ago there was the silence of the tomb, there is now the sound of excited preparations. I hear running, slamming doors, hushed calls. "They're going to leave by the back stairs," whispers Betsy, "so no one can say they saw them come out from below." In fact, it isn't long before we hear a muffled tramping on the inner stairs, at the end of the hall, and then on the tiles. The front door opens, and, one by one, with great care, looking to left and right, my neighbor's guests descend the stairs, pause a moment in front of the railing, and then, with a short good-bye, quickly move off, dispersing in all directions, carrying packages. Men and women (who knows if there might not have been women?), some in pairs, some in groups, I have no time to count them, something like eighteen or twenty people. "The packages are transvestites' costumes," Betsy explains, laughing. All this takes only a few moments. The door closes, a light goes on below, Gaylord reappears, signals the bums, and they come forward. He gives them a bottle, no doubt gin. Happy Holidays, Merry Christmas! He bids them farewell, they thank him effusively, they go off. The door creaks again, the key turns in the lock, the inner door slams, bolts are drawn shut—and peace finally reins on the deserted street. Only the snow, churned, torn, furrowed in front of the house, retains signs of the incident.

"Do you think the show is over?" Betsy asks. "How could it be? The old guy will soon be back with the police. Then the second act will begin." I am seized by a frenzy of excitement, eager to know what will happen next. "Stay here and watch while I go make some coffee," I tell her. The house has gotten cold—it's past two o'clock—and this demands some restorative. I run to the kitchen and have barely put the water on the stove when I hear a whistle—Betsy's signal. I return to our observation post just in time to see Dr. Crosby screech his roadster to a halt right in front of the iron gate. He jumps out on the run, followed by his reluctant son. The street deserted, the older man looks around: "Where are those bums?" Furious with clenched fists: "There're no police. The police only show up when you don't need them!" Casting a crazed look at the building, he runs to the door, snarling incoherent words and again begins to shake the grillwork: "Open the door, you fag, you scum, you queer! Open the door for your father!" He seems capable of bursting through the iron bars. I want to open the window and do something. "Don't even think of it!" Good God, all those people, the whole neighborhood listening, and nobody does a thing?

Just then, I recognize the voice of my neighbor, shouting hysterically from inside:

"Go away, Dr. Crosby! Go away! Or you'll regret it!" There's a chilling parricidal threat in the homosexual's voice. "Open the door, you wretch, you degenerate!" The old man leaves the door and throws himself at the windows below ours. I hear a splintering of glass. Through the bars, the old man breaks all the windows with his fists. I feel myself turning white. Betsy is trembling, her hands are icy cold, she taps her feet with nervousness. "My God, this is going to end badly." Inside the house there are piercing shrieks. The young man comes running from the street to grab his father, to hold him back, to drag him away. The older man throws him backwards against the railing. I hear the lost voice of the teacher, below: "Leave me alone! Leave me alone! I'll make you pay for this! Get out of here!"

I foresee it all: Gaylord trying to hold back his friend who wants to get to the window to... And then I hear the shattering of china, the thud of a body, a suffocated snarl: "Come on you wretch, you queer! Come on out, come and hit your own father!" They join in battle through the bars. Outside, the young fellow returns to his task, trying to grab his father's arms locked on the bars. "Daddy, Daddy, look what you're doing! From the shadows on the trampled snow I now see what is going on. Betsy twists her hands in horror. I lift the window with a shove and lean out. The older man, his arms reaching through the bars, is furiously shaking someone who is inside the house. I hear a muffled voice, a rattling breath—maybe he's got his hands around his son's neck and is trying to strangle him. A voice screams out: "Help! Help!" The young man tries desperately to pull his father away. I'm just getting ready to jump out of the window myself, when I see an arm emerging from betwen the bars below, waving a dark object. The old man gives a bellow and steps back staggering, supported by the younger son. Betsy drags me inside: "Oh God, shut the window, please!"

At the end of the street the scream of a siren tears at the silence, then another and another. Police cars converge from all sides, in a *smorzando* of sirens. From one moment to the next, the sidewalk and the space in front of the house are filled with police and other people. (In the seminary there isn't a single light: all is turned toward Eternity!) The headlights fill the street with brightness and cover the snow with elongated shadows. Dr. Crosby lies motionless on the ground. He seems red, but then suddenly turns white. The doors are opened, the officials enter the house. At around three the ambulance arrives. The intern makes a summary examination of the body, while the police keep the curious at a distance (among them I make out the three bums from the docks, who have come back again). They lift the body on a stretcher, the door of the ambulance slams shut, the younger son, forgotten, sobs against the railing. And then I see Crosby come out from below, supported by his friend, in tears, with his neck bandaged, dragging his leg. And I feel sorry for him. Some Merry Christmas we're going to have. This night I won't sleep a wink.

As we sit and drink coffee, I say: "I had a feeling I wouldn't be able to do my work on Spinoza in this building." "Work? Spinoza? You'll see, one of these days we'll all be out on the street. Once the police enter a house..."

(December ____ )

The old man survived after all: a near stroke and lacerations of the scalp. The one who stayed in Bellevue was my neighbor, on account of an "attack of nerves" and an inexplicable lesion of the trachea (strangulation, say I).

Betsy was right. Today we received a notice from the rental agency: all of us have to be out by the end of January, they're beginning a major renovation of the building. And I, who was so happily installed here!

When shall we meet again, my dear Spinoza?

*Translated by* Alexis Levitin

## YEARNING FOR DONA GENCIANA

As I look out over the Avenue from my garret and my refuge, I can sure tell you, Mr. Apolinaire, things have really changed around here. Before, people used to live here like they were living under the open sky. You've no idea. I don't know how it happens, but the days pass slowly, and the years go by fast, and you only realize it when it's too late.

It was in the early days of the Republic. I was still in short pants with my shoes stuck in the mud puddles, and was beginning to wrestle with Latin grammar and the verb, *Amar*. The Avenue was brand-new then, like the regime. It began way down there in an alley alongside a sinister-looking, muddy river where flooding between the river banks and the slim buildings sometimes occurred, and it became lost up above, among the walls and narrow trails. The houses were modest, nice and clean, and had façades made of vulgar tiles; others were painted in various colors. There were vacant lots of viscous clay where the common people went to "reign" and the carts got stuck in the mud that went up to the axles, which made the drivers swear like all get out. The trees were fragile and green, with youth and hope. In retrospect, those turbulent days were so calm. This wasn't an Avenue, it was a country lane. The world ended right there at the bullfighting ring in the plaza, a ramshackle enclosure, and far beyond it there was poetry, silence, bucolicism, and *fado* taverns. The nights were awash in peacefulness. The breeze would bring down from above a fresh smell of humus, manure, water, and vegetables. The pensive young ladies, filled with Júlio Dinis and fried fish, would finger languid pianos like guitars with the windows wide open, or else they would sit on their balconies, dressed in diaphanous, swirling clothing, and listen to the voices of Don Juan office-workers wailing the *fado* in the streets:

Oh pale dawn,
I already yearn for you.

The moonlight would flood the night, cascading through the windows, coming to meet us in our beds. The incandescent gas lights were few and dim. A remnant of Caesar and the embittered tubercular poet, José Duro, hovered in the air. In the dead of night, which was around ten, the barefoot newsboy would come by, still panting from the marathon he'd run up from the Baixa, hawking the paper, *A Capital*, and his voice had the tone of a lost world. And I, in my cold adolescent bed, would follow his steps in my mind. I would feel a tightening in my throat and an irresistible urge to cry. By midnight you could hear a pin drop on the little stones of the sidewalk—sometimes it was a dead man who would topple over, shot. In the wee hours in the street below, the oxcarts would roll by on the way to market laden with potherbs. The drivers in their great capes would sleep sitting on the shaft poles. Old carts would go by weighed down with gypsies and transient women who went to get an early start in the vegetable gardens. Júlia Mendes had only just died a little while before.

During the day, funeral processions would pass by in the winter mud or summer heat, burying the dead to the music of Chopin. Everyone came to the windows to see the Voice of the Worker carriage jolting this way and that in the potholes of the

114

future pavement, covered with flowers that came from Figueira Plaza that were wrapped in rolls and stuck on the sides so that they waved up and down in the air like plumes. "Look at all the flowers," some people would exclaim with this, our secret admiration for luxury in death; or if the carriage were white, "It's an angel, that one's going to Heaven." The Avenue was a great artery through which coursed both Life and Death. All the great civic parades would come by here, too. The memory of Propaganda rallies in the open air is still fresh in my mind—our feet were planted in the mud, but our heads were held up high in the sun. And all the flags! Afterwards, years later, there was still an occasional violent Sunday with running around, cheering and booing for this and that, blows with the flat of a sword, or an occasional shot for something else. I can still see that fellow countryman of mine—he was right over there at that corner, all alone and clinging to the lamppost, laughing, white all over, and a nickel-plated revolver in his fist, confronting the multitude that was bearing down on him; he was an "ant." He scared everybody off.

The troops would parade, the Navy, all in white uniforms, the elegantly outfitted heroes, a brass band out in front playing a well-known melancholy march by John Philip Sousa. "Here comes the Navy! Here comes the Navy! The balconies and windows would fill up. It was a festive occasion, hearts beat with conviction and passion (what do they beat to today?). All this came from far away and would pass quickly, like dead leaves on a gust of wind. Our moonlight world of dreams and stagnation remained.

During the revolution (how terribly innocent we were!) echoes of the fusillade and cannonade rumblings reached us. The Avenue (numbed but remote from that epic road) would listen: there were specialists who could recognize the voice of Adamastor, of the Rotunda, of the Alto do Duque. "Listen! They're going to shoot in the trenches now!" On the street corners or at the door of the pharmacy, groups came together and dissolved, discussing the events, anxiously surrounding anyone who arrived from the Baixa, from the tumult, from life. At dusk the Avenue was suddenly deserted, abandoned to the streetlamps and patrols. One could hear the whistling of a stray shell in the dark that sounded like scratching on silk. The Avenue would go to bed, tranquil and remote, to sleep, to love, perhaps to dream, confident in the following day, in tomorrow. There was a tomorrow everyday then, Mr. Apolinaire.

Oh, if you didn't know what the Avenue was like in those days, I tell you, you didn't know anything. On the eves dedicated to the Popular Saints it was *de rigueur* to have fireworks rain from the balcony, colored matches and sparklers glitter, noisemakers and serpent firecrackers howl, and pistols explode amidst cries of wonder. The smell of gunpowder and burned artichokes filled the air. People spit mouthfuls of water into the street, little name papers were tucked under pillows, and questions were asked to the stars—"Whom will I marry?"— in the hope of hearing the right name, or any name shouted out in the street.

Perhaps the courtships were banal, but they were filled with good intentions. A marriage around here was a happening in which, to a certain degree, all of us participated. We even had a romantic-love suicide complete with a farewell letter and a eulogy in the afternoon paper. You knew everybody's family history, the background of the children in the neighborhood, their habits, likes and dislikes. On starry, sorrowful, sentimental summer nights, celebrated groups would get together in a neighboring garden to sing innocent ditties, "When I go over the bridge I will look back," or else, "On board, no one is afraid here, nobody has any qualms..."

There were whisperings, ardent hand squeezings, secret little notes, intrigues and jealousies, a giddiness in the air. Yes, some girls even had the audacity to meet *him* in the shade of the garden. Others would court their beaus at the lower windows of their own homes until late, in murmurs or even wordlessly, in an idyl all composed of gestures. There were the early morning girls who went to high school, the Conservatory, or Normal School, and those without any definite future, some of whom never returned. The little seamstresses would go down into town early in the morning as fresh as rosebuds, and would come back up quite late, dragging their heels in their worn-out sandals, all wilted, pursued by the hawks... the little boys would play in the street, they would get into mischief, and learn swear words, and their mothers would scold them. Everybody knew everybody else from grade school, from high school, from loafing around. The world was a long way off.

Then the streetcars came and the streets were all torn up for many months. It was progress, civilization at your doorstep. I still remember the very calm afternoon when the first one went by, with a pennant hanging from it that read, "Experimental," slowly groping along the new tracks, so filled with people that it looked like a cageful of starlings. It was a happening. Business picked up. Some people even clapped! The street urchins in the neighborhood learned to get on and off while the car was still running; some of them got crushed. The marriageable young ladies would go to the window to see who was getting on and off and maids would come out with footstools so that their mistresses, holding their skirts high, could mount the running board from a vertiginous height. At that time there were still places on the streetcars, Mr. Apolinaire, and the "peoples' cars" and "Chora cars" were in competition with each other.

The vacant lots disappeared, the Avenue seemed to have reached its natural limit of growth. Once it reached the plaza, it stayed coiled up there for many years. Some streetcars went spinning around the Plaza, screeching on their rails, others went on out to the vegetable gardens, to infinity. In the meantime, the movies were also invading us with their films full of passion, terror, lies in the form of serials: *Mysteries of New York, Phantoms, Barrabas*... (Lida Borelli and Pina Menichelli also appeared, but infrequently, making people cry over impossible love.) A fiction alien to this place, the times, and the customs was introduced here that helped to corrupt the neighborhood. Love degenerated into a series of manipulations with listless intervals of waiting, all in the crude light on a zinc roof or on stucco rosettes, with an out-of-tune and myopic piano trotting alongside a West that never existed except on celluloid. But people accustom themselves to any number of opiates.

The European War, as we called it in our naiveté, arrived and cast a gloom over the Avenue. The gas lights died out. They were replaced by bleak petroleum flames. At nine everything here was like a cemetery. The guitar strumming had ended and all was hushed. People stayed at home at night, stabbing little paper flags into maps, dreaming of Victory, another fiction. Several youths from this neighborhood were drafted and some died in Africa or in France; but no one ever remembered to erect a memorial stone at that corner: "To the Youths of this Avenue; they died for their Country and for Civilization." They were quickly forgotten. The solitude of the nights was given over to the paperboy from *A Capital*, whose breathless voice got lost in the shadows of the sad and muddy new streets, like a mute appeal to the people who were sleeping or making love, or dreaming in the dark to save *pitrolino*. Vendors dressed in white would go by, carrying inside their pear crates a ghostly acetylene lamp that flickered in the wind, with their long and piercing cry, "roasted pears, fresh from the oven." It was like an evocative issue of the magazine, *Estevão Amarante*. Even ephemeral girls who sold souffléd Irish potatoes used to come around here. Where did all this disappear to?

There followed the crisis, defeat, shortages of consumer goods, waves of assaults—police whistles and cries for help in the dark. That barefoot corpse, I'll never forget him, with his eyes wide open in the light of the torches, clasping a codfish.

Through all this, however, one thing remained unalterable: it was Dona Genciana.

Few people around here remember her anymore, but I shall certainly never forget. I don't forget anything. If anyone wants to know the entire history of this place, all he has to do is come knocking at my door. You can see the house from here. It's that tall street-level building with the two windows with window seats.

There are some women of whom it can be said that they were born to a sedentary existence of intimacy and contemplation, either in the harem, or within the bosom of the God-fearing family. Seen in the street, nobody ever pays any attention to them: their heavy, clumsy shapes, their overflowing figures, their dresses that are vulgar and out of fashion... They are like fish out of water. That's how Dona Genciana was made, to reign within the setting of the harem or the hearth and home. If only you could have seen her there at the window in her starched ruffled housecoat, her black hair all wound up in curlers, elbows on the windowsill, ample breasts nestled like two doves into her curvaceous arms—you could only have admired her like all the rest of us did. She suggested freshness, coolness, relaxing baths, comfortable mouthfuls of Botot water, soft mattresses, pleasant nights. Seen from up close, she was neither young, nor beautiful, nor elegant. She even had a flat, reddish nose. But her eyes were black and generous, her skin ivory white and fresh, and her hair was lush. And this abundance of flesh, added to the vivacity of her eyes and the lace and ruffles, enchanted us so that we were wont to call her a "fine figure of a woman," "a sexy lady." Every inch of her radiated a mysterious, captivating magnetism that was worth as much as any beauty. There wasn't a serious man, head of household, policeman, or mere night watchman, who, on catching sight of her, didn't feel an irresistible respect, a wish to greet her, to strike up a conversation, to talk about inoffensive, familiar, and even confidential subjects. Even the Chora coachmen, who passed by tumbling into holes in the pavement, greeted her in passing with a lively crack of the whip. "On to Bethlehem!" She would smile at such homages and would return the compliment.

When the streetcars appeared, creaking on their rails, the conductors and brakemen would slacken their pace—pfff—and would extend to her a cordial, friendly gesture. If they went by during off hours, they would stop for a little chat. Anyone could see perfectly well that she had neither prejudices nor preferences. This way she made many friends and was a locally popular figure. She became the center of the neighborhood. Her eyes brightened this stretch of the Avenue, and her mouth smiled gently. She had a native honey in her voice and a tropical coyness in her manner that made her even more intriguing. Certainly this mixture of exotic characteristics both attracted and intimidated me. As an adolescent, I very much desired her, dreaming of her with a Biblical sensuality. But I was afraid of her. If I happened to pass under her window, I would falter, stammer good afternoon or good day, and that was all.

Dona Genciana was from primeval times, that is, she had lived there since the times of the vegetable gardens. She must have been around forty and a "widow." Even today I ask myself if she could have been, as they said, a "Brazilian" or, perhaps, a "returned Portuguese." There's always an overseas past in these mysterious families. I got into the habit of imagining her with a parrot in a cage or a little monkey tied to a stake in the backyard, a metal ring around its waist, perpetrating melancholy mischief. But there was no monkey, no parrot.

She must have had some property of her own somewhere in order to carry on like that at the window, making calluses on her elbows, not lifting a finger. But if she had any money, no one ever saw her with it; and she did have debts, plenty of them. Right there from the window she would send messages to the local stores, or clap her hands to call the apprentices, who would come running. She'd chat with each one of them. She would discuss the bills, which were rarely paid, with the creditors. When a creditor griped, she always had this answer, "Don't worry. I'm expecting a remittance from Brazil." But it seemed the "remittance" never arrived. With coyness, gleaming eyes, lace and tinkling bracelets, she placated the fury of the bill collectors, baker, milkman and corner grocer. She was an eloquent and beguiling woman, and they, fascinated, were resigned.

Besides the debts, she had three children who somewhat diminished the brilliancy of her eyes and the freshness of her soothing breast. But after all, this proved that her entire love life had not been in vain. The eldest, Epaminondas, grew up fat, insolent, and cowardly. He would insult other kids from afar, and then run home to Mama. A vagabond, he played hooky from school and his mother beat him. It was he who one day offered, for a few cents, to take a love letter to that little blonde in the next street, Constance, that I was courting desperately and mutely. She used to laugh at me. In those days I was already a serious young man. I was about fifteen, she would have been the same age or a little older, and Epaminondas, nine or ten. He delivered the letter to her... but did he really? She never responded; she kept smiling at me provokingly and slamming the window in my face. She was one of those who disappeared, never to return. Moreover, I was at the door of a bookstore in the Chiado one afternoon many years later, when I saw her walk by, an elegant, fully formed woman. She stopped, smiled, spoke to me; she wanted me to accompany her to Ferregial Street. I told her I was waiting for somebody (a lie); I blushed, got all flustered, and was horrified. How many years had I waited for an answer to my pure, lyrical love letter sold for a few pennies, waiting so long that my ardor was cooled in the moonlight. And now suddenly, right in the middle of the Chiado, and me without a dime, that invitation to disenchantment, to the ruination of my fifteen-year-old's dream.

I would rather not have seen her. I preferred to have died chaste.

The youngest child, Júlio, was pale and very thin and kept to himself. He suffered from chronic bronchitis and coughed a lot. He didn't even seem to belong to that exuberant family. The middle child, Mimi, was a very precocious child. She was always over at the neighbors' houses, in Dona Elvira's guest's bedrooms on the third floor, eating rolls, swiping forgotten coins, or playing in the street or in the shadow of the balcony with the young pups who would argue over her. She would especially approach the older ones. And I, tall, gangling, and solitary, I would sit her on my lap, when she would show up around the house, and read her stories. Her generous eyes had a mature languor in them. One day she grabbed me with her little infantile hands, and very serious, kissed me on the mouth, a woman's kiss, hot and passionate. From then on, whenever she came, I would be all in a quiver, my mouth dried up, my voice broke, my legs went weak. I'd whisper meaningless babble to her, sweet nothings. Things a timid, repressed, very serious, half-grown boy would say. She'd look at me, blush, all very silent. I didn't know if she understood me. Then she would slip to the floor and with a puzzled look on her face would silently leave me in an intolerably excited state. I would wait entire afternoons, pretending I was reading or studying, my senses on fire.

The neighbor women detested her. Dona Elvira got upset one day and finally kicked her out of the boarding house: the kid was a thief, a depraved scrap of a child, she had all the cunning of her mother. She didn't want her there in the house, always nosing around the guests, a girl that age! She should be keeping to her embroidery. (Could it be Dona Elvira was jealous?) The fact is that little girl was possessed by the devil.

There was also the Professor. He was a scrawny, shriveled-up old guy with a very thin face and gray paint-brush moustaches, cured by cheap cigarette smoke as were his long-nailed fingers and ink stains on the front of his dirty shirt. He ran errands in an old cutaway coat from our grandparents' time, and he took care of the children. I don't know what he taught them; he was like a schoolmaster in a farce, cranky and pensioned off. He only spoke to strangers to ask to "borrow" a cigarette. He belched up wine and embedded nicotine. Nobody in the house showed him any respect, and he would answer in a cavernous and irritated voice, "Go straight to hell!" He had returned from Maranhão with the family perhaps; he was a leftover from its past grandeur. It was rumored around here that besides being a pedagogue, he had been, in former times, a husband and father, reduced now to a mere domestic appendage. The fact was, little Júlio looked immensely like him. Packed off into a corner of the kitchen, he'd drink and mumble, belch and drool.

Now one day, almost overnight, Mimi grew up and stopped going to the neighbors' houses. How fast that little girl grew! At fifteen she was a mature woman. She never again played with her little friends on the back balcony; they remained children. But she acquired curves, an inviting look in her eyes, serious demeanor, and the freshness that her mother used to possess. She was promising. "She's the spittin' image of me at that age." Dona Genciana would say, seeing herself reflected in her creation. Mimi went to live in the adult world. She would greet me disdainfully; sometimes she'd even pretend she didn't know me. And I was stupefied. Perhaps she was getting even with me and bore me a grudge. I watched her blossom and desired her from afar, dreaming of the uninhibited days when I used to sit her on my lap and make her blush with whispered tender words and my timid adolescent moves. Just the memory of that kept me from sleeping and made me toss and sigh in bed. I would tremble, and not only with remorse, oh no. With her, I entertained the fantasies of my solitary, sober hunger. But there was in her, how shall I say—the innocence, the ingenuousness of a libidinous animal.

Dona Genciana, in a pink, lilac, or sky blue lace-trimmed housedress, received many male and some female friends, always at night. They laughed and had a good time on into the wee hours; the lady of the house, always very dignified and erect in her somewhat impenetrable corset, would pat the curls on her forehead, strum *fados* and sweet popular songs on the mandolin, beating time with the heel or toe of her slipper. I know only from hearsay what these get-togethers were like because I was never invited. I would walk by, eyes downcast, very serious; good morning, good afternoon, and that was it.

The little boy's cough, poor thing, was getting worse; all night long grating on the neighbors' sleep in his narrow box-like room off the inner patio. I can't count the nights I was bothered, tossing and turning in that bed (by then, an orphan at eighteen, I was living in Dona Elvira's boarding house on the top floor), unable to sleep a wink, hearing the little boy's exasperating cough. Little Júlio would burst out coughing. Epaminondas would run around on the streets like a vagabond, precociously drunk and provoking. Mimi would go out with her boyfriends, the bums, and the Professor, always with his coat in threads, seated in a corner of the kitchen, would cry and belch out his longing for Maranhão into his cup of red wine. I, upstairs, would dream about Mimi, observing her growing forms. How I wanted her! It wasn't that I was in love with her, it was the image of her white and tender little body, full of precocious venom that intoxicated me like bad wine. Why was it she didn't come over like before? Since we were neighbors, everything could be so easy. There wasn't a soul who could drag me away from the place, from the building. Why was I waiting? I never did leave.

Some years went by like this, and nothing happened. Dona

Genciana, white, jellyfish flesh, her teeth (dentures?) always showing in a broad smile; I felt she would consume me with her carbuncular eyes. But I was frightened of her. It was the daughter I wanted. Until one day there appeared at the house a sergeant, Cerejo, from the Quartermaster Corps. He wanted the little one, a tasty little mouthful of a woman. Soon, it was whispered in the tobaco shop that a "courtship" was ensuing. He could have been her grandfather. He was immaculately bald, short and fat, with a bulging belly and an abrupt manner; a soldier in the style of the old National Guard, a fat, jolly guy who could drink you under the table. So what? "That's the stuff a real provider is made from," Mama said. I was tormented with jealousy. But the die was cast. Ah, if I had gotten along with the mother! A timid guy, a loser. Under the very same roof, the flame about to ignite the strawpile. The courtship caught on, it became public knowledge. Who would have thought it? But that little girl always had an inclination toward older men. I—with this pride of mine, keeping my own counsel, incensed by my idealism—couldn't even look her straight in the eye anymore; at most, good morning, good afternoon, and always with eyes downcast. (I know very well what they were saying about me in the neighborhood. It wasn't anything bad, rather it was—it hurt more that way—"A respectable young man, he doesn't raise his eyes to anyone." Oh, I raised my eyes all right, but no one noticed it out there.)

Cerejo would arrive early, breathless, loaded down with packages, bottles of fine sweet wine. They would dine on the back balcony. Night would fall. Sitting at his side, fresh and like a dream, Mimi was pursuing the bald and boozy, chubby old sergeant. Everything was very proper, everybody could see that, there was nothing to be said. Upstairs among Dona Elvira's vases of begonias, nasturtiums and scented mallow, I would listen, bite my nails, smoke exasperated cigarettes. Limp conversation, muffled murmurings interspersed with coy giggles and long, disquieting silences. Inside the house the little brother was having coughing spells, and Dona Genciana kept strumming the mandolin and gossiping with her big buddies. The night would wear on. From the large unkept rose gardens came the strains of *fados*, arpeggios on the guitar, crying, scolding, arguments, the clinking of china, and gurgling from fetid wash basins. And they kept cooing away. Fairly late, Dona Genciana would come to "serve as acolyte" (in Dona Elvira's words, who couldn't manage to drag me out of there). The little girl would fall silent; Cerejo's and Mama's voices would rise in tone and animation. They would speak of practical things, politics, military life, and I don't know what else. Sometimes Mimi would cough a bit. "It's being out here in the damp night air," Mama would say. "Go inside so that you don't catch anything. The cool night air is bad for you. These young people..." Mimi would obey, and Mama would stay to keep the sergeant company; they were like two old friends. Silence would fall in the gardens, which were plunged into darkness, like a canvas over an empty circus; the lights would go out in all those buildings honeycombed with windows, human anthills; the stars sparkled more brilliantly in the narrow corridor of the sky; you could hear people snoring, sometimes a late clinking of china, and the voices on the balcony lowered to a murmur punctuated by muffled laughter with lingering pauses. Around midnight, or one o'clock, Cerejo would get up to go home since in the early morning he had to be at his post to weigh out the troops' beans and codfish. He would go to Mimi's room, linger a few more minutes to chat with her. Seated at the edge of her bed, he would give her a kiss, until tomorrow. Dona Genciana—"Child, don't go near the window!"—would say goodbye to the old boy, who would catch the last streetcar. Then she'd stay there enjoying the fresh air and gabbing with anyone who passed by. Mimi in bed was crying, she was having coughing fits. Such a flawless little girl, so ill-used. Some days, in the afternoon, violent altercations arose between mother and daughter. There was shouting and tears. Afterwards, Mimi coughed quite a bit and everything fell back into an honest peace. There wasn't anything extraordinary in this. Heated discussions are heard in all households. And there, everything went on with a maximum of publicity with the windows wide open so as not to fuel the gossips' fires.

The Professor was senile and useless. When one of the

rooms became vacant, Cerejo moved into the house bag and baggage. He shouldn't have wasted so much time moving in, he explained at the pharmacy, and as there was a streetcar at the door that could take him to the Commissary in a flash, and so on and so forth. Besides that, Mimi's cough was worrying him, his presence in that family, "in lieu of a man" was indispensable. So he stayed. In the meanwhile, little Júlio was getting worse. He called and coughed, coughed and called. Nobody seemed to hear. The friends arrived, they opened bottles of fine wine. Dona Genciana plucked away at the popular songs of another era—Maranhão in the dust of Lisbon. Strains from the mandolin floated out through the window, voices and laughter. One day it was rumored that the little boy was very ill, he had spent the night coughing up blood. The Professor left the house, bewildered and crying, drooling, and tottering on his weak legs to call for the doctor. Two hours after the doctor arrived, the child was a cadaver, as they say in the police reports. It was then, I should say, that Cerejo rose to the stature of an authentic father of the family. Yes sir, let us do him justice. His voice echoed throughout the house in a commanding tone: "Listen!" He gave orders as he would to his troops, quickly, movingly, looking like a great white and gilded gun-carriage in his uniform, carrying armfuls of flowers, helping the undertakers, receiving visitors and condolences, offering glasses of wine and distributing the mourners into the carriages with his resplendent head exuding perspiration. The hearse disappeared under all the flowers. The street and the windows were black with people watching the spectacle. There was lamenting and sighing everywhere. Dona Genciana really had a lot of friends. It's at times like these that they come forward, isn't it the truth? The men from the Railway sent a delegation with a huge garland of immortelles. A burial unprecedented in memory, not even on an Avenue so frequented by corpses. Mimi, very pale in her black dress, bathed in tears, went in the same carriage with Cerejo and Mama. I had never seen her so seductive. The Professor, poor man, stayed in the kitchen, moaning and drowning his sorrows in his port wine. He didn't have anything to wear but his worn-out coat, so he didn't go to the burial out of shame. Epaminondas didn't make an appearance either. Rumor had it he was in the shadows in Limoeiro, I don't know why.

For a time, the laughter and the strains of the mandolin all stopped. But it wasn't long before Dona Genciana appeared again at the window with her usual natural freshness and dignity, her eyes just slightly red, and a sweet and sad smile on her face. Everyone respectfully greeted the mother in mourning whose heart had been broken. But little by little, everything returned to normal, the visitors returned, the bottles of sweet wine, the arguments, and the tears. There were nights when you couldn't catch a wink of sleep in that building. Now when Cerejo left in the morning, always in a hurry, with a thick briefcase under his arm, waddling out to catch the streetcar, it was always Mama who went to the window to see him. Mimi stayed in bed until later because of her cough. Mama and Cerejo exchanged many tender goodbyes, there was much waving of a lace-trimmed hand, jingling of bracelets on plump arms, and little kisses thrown on the fingertips pressed together like a cabbage. No one thought it odd because she'd been known for her tender goodbyes for a number of years. He went out into the world, a respected man both within and outside of the service, with his cigarette lit, reading his paper. He was seriousness in the flesh, fat, dressed like a civilian, always in a hurry. He was so decent-looking he even seemed like some kind of a department chief. He held an ambition of being promoted, but the ungrateful regime wouldn't reward him, so he adhered to the Opposition. Now whenever a civil procession passed along the Avenue, bald and vibrant, Cerejo got out there and cheered on the Radical Republic with a flag hoisted at his side. (Dona Genciana withdrew; she was a "reactionary" or a "Brazilian"; she didn't want to get involved in politics.) Who could doubt such an upstanding guy, such a good lady, so affable, so eloquent, so neat and tidy? When she spoke of Cerejo, she always said emphatically, "my daughter's fiancé." There was respect.

As for the Professor, he disappeared, and was never mentioned again. It was as if no one had noticed. Nobody thought it odd either that Cerejo began to sleep in the front room, which was more airy, and in the double bed beside Dona Genciana, of course. The only blot on that family was Epaminondas. The cowardly and deceitful boy had turned into a depraved and bloated good-for-nothing bum. He started living with a tramp from Alto do Pina, and once in a while made scenes at his mother's door—to reclaim his money, his "father's inheritance"... this expression had a somewhat burlesque and scandalous connotation. Processions moved along the Avenue, pilgrimages for the heroes in the cemetery (where there are always many more heroes than there are out here), and the sergeant would cheer the Radical Republic from the window; below, on the walk, Epaminondas, drunk and acting like a bully, would make obscene gestures in the direction of his "stepfather" and to the flag, and would urinate against the wall. He didn't even seem to be the son of such a well-behaved lady. He had gone from job to job, until one day he messed up and went off to cool his heels in the can. Then came the mistress—dirty, ragged, greasy hair, obscenely pregnant, whimpering under the window. Nobody paid any attention.

Mimi coughing, the mandolin tum-tum-tum until midnight, one o'clock, and Cerejo snoring with a rumble. He was a good bit younger than the lady, but simple-minded if you listen to gossip. The wicked tongues wanted to drool over him—they said Mimi was wasting away from grief, knowing what was going on in that house, her Mama thick with her "fiancé" while she sweated and coughed in bed, abandoned, as the youngest boy had been, may he rest in peace. But as another saying goes, an honest woman doesn't have any ears. And Dona Genciana explained everything so beautifully from the window to the street, "My daughter's fiancé is a gentleman. He has behaved like a father, he's never come up short on anything: eggs, prescriptions, fine wines, everything. Only a person who's never had an illness in the family doesn't know what trouble is." The one who now took care of the little girl was Marocas, a live wire of a lass, twenty some years old, uninhibited and outspoken, very intimate with the household. Her men friends would sing to her:

O Marocas,
don't touch me,
because you excite me,
because you make me want to fuck...

A real good-looker of a female with plenty of tasty-looking flesh, swaying hips, and some white skin showing that made you lick your fingers. What she must be like under her clothes! Just looking at her you could tell she was a flirt. But she never even noticed me; I was very serious. This Marocas always liked to make love in the dark of the stairwell. When she dropped one guy to pick up another, she always left the poor sucker just skin and bones. She would also sometimes keep Dona Genciana company at the window.

Well, they had postponed the event out of mourning for the little boy. A few months later they were hitched. Dona Genciana and Cerejo, for God's sake! A simple ceremony, unassuming as befit the circumstances. Lots of friends, wine and sweets, the mandolin, tum-tum-tum. Epaminondas showed up without being invited; he called the sergeant and his Mama some ugly names, he bellowed that his kid brother had died of neglect and now this shamelessness going on with Mimi sick in bed. What he wanted was his "father's inheritance." And everything went on as before, still water over mud.

Around this time, I confess that, now that I thought I was grown-up, I suddenly suffered a great repugnance for everything, a kind of systematic deception. I had left high school at mid-semester. I didn't see any future, life didn't offer me anything but Protest. For lack of anything better to do, I set out resolutely to embrace the schemes of Intemperance (the term sounded better to me than Anarchy). Destitute of any hope of personal future, I dreamed of pulverizing the nothingness in which I lived. Things a twenty-year-old would think. Now that Sampson is dead, let everyone else here die too. I fervently read Hamon, Jean Grave, Kropotkin, Bakunin, Sorel, and especially Proudhon, almost all of it in the worst translations, that abased the authors' principles even more. But I hated the Utopians, the Socialists, the Communists, all those who wanted to reorganize society on new bases. For me, it was the human material itself that was rotten. All this had to go up in smoke. I gnashed my teeth, I had a sinister glint in my eyes when I looked in the mirror. I wrote incendiary pamphlets that I read to my comrades in the out-of-the-way pubs in Baixa and Bairro Alto. Deprived of affection, in my solitude and resentment, I dreamed, above all, of Free Love; a revolution that would give every man the right to possess whatever female he desired whenever he wanted her. This was really the only Law my intolerance would admit. I allied myself to underground groups. I propagated my faith, and I even made or helped make bombs. I had a frayed bomb manual I'd inherited from my father, a former Italian revolutionary and good bourgeois, who didn't leave me anything else.

One afternoon, I was at Zola Araujo's house by Escadinhas do Duque, filling little round bombs and pineapple finials, the kind they used to use as ornaments at the ends of banisters, from where we had pilfered them, now that inflation had put an end to the concierge. They certainly were handsome, about this size. They actually resembled hand grenades; it felt good to squeeze their coolness into the palm of your hand and think of the explosion they would make... We were working at the kitchen table, a dark cubicle, when suddenly the floor began to dance under us. It was one of those Lisbon earth tremors that no one paid any attention to anymore. We continued filling the pineapple and the little round bombs—on one side, the empty ones, on the other, the full ones, in the middle the fuses and explosives. But the floor slipped from under our feet, it plunged down and pitched, the table began to dance too, and the bombs on top of it started to shake, jump, and collide with one another, threatening to tumble to the floor. All we needed was for one of them to fall off for everything, including us, to be blown to bits. It's curious. It seemed so simple to us to reduce the world to rubble, but the imminent threat of our own destruction left us frozen with fear. In the circumstances, it was easier to be a hero than to flee, so we stood there with all the blood drained from our faces, opened our arms in an arc, and leaned forward with perspiration running down our faces, our eyes wide open, and our hands joined together. We remained like that for several seconds that seemed as long as the eternal night, holding up the bombs, rocked by the spasms of Generous-and-Good-Mother-Earth, until she was surfeit with torturing us and calmed down again. Only then did we breathe. Zola (poor bastard, he's still there) broke down and began to laugh and cry at the same time like a lost soul. I had to bring him to his senses with a slap in the face. In no time we had the bombs arranged in a trunk under the bed and went running out into the street to temper our nerves in a dive in Trinidade with a lot of hot air. I swore, never again. By chance, some time later, the police made a search of Zola's house and confiscated the bombs that by then had all rusted. They never got the opportunity to implant either intolerance or Free Love.

One night... how fresh in my memory, this all still seems. I can still remember returning home late, intending to get something done, to take advantage of the rest of a day lost in idle gossip, waiting for The-Day-That-Will-Never-Come in the cafe, in the Archive, where one is suffocated by idleness, decadence, and drowsiness. The Avenue is deserted, the sky heavy and low. Dona Genciana, as usual, is at her window, and I am still trying to avoid her, so I hug the wall. I raise my hand to my hat... If she grabs me I'll be stuck there talking to her forever. But there's no way to avoid it.

"Calm night, isn't it?"

"Yes, but a little muggy. We're going to have a thunderstorm..."

"But a thunderstorm will cool things off. And the crops really need the rain."

This time of night and she's asking for a conversation. The crops. Yah, go on, Dona Genciana. To cut the farm bulletin short, I let out a rude and resonant yawn.

"As for me, this weather saps my strength. I can't get a thing accomplished during the day. Can you believe it, here I'm still going to see if I can get some work done."

"At this time of night. That'll ruin your health. You're so thin, what you need is fresh air, a tonic, an affectionate and loving companion." At times, her sensuous, mellifluous voice still takes me unawares, its cozy and maternal tone, like a religious sin. I shiver. What does she mean? I see her in the dark, her generous eyes where a remnant of her youth persists in gleaming. How many years has she spoken to men like that? She must be well into her fifties... Can she possibly know I've always had a thing for her daughter? This conversation is taking a turn... so abruptly I cut it off.

"That's right, I'm going to go upstairs and get some air; when the window is open, there's always a breeze."

"Be careful of drafts!"

Her husband has surely been snoring for some time, listless in the double bed. Mimi is coughing in the little room off the inner patio. And Dona Genciana is out there by herself, flirting with whoever's walking by.

"This urgent little job can't wait. I'd better be getting along. Excuse me."

There, I'm finally able to disentangle myself and go stumbling up the dark stairs to the first floor where I have my poor, naked, and intolerant bachelor's room, the pool where my dreams, disilusions, and frustrated ambitions ferment. I tiptoe in so I don't wake up anyone. All the lights are out. Working people, they're stretched out on their beds, all done in... there's someone snoring somewhere inside. This house oppresses me, it almost suffocates me with its blackness and stagnation. And an absurd idea comes to me: to have my own house, a hearth, a teapot waiting for me, tenderness to cuddle me. My salary couldn't provide enough for that, better not even think about it. My hopes for a raise... "When things change," they say. How many years have I been crawling around here. I stop to listen at Dona Elvira's door; she certainly must also be asleep. I go to my room, I open a window, I undress in the dark, slip on my striped pajamas and go barefoot, groping down the hall to the bathroom to take a shower. Afterwards, I return noiselessly with goosebumps from the water evaporating from my skin. But the street-sweeping machine has just gone by in the wake of a somnolent mule, and from the street there rises a choking dust that smells like dung. This happens every night. May lightning strike the city health department dead! Dona Elvira's right. "You can never open a window around here because the Town Council fills my house with dust, but if I shake out a rag from the window, they slap me with a fine.''

I sigh, shrug my shoulders, and close the window. I go and turn on the oil lamp and a sad light illuminates my iron bed, wardrobe, the boards of my bookcase loaded down with tattered books, the pine desk covered with papers, and two unmatched chairs. When I look at this disarray that reflects the disorder of my imprisoned spirit, I feel bitter and dispirited; I can't think of a thing to write. I can't even remember what I was thinking about while I was daydreaming on the walk up from Baixa. I light another cigarette and reopen the window. The dust has settled, the sky continues overcast. If it would only rain, or if a thunderstorm would break, or if anything would happen—the northern lights or a fire or a cataclysm. Summer in Lisbon, solitary and without any prospects. Is that what awaits me? How strong you have to be to resist it. The city sleeps beneath the leaden, imprisoning sky. I evoke Bakunin, the Commune, poets, I don't know...

Across their way on the fourth floor balcony, the lyceum tutor is declaimng to his mistress in large, eloquent gestures, an arm around her shoulders. Perhaps he is speaking to her of invisible stars. Then they kiss each other with a resounding smack, close the window, and disappear. Happy fools. Everybody has his consolation, except me... below, Dona Genciana is talking in a low voice to some stranger. What a devil of a woman. Carts and coaches going by and there she is shooting the breeze. It's getting on toward 2 a.m. and she's glued out there in her ruffled housecoat. Waiting for whom? For another Maranhão of her dreams to draw her inside and get stuck there? (And me stuck up here?) All this aggravates me, this mediocrity and monotony, these amoebas oscillating in a stagnant pool. Enough. I throw the glowing cigarette into the street as if it were a petard and withdraw. I have completely forgotten the words I came to compose. There's nothing to be done about it. I turn out the oil lamp and stretch out on the bed to reflect. If only I could sleep. It would mean freedom for a few hours. But tenseness and dryness assail my throat. The heat, the coffee, the bitterness of the cigarettes and the thoughts drive away my sleep. Everything in life is sour, the bad taste in my mouth, the loathing for this cheap boarding house, the desperation and frustration.

I turn twice on my stinking, creaking hard pallet, but I can't get to sleep. So I light the candlestick and grab a book. I always have a dozen of them at the head of the bed. But the happy books irritate me and the melancholy ones infect me. They speak to me of action, of distant countries, of people with life and significance and all this sick stagnant existence, without departures or arrivals, without a beginning or an end, becomes even more hateful, as it stimulates an undefined desire. (Someday we must get away from here, do something...) At other times, these books are like a trampoline where I hurl myself jumping into a world of unconnected thoughts of obsessive desire, into a fiery sky streaked with black. I persist in reading; but this devil of a Russian bothers me, the more I try, the harder it is for me to make it past the first line; I read it and reread it ten times while the rebellious spirit within roams and battles, but where? My disconnected thoughts are like acrobats lost in a sky of starry trapezes.

I hear Mimi coughing below, a cavernous, gasping cough that seems to come from the bottom of her insides and shatter them into little pieces. How she coughs. I don't know how she can take it. She goes on like this night after night. It was the same thing with her little brother, who's now in his grave. And her mother out there gossiping. Nobody pays any attention. Is it possible to live like that, unaffected by suffering even when it's right at your side? Perhaps when you're used to it, you get hardened. They say it's their family curse. Cerejo is snoring away, all worn-out, the milksop. The neighbors are grumbling, they curse, and bang down their windows. They want to sleep. It's stifling in these rooms, and the dismal inner patios are reeking of leaky water pipes. There's only one thing to do, close one's ears and conscience (he who has one). And me twitching around, wide awake. I throw down my book and blow out the candle. The air in the room is filled with the nauseating and pungent stench of the wick. My body weighs me down, it slides away from me as if I were on an incline. I thrash around constantly, inexplicably uncomfortable, looking for the "usual position" if such a thing exists.

134

The reddish reverberations from the street torment my brain. But even when I close my eyes, I can't find complete darkness; it is a copper-colored night, crossed by malignant gleams. The city is drowned in silence, but even it is abominable to me. Ah, how much better for me to sleep in the middle of the day, in a corner of the cafe, cradled in the bustling noise around me or even in the Archive. I itch all over, the roar of the water tank fills my ears, the blood courses hard through my temples and my limbs—the suffocating heat, smells, dust rising from the street—all this has united against me. As if that weren't enough, now my stomach is growling from hunger. Infuriated, I get up and go close the inside window shutters. I stand there somewhat calmer. To think that in this very room, in the wintertime, my teeth chatter from the cold and I wake up with frozen knees. Two o'clock sharp, and I'm here like this. I hope the Archive opens late and the work isn't a killer. But now she's coughing again, sweet Jesus. I don't dare dream anymore of her white and tender body that used to fill my nights with consoling images.

The murmur of voices and the creaking of a bed float down to me from above. The actress who lives upstairs is primed. That's the bullfighter who's come back from Spain (if it isn't some other visitor who's stayed the night). Whenever he's in Lisbon, this lovemaking goes on. The last time there was a hell of a scene right in broad daylight. The actress trembling on the landing, screaming "police," and the neighbors clustered around; and the bullfighter, a real fop, running down the stairs with his hat pulled down over his eyes and a package under his arm. And her, on the landing, with her hair uncombed and no makeup on, deep circles under her eyes (she seemed even older), a split lip running blood from some punch he'd given her, crying out, "You lout! No good thief! This time he's even taking my jewels away from me!" In front of everyone in the building. Afterwards, of course, they made up. They make love furiously and in the intervals they fight each other like beasts. She's the perfect woman for him. A comedy actress, unemployed in life, which is the real comedy... He's an amateur bullfighter, or something like that, with an aristocratic name and effeminate mannerisms. He uses her right. The jewels are in the pawnshop and now he's dominating her. She, who's even toured Brazil, in the hope of snagging a "Colonel." They must have had a reconciliation. This is promising. A mosquito falls on top of me in a choppy flight like a tuning fork. He's probably carrying malaria. I already know what their kind of music is like. They come from those big, sad, overgrown backyards where there is always stagnant water lying about, uncovered wells, and poorly draining sinks. I shoo it away and wipe the perspiration on my forehead. If only they wouldn't buzz, I would resign myself to being eaten up.

Someone just jumped out of the bed downstairs, barefoot, and is dragging a resonant object across the floor. Damnation. The bed begins to creak again, I hear muffled voices, a giggle... I pretend to cover my ears, that I don't want to hear, but I remain rigidly fixed by the needles of my attention to the stucco flowers like a toad on the top of a dissection table. I almost don't even breathe in the effort to hear what's going on in the bedroom of the unemployed actress and the aristocratic bullfighter. I'm not downstairs anymore in the sticky heat of my bed. I'm up there, hidden like a thief, stealing a love scene under that other bed that creaks and moans.

A car passes along the Avenue like a trumpet, honking deafeningly, full of bohemians and other rabble. Riffraff. I follow it with furious attention until it is lost in the distance and silence returns to shroud the place. I am dying with fatigue and tension; I need to sleep, but it is impossible. So I stand up in the bed, twisting and panting, supporting my hands on the wall, stretching my neck out and crooking it nearer the ceiling, nearer to them, listening avidly. I don't want to miss a thing going on in the intimacy of that bedroom that doesn't hold any secrets for me anymore. Jesus Christ, how these people make love! It's enough to bring the house down. She moans louder and louder, she cries out, she says things in a choked-up voice, like someone begging for death or salvation, she lets out a piercing scream, after that a rattle in her throat that is drawn out in a convulsion, the afflicted murmur of a person either lamenting or blessing. It's like a death agony. My legs tremble like saplings. I burn with fever and I perspire. And now silence. One of these days, she'll stay in his arms. And what does it matter to me?

When she comes down the stairs in a cloud of perfume, all made up, in her tailored suit, her thick and robust legs, her full breasts, her laughing green eyes, moist and sensual mouth, and elegantly greets me, can she possibly know that I hear everything and follow it with all the agitated desire of a serious young man? I shouldn't stay here another day, but I can't live without this blindman's spectacle. I go home every night in the hope that they're there. Someone's getting out of bed—I know the fast and heavy walk. The door squeaks open, she's on her way to the bathroom...

I lie down prostrate. It's getting on to 3:00 a.m. and I definitely won't be able to get to sleep tonight. Now the only thing left to do is to wait for daybreak. I intimately curse my neighbors. Why can't these people go to bed on time? Don't they have to get up early? Why can't they make love in the daytime? And I tolerate them; solitary, starving, gnawed with envy and insomnia on my hard and stinking straw pallet. Above the battle for Love, and below, the struggle for Death. Between the two, immobile, helpless, I grapple with insomnia. I try to recite poetry, but I stutter mentally, I forget the rhymes, I transpose stanzas. And that devil of a mosquito won't leave me alone! I light a candle to see if I can catch it. It's poised right over the head of my bed in a tactical position, the bandit. They're so clever! A female. Cautiously I raise myself to my knees, spit in the palm of my hand, wait for it to settle down—and zap, I smash it against the wall. The blackguard, she's already sucked a drop of my blood, but wasn't satisfied.

What the devil do I hear? In the next bedroom someone makes a sudden movement in bed. I hope I haven't awakened Dona Elvira with the slap on the wall. And with the image of the actress, thirty-five vigorous years old, eyes like green flames, the performing arts, is now coupled that of Dona Elvira, voracious and skinny as a rail. A lean sardine for my hunger. Under the same roof... I turn in the bed, my spirits low. Why must I listen to that? It seems that even my bones are throbbing. Upstairs, silence. They must be sleeping, satiated. It won't be long before he breaks out into a snore. And Mimi, downstairs, coughing again.

I knew it. Dona Elvira's awake. Who knows if she also heard the scene the neighbors made. She carefully gets out of bed. (I've accustomed myself to recognizing in the dark all the little noises in this house.) I can see her feeling around the little Grandela rug with her feet looking for her slippers. She's going out to the hall... she's gingerly crossing the parlor... she's stopped at the door of my "seperate" room. I don't know if I hear her or if I'm just guessing. I'm all tensed up. My heart is making the metal parts of the bed ting. I can tell she's listening... she's scratching very softly at my door (the usual signal) so that the other boarders don't hear. As I don't answer, she silently opens the door halfway (she's had the hinges oiled so they don't creak), and she whispers through the crack.

"Did you call? Do you want anything?"

Such innocence! I pretend I'm sleeping. I don't move a muscle, but I think that even the walls must hear my wildly beating heart. Through my eyelashes, I perceive her shadow in the dim light of the open window. She's closed the door, she's coming closer, bending over me, spying on my immodest seminudity. I hear her breathe harder, I sense her sharp and stimulating smell, a vague, salty aroma... and suddenly she lets out a surprised exclamation. On that sweltering, exciting July night, she falls on top of me with all the weight of her incontinent impulse, she presses the entire length of her spare and convulsed thinness against me, nude beneath her open robe. Her mouth ravages mine with a whimper, her breasts, so round for her skinniness, crush against my flat chest. I don't say a word. What can I say? Everything is nocturnal and clandestine between us. What misery! Ah, but bless her, skinny Dona Elvira!

A thunderclap finally rolls slowly across the sky. The rain lets loose with a happy stomping on the sidewalk, and on the browned foliage of the stunted trees. A fresh smell rises into the washed air. I'm already breathing better. Dona Genciana was right, a thunderstorm does cools things off. It's going on 4:00 a.m... Mimi's coughing has stopped. The building is sleeping. An immensely peaceful feeling relaxes my fatigued body. My lost thoughts come back to me. I'm hungry, so what. I jump out of bed, open the window wide, light the oil lamp and sit down to work. It will be daylight in no time...

Mimi had been dead for two years when I heard through the grapevine that Dona Genciana was in bed with an ache. I was concerned, given the number of people in this country with a variety of conditions who die of this mysterious "ache." Moreover, I was perturbed because I had never in all these years, heard it mentioned that the good lady was ill, so I made sure I ran across Cerejo on the stairs.

"I hear your wife...?"

He explained to me in moving and precise terms that it was a tumor. But it had been operated on, and she was out of danger. I congratulated him and, even though I was satisfied with having performed my duty, I was left with the impression that something was beginning to collapse around us. It wasn't long before she returned to the window, paler, emaciated, and gray (perhaps she wasn't dyeing her hair anymore), but always dignified and fresh. Life went back to normal, friends, Marocas, partying. It was a year later, not even that long, when late one night, I heard groaning. It came from downstairs. It stopped for a few days, then started up again. Dona Genciana disappeared from the window and the ex-sergeant (he had left the military and was established on his own and no longer cheered the Radical Republic) was going around looking worried and depressed. This time it was on the streetcar:

"So your wife is ill again?"

"She is. Just imagine, one Sunday we went for an outing to Mafra, a very good picnic, organized by the girl, Marocas, and on the way back, my wife slipped on the runningboard of the truck and did something."

"Did something?"

"Yes, to her back. It seems she dislocated something and now she's in a lot of pain."

The pain did not abate, and one day the final blow: it was cancer. The martyrdom lasted for months. Day and night there was moaning and groaning, entreaties, enough to drive you crazy, right under my room. Marocas, who was very dedicated,

settled into the house once and for all, to take care of the invalid. Since nobody looked after anything, she assumed effec-
tive command. That girl went around in a whirl. She was such a
live wire. Cerejo needed to sleep because of business, so he
moved into another bedroom in the back. Friends still came by.
Dona Genciana, alone in the double bed, devoured by pain,
moaned, called for her husband, and he came or didn't come,
depending on the circumstances. There were nights when he
would snore like a saint, and she would moan and call. They
grew accustomed to it and finally not even Marocas would
answer. They slept. Only me upstairs, unable to catch a wink of
sleep, listening to her. Whenever they gave her morphine, I
think she'd drop off for a few minutes, but would soon begin
again. I still ask myself today if she groaned exclusively from the
pain. Or if the suffering didn't also come from a certain
understanding... the pious tongues, with Dona Elvira in the
vanguard, started clicking again. What was Marocas doing,
what was Cerejo doing, always hidden in the back whispering to
each other on the balcony, and the poor woman suffering in a
bed? For months! I don't even know how I was able to sleep at
all. Fortunately, the actress and the bullfighter had definitely
separated, and she was on tour in Africa.

Until one day, for the first time in all those years, I dared
cross the threshold of that apartment to see Dona Genciana.
She was a shadow of her former self, almost unrecognizable,
her hair all white and sparse, her eyes closed. She partly opened
them to see me, she grabbed my hand vehemently, she tried to
say something, and the tears ran down her face. They buried her
a few days later. Marocas made a stink at the funeral procession. She had her reasons. Once again, Cerejo behaved like a
gentleman, the father of the family.

The house was consigned to the two of them. Of the family
members, only Epaminondas was left, and he continued his life
of idleness, now separated from the tramp. One afternoon he
came to reclaim his "mother's inheritance," the house and the
furnishings. But the house belonged to the widower, and there
was nothing to be done for him. Epaminondas created another
scandal with the obscene gestures, pissing all over the wall, and

then disappeared. But this Avenue was beginning to take on an impersonal aura, and nobody paid any attention to him. Cerejo put his shoulder to the wheel of a new life: paintings, furniture, remodelling, new plumbing. He even installed his Commissary there and put up a nameplate. He asked Marocas to stay on and take care of everything. She stayed. A year later they were married, two little doves. The gossips fell silent, and everything returned to its former peace.

Sometime later I heard that Epaminondas, on returning to Limoeira, had died in the infirmary, gushing up blood. His mistress was in Mónicas, doomed by the abortion. And suddenly I realized that Dona Genciana's family line was extinct.

It was around that time that I decided to take a new course of action, leave behind my scruples and idealism, and face life in earnest. I took up with a learned major who used to show up around the Archive, I wrote two trite pieces for a feature newspaper, and managed to be promoted. I told Dona Elvira to go jump in the lake. I moved out, but continued to frequent the tobacco shop, the eternal center of gossip on the Avenue. Marocas, it was now said, was making life miserable for Cerejo. Nothing would surprise me, she was a real hot tamale. They said she had lovers in the house right under his nose. The man lived on a few more tormented years, debilitated, who knows if out of remorse, until one day he kicked up his heels from pneumonia. Marocas became sole proprietress of everything. She put up heavy drapes, and still receives many visitors, but she never opens a window. She's also rented the floor above, the one that was Dona Elvira's. A complete transformation. Things have really changed around here.

As I look up this Avenue that was so peaceful and removed from the world, I can hardly recognize it anymore. If you want me to tell you truthfully, I feel a yearning. Before, there was an almost painful honesty in all this, an honesty of appearances. It was provincial, but sincere. Then some mysterious fungus appeared around here. New faces, different customs, rooms to let, suspect houses. Mothers in nylons who leave all by themselves in the afternoon and only return late at night or at dawn in a taxi... a crossroads of disintegration. I don't even want to look.

It nauseates me, all this cheap Babylonian *ersatz*, this branch of the Baixa, stingy on compassion. Now the dead go by on gasoline, without the aid of Chopin any more; there are no more processions, parades, or animated bands. The Popular Saints have become bureaucratized and have emigrated from here. Even the moonlight seems different, distant, dimmed by the illumination. The nights are stifling, the breeze from the gardens has been cut off by the new high rises. Construction, construction! There are those who like this, and even those who call it Progress.

An odious racket rises from the street; the cafes, down there in the Plaza, are always filled with apathetic young people reading about soccer. You can hear the loudspeaker barking. The bar over there vomits out shellfish, peanut shells, and lupine seeds. It overflows with riffraff, young bucks who talk only about business and dealing, a solid block of cars in the street, and females to buy and sell walking down the Avenue.

Where are the vendors' cries, the singing, the strains of the guitars, the love affairs, the alarms, the innocence, the dust of the old times? Where are we ourselves? Yes, living under the guise of a promoted and disillusioned office clerk, where am I? So as not to lose myself, nor to miss a step in life, once in a while I still raise a corner of the curtain and stand there looking at what for me, for those of the old guard here in this place (so few are left), was and will always be Dona Genciana's house.

*Translated by* Carol L. Dow

# THE STOWAWAY'S CHRISTMAS

In that year—so long ago in time and in the ways of men that we sometimes believe that we live in another world—December ran much less to cold then usual along the Atlantic coast. Foggy, rainy, and even warm, as if the Gulf Stream, before moving away on its course to Europe, had decided to come close to the shore for the purpose of better protecting and warming the coast from the icy waters of Greenland.

Christmas was approaching and still no snow. Well, anybody knows that a Christmas without snow or cold is no Christmas at all. There are no sleds screeching down the hillsides and roads, no snowmen with old hats on their heads and pipes in their imaginary teeth, nor any snowball fights. And in the still unfrozen reservoirs and lakes, ruddy-cheeked people are not seen skating and holding hands, their hair flying and their scarves fluttering in the wind. There are also no cries of joy in the crystal air, nor the tinkling of sleighbells that fill the starry nights with a festive echo of happier times.

Jingle bells, jingle bells,
Jingle all the way —

On the front lawns of the houses, no colored Christmas-tree lights shed their silent reflections upon the snowy whiteness of the ground, suggesting hospitality, warmth and friendship. Nature is soaked and dark, the harsh woods stripped bare, and the fog and rain dim the street lights, at the same time smothering the ringing of church bells which would otherwise fill the tinkling echo of the night.

Casting outside the windows their golden holiday glow, the houses, inside and around the decorated trees, harbor the usual excitement and anticipation over Santa's presents, piled up in their lush and fancy wrappings. From the street, the lonely traveller sadly takes a glimpse at the dancing couples, the happy and satisfied faces around the table, where a golden turkey presides. Christmas, as always, is homey and intimate. But without snow it loses all the earthly joy that fills the forests and valleys with echoes of laughter and cries of youth. No, a Christmas without snow, a Christmas that isn't white, is no Christmas at all. It's more like a late Thanksgiving.

\* \* \*

Well now, this story happened (or better still, began) in Baltimore, a somber, peaceful and orderly city, although much less sorrowful than our Poet imagines her to be—"A sad city among other sad cities." Or maybe because its belltowers forgot the "Raven" of Edgar Allan Poe, and no longer repeat the sinister "Never more, never more," which he believed to have heard them cry out. Nonetheless, one does have to leave the downtown area and roam through the suburbs to find the appropriate holiday atmosphere. The city's docks are gloomy, chaotic and confusing; here and there, grim warehouses and buildings, threatening to collapse, seem like old and abandoned country churches. Deteriorating ports are so sad, especially at night. But one takes in a breadth of poetry in these piers of dark and slimy moorings, where the tired and oily waves gently beat to rhythm their lovesong for the land. There are cities that seem to live intimately with the drama of the sea, always present in the daily lives of men. And nothing speaks so much to the wandering and lonely heart than this eternal call of the sea alongside the docks.

It was by one of these half-crumbled wharves that the ship anchored on the morning of December 24th, having come from the sun and the open and blue sea of Africa and the Tropics. It was an old and narrow cargo ship with a tall, smutty smokestack and large rusty patches on the hull, her waterline a few feet above the waves. One of those obscure wrecks that sluggishly roam the seas, limping along in search of trade. On deck there were badly washed clothes hanging out to dry on the rigging as well as a few mangy seamen, elbows on the railings, gazing at the strange land. One of those ships that could have inspired a sad story by a Joseph Conrad or a Pierre MacOrlan.

It carried a small and motley cargo: palm oil, coconuts, rotten bananas, peanuts, a few bales of cotton, and a monkey, more or less housebroken, who had become ill during the trip and was whining in a bed of rags, complaining of the winter cold.

On board there was also a passenger not logged into the records, one who had not paid for his passage, but had been placed in the conspiring care of one or two sailors—hidden in the groaning bowels of this junk ship, in a dark and stuffy cubicle next to the coal-bins. Who was he and where did he come from? Ah, but those are questions one never asks of such thin men with faces precociously wrinkled by work and toil, hardships and foreign winds, and whose sunken black eyes glow sadly out of fear and mistrust. Would he be coming from Morocco, a refuge for so many emigrants? From the Azores? From the Coast of Africa? No one would say, even if they knew, he least of all. Illegality has its own laws, morality and connections. And silence is the golden rule for the poor people of this world. Who had put him on board? Who kept him there and provided for him secretly during the night with scraps from the miserable grub of the somewhat seedy crew? A mystery, a mystery. Solidarity is another sacred law among the men who live on the edge of life.

He had come on board in the quiet of the night off a desolate port somewhere in Africa or in the Azores, and that's all. Someone had ever so quietly guided him, taking his calloused hand through the reverberating labyrinth of the ship, and then had left him like a cellar rat. And there, in the suffocating darkness, he had crossed the endless sunlight of the tropical ocean.

The *Maria Alberta* (let's call her that, hiding her real name and serial number), after having dispensed with all legal procedures, emptied her meager merchandise on the gray deserted dock. Cranes squeaked, pulleys squealed, booms performed their staggered acrobatics in the ashen air, and the cotton bales were literally swept into the warehouses by the wind. Nightfall came early, everything again fell silent, the watchmen and the dock officers, almost all, went away, and the *Maria Alberta* vanished out of sight and mind into the darkness, like a tired, sickly horse at the back of a stable.

It was Christmas Eve and each man looked for his own refuge, his family, if he had one, or the smokey corner of a low-ceiling barroom, with dishevelled and drab women sipping bad whiskey and a jukebox rattling away hot and sunny melodies, suggestive of Californias and coconut groves that exist only on film or in dreams. For men who crawl along the surface of the world and life, there is no other refuge except this, a rented bed and some borrowed affection.

Silence dripped on to the pier and the warehouses. A few lights were shining, but very few made it through the thickness of the fog that was turning into rain. The anchored ships' masts lost themselves high up in the polluted sky. But somehow the mist around the docks always creates a cloak of shelter, a shade of protected secrecy.

The captain, in street clothes, went ashore and on his merry way. He had some business to deal with in Philadelphia. Right after him went the first mate, then some officers and helmsmen, the orderly, and even some sailors. A few of them took along a small bottle of unsavory moonshine, which they hoped to use to grease the palm and invite the good will of the guards and customs officers who let them pass through without the mandatory frisking or checking of their packages.

The customs officials—well paid, well nourished and well

bundled up in their warm and smooth uniforms—looked with a mixture of pity and surprise, or rather mockery, upon those poor, scrawny and unshaven sailors who were shivering inside their patched-up thin outfits of denim and faded cotton, one or two of them wearing a fairly threadbare jacket, and on their heads a knitted cap or a Basque beret. What in the hell kind of contraband could these wretched souls be transporting? Certainly none of them would be carrying any gold, diamonds or cocaine.

The officials would accept the customary bottle and let the men pass through with a "Merry Christmas," and then return to their card game and whiskey. The sailors would smile, rub their frozen hands and disappear into the dark in their rolled-up pants, confident that they had hoodwinked the Treasury Department's security. What in the devil were they going to do in the land of dollars on Christmas Eve with their skimpy seafaring wages?

\* \* \*

In the dark of night, the stowaway climbed up from the bowels of the coalbin in order to hide in a skylight on the main deck, where there was enough space for a man to lie down. (Many others had travelled in the same spot for days and weeks, and one of them, in the light clothes he had on from Brazil, had been caught in this hiding place by a hard nordic winter and had become debilitated for the rest of his life.) He hadn't eaten since the early morning when they had brought him the usual bitter coffee and chunk of bread. Hunger was gnawing at his stomach, and after the stifling heat of the boilers, the wet coldness of the night went right through him.

Boxed in there, he heard voices, captain's orders, people who were going down the gangplank—steel echoes of the emptied ship. He waited until everything became quiet. The silence was almost complete and he felt increasingly impatient. What in the hell were they waiting for that would make it safe for him to leave that hole? Would they forget about him and leave him on board alone in that coffin to freeze to death? Night was approaching with an exasperating slowness and he was in a hurry.

He tightly clutched the bag that held his few belongings.

He had glimpsed through the night air the outlines of the hangars and warehouses, some buildings in the distance, as well as the dead light of the city. He was in America, just two steps away from a job and his livelihood, a leap away from his destination. And his heart thumped with anxiety. He had settled his accounts with the two mariners who had hidden and fed him on board. (If there were somebody else in cahoots with them, that was no concern of his.) He had a few dollars left in the bottom of his pants pocket. Along with these, he squeezed into his sweaty palm a worn piece of paper with an address—that place lost in the vastness of the unfamiliar America: Patchogue or something like that on Long Island, to the right of New York. How many miles would that be from Baltimore, and how long would he have to trudge blindlessly to get to this destination? And that notation with some numbers, maybe of houses or streets—who knew what; all he knew was that he didn't understand anything. He knew nothing of English. He only knew that there he was waiting until they made arrangements for him, so he could start a new life, or else... He was making his way toward those people, immigrants of the same breed, who would try to get him a job and a hideout. He didn't know anyone else in this immense country, now wrapped in darkness and fog. It really bothered him to think about all of that while he was there immobile and powerless to do anything. If he could ever get up there! But here he was with a cringing heart aching in his skinny chest.

How many years had he been dreaming of America. He came in search of her as four hundred years ago his more fortunate ancestors had come in pursuit of Terra Firma, the El Dorado or Xipango. They hadn't needed any passport; the world was then a mystery, but free to the curiosity and ambition of all. Yet here he was travelling secretly, even though gold was not his quest. And if one wasn't shaking gold dust from one's feet, it was still possible (in the words of some German he had met and who had returned from there) for the fellow with his nose to the ground to run across a lost penny or two. And besides, he had two arms and knew how to work a pick and shovel.

148

The dream of the New World still hadn't died in the hearts (or rather in the stomachs) of men. It was coming true for him by the quickest route, one that was far from being the least risky—stowed away on board a rotten cargoship, a rusting piece of junk that wheezed and hobbled along.

* * * *

The hours flew by and he dozed off. Suddenly he awoke with a start and clasped his hands around the bag. A husky voice whispered into his ear:

"Jump out here, Suh Thomas."

The skylight was raised. With his stiff legs he shot out of the hiding place, but when he tried to stand up, they gave way. He couldn't walk. His stomach was aching, his bladder bursting, and he was dying of thirst.

"I can't move."

The seaman muttered something, some swear word for sure, and then he began to rub him up and down vigorously—his back, legs and arms.

"Here, drink a shot of this moonshine."

"You can't stay here. See if you can pull yourself together. We have to take advantage of this break; there's nobody walking on the pier."

He drank, his limbs came to life a little and he could walk. He went to relieve himself alongside one of the lifeboats. Restless, the other guy, while smoking, would hide the glow of his lit cigarette in the cup of his dark-skinned hand.

"Here take this food for the trip. And be careful now, huh?"

He felt the warm parcel of the rations that the other guy shoved into his hand. Through the dark, they made their way toward the poop deck. The gangplank had been removed, but even if it had been there, at that late hour it would have been dangerous to disembark in the open. He saw himself forced to climb over the railing and go down by a mooring rope like a big sea rat.

"Put your rations in the bag, man. And see that you hang

it around your neck. Otherwise, how are you going to be able to climb down? Don't be afraid, go on ahead.''

This was going to be the hardest part. Once on the dock, it was one eye ahead, one in back, staying in the shadows and against the walls, becoming a part of them and fading into the darkness. Then, once outside, it was just a matter of walking.

The seaman shook his hand. The dim light from the city in the distance made the watery abyss down below even darker. He fixed the bundle to his back and felt faint. How high would he be from the dock? The mariner held him, then helped him climb over the cold and wet railing; he grabbed on to the rope. From above he heard a murmur:

"God be with you. Good luck.''

He was all alone, clinging to the rough, thick and soaked cable. A few meters down below was the invisible dock, terra firma, liberty, and the bread to be earned by the sweat of his brow. Would he know how to reach it? He would have to be brave. Yes, but he was so tense that you couldn't put a needle up his you know what. It was as if he were now between the sea and the sky, praying to the Lord for all the help he could get.

Slowly, with the bundle hindering even more his already shaky movements and his legs all tangled up, he went sliding down backwards, the palms of his hands scratched and burning. The weight of his body kept pulling him down. But he was thin, and he finally managed, overcoming the gravity, to straddle the cable.

All he had now before his eyes was the dark hull of the ship from which he could not divert his gaze, as though it were stuck to his sight. Down below, the black water quietly slapped against the wooden pier which creaked ever so gently. The water was now his deepest fear, and perhaps it would become his grave. If he were to look down, he could get dizzy and then...

By the angle and sway of the cable, he could see that he was closer to the pier. But he couldn't see an inch beyond his nose, only the blackness of the hull. He gripped on more firmly, freed one leg with difficulty, and with it began to feel for the ground. But it had to be still beyond his reach. He rested a bit. The sweat trickled down his face and soaked his back. If he were to fall down there, he'd really be a man of the sea. Nobody would notice and if they did, from aboard ship no one would ever come to his rescue. Not even from the deserted pier. On the following day, or God only knows when, his body would be fished out, half nibbled at by the fish and crabs, or bloated and stinking, water and mud dripping out of him. If this were to happen, he would be one more missing person, or an unknown corpse that nobody would come to claim. Far away, his family, to whom he had not written in about two years, would continue to wait a little longer for him, or for some news. But they would end up forgetting him. On board, nobody would know a thing, or else, they would keep quiet. As for those at home, so far away, what did he matter to them now? They would coldly say, " He probably never even got to sail anywhere." That would be his whole epitaph and funeral. After a short spell he tried in vain to touch the ground with his legs, then he slid a little bit more. With his body practically in a horizontal position, swinging on the rope, he didn't know how to defy the law of gravity in order to regain his balance and the upright position. Even though his foot might hit against the edge of the pier, how was he going to free himself from the cable, spin around and jump in order to land on firm ground? His body refused to let go of the support, to straighten up and to brace itself for the jump. A few more minutes—how long would his strength last?—and a fall now would be fatal.

He had a very clear view of his considerably hopeless situation—the black jaws of death waiting for him down below like an insatiable shark. To himself, he cursed the ill-fated hour that got him into this fix. Since he wasn't a sailor, he didn't know how to climb a rope or how to swim.

He pulled himself up a little more, slid down a bit, and with one desperate try finally managed to touch the ground. He felt as if the torch of life had come from this touch, warming his limbs, rekindling his body. The wet and slippery wharf was within his reach. But what was underneath the rest of his body? Would it still be the water or was it already the pier? Straddling the cable, all tightened up and aching, he thought for a moment. Then he freed the other leg and swung both of them in search of the ground. The thin soles of his shoes slid as they skimmed the sticky surface, throwing his body off balance. If he were to put his weight on them, he would definitely slip and take that one final dive. Sweating bullets and shaking from the strain of having to hold on, he stayed there, for one moment, with his feet hanging and completely still.

To climb back up—he wouldn't even think of that—he no longer had the strength; and if he had, on board they wouldn't let him get on and stay. Now he had to go through with it and escape or die. Like a stubborn fly who flaps around to get out of a trap, he began to try and find some support and, as he did, shouted out loud:

"Freakin' luck of mine."

It was when he felt something hard—a hand or prongs, grabbing him fiercely by his loins and giving him the feeling of a red-hot iron—that he had a brief moment of resignation: I've been caught. But curiously at the same time he regained his composure and hope.

He felt drained and did not resist until he managed with some difficulty to stand on his feet and straigthen up, still clutching the bag. The hand holding on to him was as hard as iron, grabbing his clothes and flesh, mortifying and hurting him. With a jerk, it almost lifted him off the ground. Raising his eyes, he saw before him a huge dark figure, a uniform with brass buttons, a rain slicker, glittering from the wet air, and a white metal badge. A police officer with a round and hearty red face leaned toward him.

"Stowaway, eh?" And the hand shook him vigorously as if wanting to wake him from a stupor. "Stowaway?" he repeated and laughed. "You speak English?"

What can a man say in a situation like this? They had advised him: no matter what happens, don't say boo. Play dumb. But with that big hand, one didn't fool around and so he answered:

"I no eespeek inglishe, no eespeeke."

The officer had a good laugh and began again to shake him.

"No eespeek. No eespeek."

152

Small as a mouse, shivering cold in his suit of clothes (who knows, if angered, the officer wouldn't give him a shove and throw him in the water) the stowaway, awaiting a decision, stared at the brass buttons and the long shiny billy-club.

The policeman said something else that he couldn't make out, and tightened the grip on his shoulders as if he were planning to crush them out of sheer sadistic pleasure. Then, he forced him to make an about-face toward the land, and braced his enormous flat hand on the man's back and pushed him forward.

"Run."

The man didn't have to understand. He ran. He ran without knowing where he was going or thinking, or whether the officer was about to shoot him in the back, like a dockyard thief who disregards the order "Halt," or whether he was really sending him away, free, without arresting or forcing him to return to the ship. He ran blindly, laughing and crying, biting his words without a sound, stumbling over something at every step. Running into walls, crates, bales, rigging, machinery, he was confused and lost, unable to find an exit from the dark maze.

Far away in the distance the policeman yelled at him:

"Merry Christmas."

The stowaway stopped, vaguely understanding, and only at that moment did he remember that it was indeed Christmas Eve. Then, all choked up, he jumped over a wire fence, crossed some railway tracks and suddenly began to run less anxiously now that he was in the clear.

In the distance, the brighter glow of the city guided his way like the reflection of a mysterious and obscure star, or a warm hearth, beckoning him to the Christmas banquet.

*Translated by* Nelson H. Vieira

# STEERAGE

(Shipboard Journal—1935)

Of this voyage on the ancient *Arlanza* to Southampton, I shall always retain an indelible memory. At the docks I leave my handful of friends, who, through time and space, will probably diminish and fade unto full forgetfulness. Aboard there is no companion, who can assuage and lessen the wounds of those burdens that dog my steps or solve the enigma that awaits me on the other side of the Atlantic. Life is a chain of unresponsive sphinxes, and one must run alongside them, always advancing, in the belief that somewhere there exists an answer. Solitude causes me pain, but the attention I pay to those who are my fellow voyagers in misfortune helps to dissipate that pain. Among them, I soon forget my pain—almost.

Only those who have made one of these translantic crossings can have any inkling of the barriers that separate men and classes, even in an ocean-going tub. And there are only a few of us, here, no more than fifty. What would it be if there were 200 of us, or the 400 of full capacity, only God knows, piled up in that feculent asylum which is the immigrant's steerage.

The *Arlanza* returns from South America to Southampton with calls at Madeira, Corunha and Cherbourg, carrying in its mercenary belly a handful of the saddest breed of voyagers: those returning immigrants, who in the distant past sailed off in a ship's hold, and who, years later, return to the land of their birth, in the bowels of a floating sepulchre that a veterinarian might have condemned as unsuitable for slaughter-house animals. Upon departure, they had carried with them some hope at least; now even that is gone. Many of them, along with their great dream—their one luxury—have lost health and strength, their only wealth.

Along with these, the returning immigrants, there are other Portuguese—some who have embarked from Madeira, some who, like me, have boarded ship in Lisbon—all of whom now go to England to catch the ship for the United States. In this fashion there come together two currents of people who, despite having their destinies and the state of their souls in opposition, drift in the same sea of woes. One of the currents, still warm from the sun of illusion, moves westward toward the more temperate, more prosperous latitudes of America; the other current, returning from the equator and the tropics, chilled by disappointment, battered and broken, scrofulous, to be scattered throughout every corner of that Christian, occidental world of ours. Human currents, in a restless, perpetual maelstrom within that other Sargasso sea which is life.

While we move under the sun of coastal Portugal, all goes well; but as soon as we sail past Leixões, it rains. It's cold (and it's July). The majority of the travellers, some of them ill, all coming from lands of milder clime, disappear into the deepest cavities of the ship, wherein reign all those smells—enemies to man—that are steeped in twenty years' use: cloying food, creosote, vomit, spilled urine. The bad weather aggravates the monotony of the voyage.

It is nearly impossible for us to walk the deck at the prow, for it is exposed, cramped, wind-swept, rain-battered, and splattered with the Atlantic's atomized phlegm, even as it is jammed with commercial cargo and the bags of the poor. The rocking of the ship threatens to wash us overboard. Only one person, an

156

Irishman, I suspect—lean, silent, dressed in denim—walks obstinately, hours on end, like a man possessed, hands in pocket, biting on a pipe. He appears to be bent on walking a path between Lisbon and Southampton. Once in a while he pauses, fixes the hoary waves, takes his pipe from his mouth, and spits toward the sea in what looks like a gesture of rage. I notice that he has fingers missing on his right hand. We are in competition, and with each turn I take, we collide. I recoil, and he, annoyed, grouses.

I would like to escape, but a rope streched across the deck separates, like a barrier, the human cattle from the world of mankind with its torrential electric light, and from which issue the sounds of tinkling cups and squeaking violins. Fearing the immobility to which, for three days and three nights, I will be condemned out of a scarcity of vital space—I, a born walker, impeded in my movements by the Irishman on a marathon—I approach a beardless steward and say to him in poor English, which he nevertheless understands all too well: "Where can I walk above ship? Here there isn't even enough room to stretch one's legs."

He looks at me courteously, standing there in the new outfit he bought for the trip, and says:

"But, sir, you can walk anywhere you please. This place," he emphasizes with a disdainful gesture, "is only for Spaniards and the Portuguese."

He has taken me, undoubtedly, for a passenger from another deck.

I am irritated, and I answer:

"Thank you. I, too, am Portuguese."

Behind me I hear the lackey murmur in English, "I'm sorry, sir."

I return to the company of the spicks dancing below to sad, interminable whining, greeting the approach of their native land, and that of the Portuguese who embarked with me, the Syrians and Poles—sick, poor, beaten—who retreat from Eldorado and the dream. I return to the smell of vomit, the stench of the mob, and the odor of creosote. I have never felt so close to all of them, so at one with them, nor so distant from that strange, hostile world above us, It's from that other world that I flee, and it is to this one that I run. (I begin to understand, with a start, what it is that moves me; it's my desire to identity with the meek of this world.) "For Spanish and Portuguese people only"—so clearly do the prestige and grandeur of an empire shine through the soul of even the last of its lackeys.

Lying in my miserable bed, numb with cold beneath my prisoner's blanket that, drawn up to cover my shoulders, exposes my feet to the cold air such that I either freeze or suffocate with warmth, I listen to the convulsions of the ship's propeller, which shake frightfully the stern of the ship when the huge undulations of the sea expose the propeller; and through the clouded porthole, I look at the billows of the verdigris sea, irritated, foam-crested, and gnashing—there had to be the inevitable gnashing of teeth—as, all the while, there run through my head the "Steward's" words. Pirates.

The rocking of a badly loaded vessel wreaks havoc with my insides. At times I have the feeling that my stomach and liver, unfixed and crumpled into a ball, throw themselves to the bottom of my abdominal cavity; at other times it feels as if they swim and climb, sticking to the back of my ribcage, seeking a hatchway to the throat. But I do not throw up. It is the third time that I have crossed these agitated straits, and never have I been seasick. That much to the good, at least. I get up, I lie down again, I try to concentrate, to read, to entertain myself, but all in vain. I lose interest in H. G. Wells when I discover that I can understand him only with the aid of a dictionary. And the light is atrocious, worse even than my English. I give him up but I harbor the anguish of ignorance.

When the ship's rocking gets worse, I hear cries and moans of children and women. Coming from the neighboring cabins, from which I am separated by a partition of metal netting with no bottom frame, is a suspicious-looking liquid running over the scarred floor of pressed cork, and, with it, the spreading smell of vomit and urine. "For Portuguese people only..."

There is no place nearby where one can answer nature's call. I must get dressed, leave the cabin, step in the flow, walk a great distance, climb up and down iron stairways through which blow harsh winds. In the corridors and passageways I collide with other afflicted beings who, in agony, stumble along, grasping the rails, clutching the viscous walls, seeking relief. I finally succeed in discovering the object of my quest, but I am losing my balance. I lose a slipper, and the wind, blowing through me, knifes me in the belly. I run back to my cabin.

At first I was given an interior, asphixiating berth, with no porthole, crisscrossed with scalding water pipes, suffocatingly covered with naval paint. (Everywhere the ship seems to be coated and recoated with paint accumulated from each crossing.) When I protested, in English suitable to the time and place, they moved me to the frigid cabin in which I now find myself, one with two double bunks, but three unoccupied beds that constantly bang together, like the chattering teeth of a sick man chilled with fever.

Out of boredom I try to while away the time by brushing my teeth with water from the bottle, water which emanates from the small tank, set in the wall, that also supplies the trickle of water used in washing one's face. It has an execrable taste. I refuse to drink it, to rinse out my mouth, or even to shave with it. I shall become a reflection of my surroundings, which are worse than a dungeon. Sordid surroundings degrade man; they demoralize him.

The "stewards" enter without knocking, without asking permission, without a word to me; it is as if I did not exist. They clean, make the beds, change the water in the wall tank. Like dogs, they bare their teeth and growl sounds I cannot understand. They are like prison guards, and I get the feeling that I am one of a gang of convicts.

From the cabin nearly opposite mine comes the soft voice of a Madeiran who goes to the United States to join her husband. She is accompanied by three small children, who look like lambs on the way to slaughter. (It is at the expense of such humble beings, devoid of any and all protection, that the pride and the disdain of authoritarian Empires waxes.) A pleasant and kindly peasant, she answers everything I tell her with a "Yeh, my lord" that knifes me to the heart. One could say that she had lost her mother tongue but has not yet discovered its mother-in-law. She looks at me with a start. Can it be that I, a "lord," am also going to "Améreca"? As if the land of opportunity were the Mecca of the hungry alone. She has already spent some years there, and it was there that her two youngest were born. Her husband is a weaver in "Bètefete." "We've separated—four years." And she returns to the great dream of prosperity, where there is no lack of bread for the hungry mouths of submissive sojourners. Yeh, my lord.

The children get seasick; they have lost their appetite. The older girl gnaws constantly on a peel, either lemon or orange. And the smallest child, with yellowish eyes, muffler wrapped around his slender neck, wears a bony smile that is meek and sad. The mother—fat, calm—has dark, kindly eyes; her smile is that of the canine humanity one sees in the poor who are inherently resigned to their fate.

"We sold our little house. All our savings went. Not even 'crackers' for the children."

Every so often she raises one of her many skirts; and out of some hidden depth, she extracts oranges or a handkerchief to wipe her children's snotty noses and the vomit from their chins before she medicates them with a swallow of sugarcane whiskey. "*Doze mil-réis* a liter, yeh, my lord. How dear it has become, and they won't let us make it anymore, as we used to. It's prohibited. A poor Christian can't even have his drop."

At meals, at my table, eat Poles, Portuguese, some lower-class Englishmen (Irish surely), an incommunicative German couple, a large Syrian clan returning from the north of Brazil with jaundiced children, and others of the same breed. At my right is seated a Polish woman returning from Buenos Aires. White, blonde, Medusa-fleshed, incipiently obese, she is right out of pulp fiction—a case of trafficking in white slavery, and right out of cheap, sensationalist journalism. In front of her sits the classic figure of the two-bit pimp. At the table, for a while, both of them try to pass themselves off as French, judging from the linguistic scraps in which they pretend to converse, with a *oui-oui* dropped in here and there. At a certain point I turn to the procurer and ask,

"*Vous êtes polonais, n'est pas?*"

He blanches, stammers, and answers precipitately that yes, but well, no. Madame is French, from Paris (of course), but he is, for all purposes, Polish, and how *was* I able to guess it.

"Oh, it's most simple. It's in your face; I'm familiar with your type, and then there is your accent."

The man withdraws into himself, the conversation falls off, and we continue to sip at that bilge that aboard ship is called coffee, though I would call it dishwater, were it not so black and bitter. Why do such people try to pass themselves off as something they are not? This poor Jew, beaten and persecuted in his native land, has no home, like so many others. The brutality of his existence has perhaps made him into the thing that we see—a vulgar *souteneur* of the byways of Buenos Aires. Now it is Paris that attracts them as a port of refuge. But for how long?

Madame has a sweet, submissive, come-hither look. She is (or rather was) actually pretty, with a delicately shaped face, softly fleshed, but judging from a glancing inspection, very much worn down by overuse. In her day she must have been a good source of income. Retired, with a little savings. Are they friends? Are they married? With her she has a little monkey, a *sagouin* I belive, that she bought in Bahia. She cuddles it on her knee. During the meal she lovingly feeds it little bits of boiled carrot and other delicacies (good for monkeys), and it soon walks about freely on the floor and on top of the table, unceremoniously sticking his four prehensile limbs in the plates of the other messmates. Suddenly, having climbed on my shoulder, it takes to pulling one of my ears, and tries to bite me. It's jealous of me for having spoken to its owner.

But, eyes lowered, she hardly replies in that broken French of a transoceanic *maison close*, where the exported echoes of official French culture are never heard. The problem is that I have no one to talk to, and my intentions are most honorable. In the midst of the conversation (in taking another helping, I had turned away) I catch the pimp, wide-eyed, signalling her. He seems to be warning her against me, taking me, perhaps, with a nose like mine, for a spy. What is clear is that the lady, whose flesh is voraciously felt up visually by the other messmates, disappears at a certain point from the table, to reappear only on deck from time to time, with her chained simian and a book in her hand, one that she does not read. "She's ill," explains the procurer. The food has made her seasick. It's a shame. Now there's nothing left at mess that's worth looking at.

It's a lie. It was my fault that in my nautical tedium I insisted on striking a spark of *esprit* in that gelatinous jellyfish despite the simian's hostility and the impressario's suspicious glances. But the poor thing had nothing about her to sustain her in the role of *parisienne* for export; and having stammered her two macaronic sentences, she decided to beat a hasty retreat. She spends most of her time in her cabin. The simian, who defends her literally with tooth and nail, keeps her company. With him at least, the poor woman can externalize those stores of tenderness that men had taught her to disguise and to hide. An animal's love is free, but gratifying. Meanwhile, her pimp, with his boxer's flattened nose, walks the deck in bored preocupation, chewing on an old toothpick, shuffling along, wearing slippers and a cloth cap pulled over his eyes, just as if he were at home.

After a skilfully conducted conversation with him (I have not yet lost entirely the habit of interrogation), held at the rail in the wildly blowing wind, I establish that they lived for a while in Southern Brazil, where certain "difficulties"—oh, nothing extraordinary, he hastens to correct himself, glancing uneasily in my direction—caused their removal to Rio da Prata. What new "difficulties" cause them to return at this time, still in their prime, to a Europe on the edge of crisis, I am unable to learn. Cautiously, upon separation, I touch discretely the pocket in which I carry my meager change.

Caged within the depths of steerage, in a kind of prow with a hatchway open to the wind and the rain, are the Galicians who return from Argentina. In reality, that place is called "immigrant" class. When at mealtime the doleful bell resonates throughout the fetid bowels of the *Arlanza,* they throw themselves, frenzy with hunger, into the tight quarters of the refectory. They eat at second sitting, and I at first. I do not know which is better or worse; both are bad.

Once in while, from the abyss below the hatchway comes the descant, the whining, and the scraping of dancing. The beer runs over; it is flat, tepid, and with no foam. During the voyage to Corunha, the men yell, argue vehemently, insult one another; they're full of protestations. They surprise me. They are not like the Galicians of my dear old Lisbon, whom I was accustomed to see as docile, smiling, and of good disposition. The New World has soured them; it has aged them.

Suddenly, the tumult increases, and I cock my ear; something subversive is going on down there in the animal pit. It isn't long before one of them—small, thin and eloquent, his beard blue against those emanciated cheeks of the tubercular, one who is quickly recognized as the "leader"—rants against the lack of consideration that victimizes them. They complain; they want better coffee, merely coffee: *"que seja café, vamos!"* Perhaps they are encouraged by the nearness of their homeland. If that's not the case, why have they waited eighteen days before registering their complaint? Or perhaps these are habits picked up in Argentina, where despite everything, the catharsis of the Scream is still tolerated. Now all of those below join in protest to support the "leader."

I ask the insolent *steward*—who, tray in hand, looks on the scene with supremely disdainful Arianism—why, since this ship has come from Brazilian ports where they burn and dump overboard mountains of coffee, are we being forced to swallow that brackish, oily swill, that brew of shoe dust and toasted bean, they call coffee. He has no answer to that question. He shrugs and says,

"In first class no one complained. Perhaps you would prefer tea, Sir?" he adds, with continued deference to my garb.

But the tea is even worse.

To the *steward* and the passengers in first class, who come to look down from the balustrade at the tumult, as if they were viewing an animal circus from a gallery, smiling and thrusting forward their cigars and cocktails (the men are in "smoking" and "evening jackets"; the women in *décolletage*, with fur wraps over their delicate, freckled shoulders)—to them any drug will do for this bony, swarthy herd, deformed by labor. *For Spanish and Portuguese people only.*

Since the protest increases in tone and assumes the abstract character of insubordination—one never knows how far the destructive furor of an empty-handed mob will go—the purser goes off to summon the officers. These appear in dress whites adorned with gold embroidery. They are impeccable, giving off the smell of Havana cigars and the aroma of first class. They smile cynically, showing bad teeth in a way unique to the nordic blond; and they proceed with rapid, formal questioning. The *meneur*, sour and tubercular, is reprimanded. He is threatened with the calaboose.

Then, intimidated by the presence of the Empire, disconcerted by the language in which they talk to him, abandoned by those who until recently were his comrades, this luckless being loses his eloquence, turns even whiter, shrugs with a smile, dissolves into stuttering explanations. He fears what might await him in Corunha, that if he arrives under arrest they will deliver him to the *Benemérita...*

Immediately there is silence below; and the spectators retire from the balustrade in laughter, exchanging comments with the gallant officials as they go.

Ah, what can one expect of these sad beings, graduates of the school of misery and humility? How create the City out of such imitations of Citizens? And they—who return even poorer than they left because without gaining anything new they have expended their irreplaceable treasury of illusions—try to drown their humiliation in the intoxication of bad beer and music. Again I hear bagpipes, tambourines and flutes. It is Galicia, which they carried away with them in their hearts and which they now bring back.

When the ship drops anchor in Corunha, all of them come up into the light of day, showing off their best rags, their rings of *ouro-besouro*, their scarves in vivid colors, their feast-day shawls. On the upper deck they pile up their chairs, their chests of battered tin, their crumpled suitcases, their bundles, all in the humidity and anxiety of disembarkation. Already they have forgotten the bad coffee. From afar they wave at the land, which responds to them. They have tears in their eyes, songs and laughter in their throats. Before them lies Galicia, all green

164

and misty, like a poem in a medieval songster, looking sad, reclusive, and mysterious. It rains. The children, sucking on their fingers, clutch their mother's skirts. And a small Syrian the color of citron, with his jaw bound against the mumps, runs about excitedly, idiotically, gnawing at a crust of bread, with gestures of abnormality.

From above, from the heavens of first class, comes a gun-blast of *jazz*. The tourists look down on the scene from their main-rail vantage; and they laugh. The baggage piles up in disorder in the launch, which dances on the waves. The women scream out of fright, the children cry. But it occurs to me that it is well worth risking one's life to escape from the innards of this monster, on which some travel and others are transported.

On the day I sailed I had already caught a glimpse of her through the open cabin door, moaning and spitting incessantly into the spittoon at the side of her berth. She was overwhelmed by nausea, kicking and flailing from time to time in hysterical fury, shouting, as two or three women tried to calm her down. She was screaming loudly for vengeance, it seemed. They said that she was dangerous. Between Brazil and Madeira she had attracted to the pestilential abyss of her cabin two poor hardup males—only to start screaming and to have them arrested. (Now they're in the can.) Aboard an English packet, an act of this nature is nearly as subversive as the protest that coffee must contain caffeine.

She is a poor Turk (or maybe a Lebanese), small and scrawny, with a recruit's fuzz above her upper lip, a bony, sickly smile, and ugly knees that she gladly shows off to the men who lazily stroll the deck now that the weather has cleared up and she can come to the surface to take up her knitting. The wretch has her story. She comes from Buenos Aires. Her husband sailed with her, intending, apparently, to return to the Levant, carrying their trunks aboard, as well as all the clutter and junk of the peddler. When he caught her absorbed in making the rounds of the ship, happy with the notion of the trip and wearing her new clothes, he slipped back to shore at the last moment. And she, desperately screaming in a language no one could understand (there were no other Turks aboard and the Syrians did not come aboard until Brazil), found herself abandoned (ugly and skinny) in the bulging, accelerating monster. No one paid attention to her drama. The *Arlanza* neither turned back, nor stopped. Then, in a spurt of madness, the luckless one took to throwing overboard, into the Rio Plate, her dresses, gowns, skirts, souvenirs—all the fruits of long years of slaving—an act of indulgence by the traveller returning home. Of what use were all those things now that she no longer had her name? She left her baggage behind, except for her carcass, saving that because she lacked courage or because she wanted vengeance against men. But after the sad experience of the first two men, all men run from her, from her goat's eyes, black and mysterious, in which one discerns the jail that looms in the sinister light of moslamic vengeance. No one wants to aid her in her quest for revenge. Damn.

The one who told me all this was a Portuguese fisherman, who was returning to America for the fourth time in order to fish like the mariners from the time of the Corte-Reais. In the past he lived there for years at a time, but now he travels back and forth, as the spirit moves him. He is swarthy, lean, direct, philosophical. He reads books; he wears thick glasses, a toothpick made of bone in his mouth, a Basque cap on his head, and fisherman's boots on his feet. He is a native of Figueira da Foz, he tells me. One readily sees that he has been around, that he is his own man, with no hangups or mental blocks. The world and the sea belong to him, without limits other than the rights of the next man. He expresses himself clearly and precisely. He looks more like a hunter than a fisherman, perhaps because his speciality was once the harpooning of whales. Every so often he disappears, so that twice a day he can shave. He then returns to the deck, toothpick in mouth, to study the sea and to size up the Polish woman:

"She's quite a piece. Oh boy, a chippy like that, and he a skinny pickle. In America, those Polish women..."

Her appearance, in the midst of his indolence, gives him rather unorthodox thoughts. When she disappears accompanied by the hopping simian, he—irritated—also disappears. Possibly he is going to stroll by her cabin door. And the pimp, a weakling, walks around. He is uneasy, pale; he sniffs danger, a rival. On board it is necessary to toe the line; business is over. They are respectable people.

He is the most intelligent one, if not the only intelligent one, of our sorry band. He looks on his compatriots, the humble folk from the Islands and the back-country hicks, with a mixture of irony and estrangement. Rural people, parish folk, thinking of bargaining for bits and pieces of land, of parcels and parcelling—they are not like him. He has no roots on land. He is free. "Dolas" and "prop'ties" hold no interest for him. When the conversation of the country folk displeases him, he frowns, turns his back on them, and goes off to look out at the sea for infinite periods of time, not with nostalgia or in contemplation, but with the studious and critical air of the expert. On the seas there is neither a bureaucracy nor red tape. He understands things that escape the comprehension of others; he is an open, liberated spirit. He can make in his head prodigious computations on the conversion of English, Portuguese and American currencies. It is not, then, that money does not interest him; he even hints that he was once engaged in bootlegging on the West Coast.

And so, this quiet, strong man, solitary and perfectly self-controlled, has, or has had, his own drama. He was married as a young man to a Portuguese woman from Gloucester, a woman of some means, who gave him a son. For some reason, which he did not reveal, they later separated; she died years ago. He raised his child as a mother would. Awake for whole nights, he rocked him, giving him his pacifier, pinning his diapers and changing the sheets and blankets of his crib. He cooked his food, and he took him out walking. When he went to sea, he left him in the care of a neighbor, an old woman. It is hard for me to envisage this harpooner of cachalots, sunburned and lean, a wearer of thick glasses, expressing a mother's zeal for her baby. The boy grew up, went to school, learned well, and his proud father sent him to college, to Harvard, to turn him into an engineer. The guy was intelligent alright. Well-mannered, obedient, always aiming to please. He never laid a hand on him, in contrast to the custom of so many of his compatriots.

"But that thief fooled me; he took after his mother. As soon as he graduated, since he had been hanging around with a high-toned bunch in Boston and Cambridge, he married an American girl with plenty of dough. It still surprises me, for such girls pay no attention to us, and he, of all things, the son of a fisherman. She must have been lusting after him, the pretty boy. He took after me, but of lighter complexion, with his mother's face. Well, he never again sought me out. Not even a card for my birthday, or one at Christmas. It has even happened that passing me on the street, his arm locked in hers, he has crossed over to the other sidewalk just so he would not have to speak to the person who made him and raised him. Go ahead and love your child, kill yourself for him. I sold my house. I sold everything. And I returned to Figueira da Foz to forget things for a while. Now I go to America, only when I long for the sea, for fishing."

He turns his face to the ocean, fixing his gaze on it for a while. Later, with neither bitterness nor lamentation, he says, "That's life. And there's nothing to be done about it. But one always finds some solace. That damned Polish woman. Man, is she a piece. And that guy, undoubtedly, lives off her."

He goes off, gloom-ridden and sullen, to shave. Of the mainland Portuguese who get on board in Lisbon, with America as their destination, some of them upset me rather than evoking my sympathy. They belong to that category of people who talk only about land, boundaries, crops, leases, rents, agreements; and they talk about electrification and improvement, which one of them calls "improvimentos," a Luso-Americanism. They are loquacious, emphatic, even like those fly-by-night Ph.D.s (they are aping them, surely), especially when, in a Portuguese tongue corrupted by poor American English, they praise the material greatness of their adopted country, because they are ignorant of any of that country's other virtues, or the progress they have just come upon in their mother country.

This next one has a father somewhere in Massachusetts, a shopkeeper (I might have known), and he spends his time wearing out my patience by displaying his prowess in doing what everybody already knows how to do: the trapping and hunting of quails, crimes of passion in the provinces, public scandals and embezzlements, which turn him on. He tells his stories with the malice of one who justifies the blots on his own character by pointing at the mistakes and weaknesses of others, as if in so doing he would be absolved. Each of his accounts he concludes in laughter: "He should have been shot, that scoundrel." It is perfectly clear that he admires and envies those scoundrels, when they evade the Law. And he narrates for me, confidently, the entire history of the Malafaias, getting it all hopelessly confused.

He likes to talk about big shots and those with influence, showing the instinctive respect of one who would emulate them. These are the ones, with their subtle and quasi-religious legal power, who attract him; he would love to be of their kind. He insists that I, a native of Lisbon, must know all the judges, lawyers, and bureaucrats in charge of this and that, of his own judicial district—as if they were in reality the *crème de la crème* of mankind, coming from a world that is superior and olympian to a Lisbon which is their deferential and ever-grateful fiefdom. To his abject veneration for Degrees one can counterpose his unconscious rancor: doctor so-and-so is a priest's son, that other guy was born in a goat crib. All have clay feet, like him. To shut him up, I pretend that I know it all and agree with everything. But he won't shut up.

Since he arrived from America regurgitating tall tales, with the semblance of authenticity in his role, in his new clothes and yellow shoes, the village made a great deal of him. They accepted him into their circle by taking him quail-hunting, and they flattered him by asking from him a few grand at interest. He tells me all about their weaknesses and failings. He also knows some fellows from his part of the country who are somewhere in Lisbon, working for the government and in politics. "There's a guy from my place, maybe you know him? He's a cop in Olivais." Well, sure. Why wouldn't I know him? What place would I know better than Olivais? Just like the palm of my hand. (In truth, how could I, a denizen of Lisbon, ignore such a suburban authority? I'm shameless, I feel estranged from my true self.) He eyes me somewhat suspiciously. Does he think[1] that I am mocking him?

He is returning now to Massachusetts, full of himself, ready to accumulate more *"dolas"* so that he can buy more land, to fill out his "prop'ties," evict the poor, rival the powerful, dazzle them, put up a "modern" house that will wreak havoc with the character of his village. He is the very type of the poor man who was born to be a rich man, or of the rich man who was born poor by mistake; he is of the essence of that mediocrity which aspires to power. He is surely the president or secretary of some club or communal society, where these licensed swindlers gather together herds of poor fools the better to talk to them of Camões, whom they're never read, and to reach into their pockets. A greedy, furtive, shifty yokel, he is the very opposite of the bucolic rustic of legendry. His obsequious eyes weigh out all of nature in inventories and shares; his soul is made up of scraps of property and bits of land. This is the dough out of which, for centuries, have come the lawyers who have permeated the culture of Coimbra, using their political power, their influence, their submissiveness and their obsequiousness. At the rhythm of the throaty *fado*, and at the expense of Portuguese life and culture, they have reduced existence to what we today find it to be in every sector. He runs around with those who rule ("God keep your Excellency"), always in line with the "Order" and the "Conservation"; his little sly, treacherous eyes shine out from the bottom of a dark well, like those of a badger looking for its prey. He is still at the stage of piling up nickles in anticipation of becoming...

There's another guy of the same stripe, but of the large size. He's short, husky-voiced, displaying himself in an immense camel-haired overcoat, which looks like an inheritance from some nabob. Only his fingertips can be seen sticking out of the sleeves; they're thick and shiny, like drumsticks. A silk scarf, ox-blood in color, puts his full face into violent relief, a face that is swarthy and hairy, and in which the nose can hardly be seen, so consumed is it by invading fatty flesh. The chops of a bore or a one-time hoodlum. He is "Amurican," and he insists on that fact, repeatedly and emphatically. He, too, returned to his homeland to acquire property, and he is enamored of "Progress." For him a few kilometers of new road are worth more than any ideal. When he talks about "dolas" and "prop'-ties," he looks like a patrolman on leave, his twitching fingers peeking out from his coatsleeves, like puppets. He worked as a pick-and-shovel laborer—"a workhorse," he says proudly—but today he is a boss, an owner, a contractor. He's very successful, sly and boorish; he is the epitome of the *kulak* rustic. And he respects only the force of money and the power of those in charge. Had he gone to Brazil in boom times, he would have returned a baron, or at the least, have received a commendation. Stubbornly, he resumes the thread of a story no one either understands or listens to: "Well, as I was saying, there's a parish committee..."

When the matter of the Great Depression is brought up, he answers, "What depression? What unemployment? Me and the old woman, we were pulling in as much as seventy to eighty 'dolas' a week." There were millions unemployed, he will admit, but, as he insists, "There's always work for those who want it"—a viewpoint entirely worthy of the President of General Motors. A great country, America. Don't even mention those workers' Unions—a gang of racketeers. Many a martyr has suffered and died so that this "worker," who hates his own class, will take advantage of all the conquests made and the privileges gained by organized Labor: unemployment insurance, disability and old age pensions, the right to organize, and contract by collective bargaining. Freedom is his orchard, one planted by others. He wants to be somebody, spouting off about everything his porcine and inexpressive eyes manage to take in. He detests President Roosevelt, he attends the religious procession in New Bedford, just as he did in his village in the hills, and he is a member of the order of the Blessed Sacrament. (Can the Blessed Sacrament know of the existence of this spurious member?) Nevertheless, he laughs at his pal's stories about priests, and he tells a few of them himself. It is that priests have about them the mysterious superiority of an authority that does not derive from money, but from something ineffable, from their Latin and their celibacy, and all these matters attract to them a feminine clientele.

Looking at these people, I sometimes wonder, in anguish, if the People exist, if they actually exist. All that in them which was originally crude and boorish has been aggravated and accenutated in the brutal ambience they encountered; and they gained nothing of the spiritual values that America had to offer them. How much longer will the simple and deprived people continue to confuse civilization with the purely material values of acquisition? When will they learn that, without spiritual values, without principles, everything else is chaos? In their idolatry of Things (which is not theirs alone, for they learned it from their betters) they continue to be regressive and niggardly in Spirit. Things, even if they improve a man's lot, do not free him. On the contrary. It is not that only suffering and abasement attract me, not that all common success is repugnant. Time will teach me to love even those, in everything my opposites, who display vitality, energy, and a capacity to survive all odds, who make me proud to belong to the same ancient stock. We are all children of the same ancestral deprivation. It is harder to love men for all their defects and weaknesses than it is to love them for their virtues, however hypothetical. No, what bothers me about them and penetrates disagreeably, like a shrieking violin or a grease stain, is that mediocrity, utter and without character, to which they belong and which they spread all about them. They are the aspirants to the power that money brings, seeing in it the real thing, the *primum movens* of all progress, including their own—a lamentable triumph.

Fortunately, there are others. An old woman, in black, including shawl and head scarf, has been moaning almost ceaselessly, wiping her cracked lips, never having seen the ocean. She comes from way up around Montalegre, the hills of Larouco. She's tall, upright, displaying that dignity of carriage so common among our women, when, aged and hardened by all the pains and cares of life, they appear to stiffen themselves in order better to withstand, like the oak, the blasts of the destructive winds. Clear-eyed, hair severely parted down the middle—everything about her reminds me of the mother of one of my dear friends, who after having suffered his loss, took on, in her pains, the very appearance of robust health. She leaves no one on earth, only the dead and her memories, and she goes to America to join a married daughter, who lives there. Like one on a pilgrimage, she brings with her a basket of provisions—a roasted capon, cornbread, cheese, oranges, I know not what else—all of it fresh and appetizing, which she offers to her fellow passengers, and to the sick children, who are frightened and greedy. She does not eat; she moans, vomits, and coughs up with a realism worthy of Gil Vicente or Breughel. "Ai, Jesus, if someone had only told me. Will it be like this until we get there? They say that over towards America it's even worse. My God. I'll never get there alive."

The men laugh cynically at her; they try to console her with words that do not convince her: "That'll go away, granny." With a gesture she shunts them aside. Each one knows what she is going through. No one on board has any cure for what ails her. The problem is that she hasn't been able to eat during the trip, three days, from Southampton. But she hasn't lost her composure or her interest in others. "I have some oranges. Maybe you would like one?" she asks me. "I don't know why I even brought them." Was it that she imagined that the journey would be like a quick hop over to Vila Real? Just thinking about food makes her nauseous. America, is it still very far? Again she belches and blesses herself. All this she does with the dignity of nobility. Her problem is solitude; and that she is going out into the world at the age of seventy-plus years to make a new start.

"Out there, what language do they talk? They probably won't understand me."

"Your daughter will be waiting for you at the dock. Don't get upset."

"She lives over by *Providence*. Do you know where that is?"

"Everything will be alright, dear."

"If things don't go good, I'll return the same way I came."

I can see her now, arriving in Providence or Pawtucket, and handing over her hamper to her daughter with these words, "Take it; these are from our place." Maybe that's why no one on board will take what she offers them.

The one who does not like jokes about priests is the little

lady from Murtosa who travels with us. She protests, tells them to shut up, and even stops talking with the man of prop'ty, furious at the "disrespect." She has with her two boys who are not hers, she says, as if with children it was always a matter of their having to "belong" to somebody. She is going to deliver them to a family in Lowell, if I understand her. And since they are joyous, inquisitive, and active (and who wouldn't be so, at their age aboard a large ship under the tutelage of someone like her?) she treats them with exemplary harshness. "Devils. Rabble. Ill-mannered gang. Goddam them." She whacks them, shakes them, treatens them with terrifying punishments when they get to America, as if the land of Lincoln and Whitman were Purgatory. But the two children mock her. They do not take her seriously or show her any respect, unless it is the respect born out of hypocrisy, that disgraceful teacher. And they continue to do whatever their vitality demands. She calls in vain upon God's Holy Name, displaying a child-killer's glare in eyes that are black and hard as glass beads. She is beginning to look like the Turk, only worse.

The good Madeiran mother remains calm and tolerant. She has a fundamentalist's belief in God, and she feels that "priests are needed," even if she doesn't know why. "Who would marry us? Who would send us off when we die? Everything in this world and in the next has its hierarchy." And she smiles good-naturedly and deferentially. The old lady from Trás-os-Montes, distracted by the conversation and finding herself relieved from her nausea, even smiles at the one from Murtosa. "Let 'em talk woman. They're men; they like to laugh. Don't you know, woman, that men want nothing to do with priests?"

The one from Murtosa makes a hex sign, and she goes off to see what deviltries the two pupils are up to. They just have to be deviltries. They'll pay for it. But later on I catch her surreptitiously looking at her antagonist with the eyes of a cow in heat. She would convert him, perhaps, by less than canonical means. She's the kind of woman who gives in only to those who oppress and crush her. A dry old maid she might be, but down deep she's of his kind.

The time passes with such disagreeable conversation.

I will find the majority of these countrymen in Southampton, spread out in suspect quarters, provided by the shipping company and the travel agents—all of them with little flags in their lapels or on their blouses so that they won't wander off and mix in with the others, just like head of cattle marked with their owner's brand. In great anxiety she looks for the *Aquitania*, one says, or for the *Manhattan*, says the Madeiran woman. The *Manhattan* has three chimneys. I see a kind of melancholy in their eyes. Can it be that the voyage has created within us a sympathetic tie? There we will separate, perhaps forever; America is so big. Treated like cattle, they are exploited even more than I, for I will sail on a luxury liner (it's the *Normandie*'s second voyage) and I'm paying less than they do. In addition, I will pass them on the way.

Her little children are sick; they are little plucked chicks. I give them aspirin; I take their temperatures. (I never saw a doctor aboard ship.) The little girl has a temp of 39.5c. Her head and throat ache, and she vomits; she sucks an orange peel. They do not drink milk.

This is the way they continue their voyage on the *Manhattan*. I do not see them again, and it makes me sorry. I do not know what secret feeling now binds me to all of them. Destiny has brought us together for a moment, and destiny has soon separated us.

The one I have totally lost sight of is my fisherman from Figueira. Where can he be hanging out? I begin to think that maybe he left in Cherbourg, chasing the Pole from Buenos Aires, who disembarked there on her way to Paris.

The fact is, though, that on the last night of the voyage, a night, as it were, dark as pitch, I came upon him in a nook on deck, his cap pulled down over his glasses, and wearing, as always, high boots. Beneath the cold drizzle of Mancha, he clutched the Pole, squeezing her in silence against the rail, as if he were trying to extract her holy essences. I just knew she had always sensed the harpooner in him. I did not lay eyes on the pimp. I saw only the little monkey, held by a chain, squeaking weakly, whether in reaction to the cold or out of jealousy, I know not. His owner paid no attention to him, nor did she feed him bits of carrot. And he was not biting the stranger. But there is no doubt that he was jealous. Monkeys have peculiar habits, I'm told.

*Translated by* George Monteiro and Carolina Matos

# A PORTUGUESE HOME

He'd been sick, lost thirty pounds, suffered from acidosis (what the devil's that?) and that Saturday I talked to him.

"Come over to the house," I invited him. "We'll have Portuguese stew."

He came for lunch. The stew was almost a casserole, the broth a sauce. He liked it, ate a lot, and even got some of his color back.

"This is what I need. Do you see, my friend? To enjoy life a bit. It's been a long time since I've felt as good as I do today."

He was in his thirties, tall and still good-looking, but with a middle-age spread. He shuffled his feet a bit when he walked. The four of them—his mother (a healthy dark-haired woman) and the two sons and daughter (the latter the youngest of the three and the only one born in the United States)—all worked. They lived together, along with three enormous yellow dogs, in their own house located in an outlying Queens neighborhood marked by broad, tree-lined streets and grassy lawns—in sum, a decent, comfortable place. They were respectable, Azorean, bearing an aristocratic family name, and very broad-minded.

The father, a most proper Portuguese more inclined to breaking than bending, had been a scrupulous translator, who thrived on patriotism and correct grammar. He had died suddenly, about a year before (what a temper), leaving them the house and, I suppose, some savings. He was the kind who'd pound on the table with his cane and tear up his translations if anyone changed so much as a comma.

"Beyond that door, only Portuguese may be spoken," he commanded.

He didn't let them make friends or bring home schoolmates.

"We were raised here alone; we don't know any Americans," Leopoldinho once told me. "And as for the Portuguese, you already know how it is with them."

They belonged to a Portuguese social club. Leopoldinho, who was the eldest, headed the Portuguese segment of a working men's organization. He attended meetings and went to debates and was always good-natured and conciliatory. He had found an escape from his loneliness. But the roughness and fanaticism of the "continentals" bothered him. With the help of an Azorean baritone, a former student of one of the famous Andrades, one who drank himself to death there, he organized a little choral group to sing album music—there wasn't any other kind available.

Because of the small-talk, lunch was over late. I had to go see a Brazilian friend, and we agreed to meet at night at the home of an American in the Village. I got there about 8:30 and found him depressed and looking pale. After a whole week of work, the day was a loss. The meeting went badly; there were disagreements and harsh words exchanged. We left together, around midnight. Out in the street, he seemed suddenly lost; he didn't know which way to go to get the Sixth Avenue "El." It stopped nearby and was his best way home; but if he missed it, he'd have to take a bus, and that was more than an hour's ride away. I pointed him in the direction of the station, a little way up ahead, at the intersection.

"I am getting absent-minded; it must be because I am tired," he said. "Tomorrow I'll sleep all day."

And he walked off, a little sadly, not at all the person from lunchtime. I wondered about it. Could it have been that acidosis?

Sunday went off monotonously, as usual. Monday we returned to the boredom of our jobs; and Tuesday morning—it wasn't even eight o'clock—the phone next to the bed rang.

"It's probably Martinson asking about the translations."

She answered. A sharp hysterical voice was on the other end.

"It can't be!" she was saying, upset and barely awake. "It can't be... just last Saturday he was... oh! my God!"

She turned toward me.

"Leopoldinho."

And she burst into tears.

I yanked the phone away from her.

"Hello, hello!"

A feminine voice on the other end stammered out an explanation.

"An emergency operation yesterday... he died early this morning."

"But lady," I was saying.

"It's no lady, this is his brother."

"I'm sorry, things are confused. I misunderstood."

I said we'd be there as soon as possible. But we didn't get there until mid-afternoon.

The brother had gone out. The mother and the sister were alone at home with the body of the deceased. How quiet things seemed. In the living-room, which was arranged like a room in a funeral-home, surrounded by flowers, the made-up dead man was smiling serenely, hands folded over his chest. Only the top half of the casket was open, so that the body could be seen only from the waist up. It was like a display box, and he looked like a wax manikin. Horrified, I followed them into the kitchen. There was cold chicken, salad and perked coffee. We ate and we talked. The dogs dozed, piled up in a corner. From where I was, I could glimpse part of the catafalque.

Dininha told me how it happened.

"He came home Saturday, after one, exhausted. 'What I

need is some sleep.' Around noon he came down for coffee. 'I'm so tired I think I'll go back to bed.' He mentioned having lunch at your house. He slept all day Sunday and didn't come down again until dinner-time. He didn't feel like eating. About midnight, before she went to bed, Mother looked in on him. She found him sick, livid, teeth chattering with cold. She put more covers on him, gave him something hot to drink, but the chills kept on. Seeing him so sick, around 2 a.m., we called his doctor. The doctor said he couldn't come and gave us the name of a colleague. The other doctor arrived after three, and, as soon as he examined Leopoldinho, he said:

"This is a case for emergency surgery—peritonitis."

The ambulance came and took him straight to the hospital emergency room, but it wasn't until seven that they could operate. We waited. And when they opened him up, they found a tumor the size of which they hadn't even imagined: stomach, liver, intestines, the right lung, pancreas...That's what was causing the acidosis, the diabetes."

"But didn't he complain?" I interrupted. "Didn't he have pains? What did the doctor say?"

"He just seemed depressed. The doctor? Perhaps he didn't want to explain. Since there was nothing that could be done, they just closed the incision and asked our permission to remove the organs, after his death of course, for the pathology museum. Such a cancer! When he woke up in the oxygen tent, he was laughing. 'Well, so it was appendicitis after all, wasn't it? And you didn't want to believe it. Just like a member of our family. I'll be alright now.' Poor thing, he stayed like that for a few hours, but he slipped away and fell into a coma."

"Don't forget, daughter," sighed the mother. "The word coma in Portuguese is masculine, not feminine."

Nervous as I was, I could hardly keep from laughing. The importance of grammar. Even with a death in the family. What a thing it is to live away from one's country.

"He caught a post-operative pneumonia," continued Dininha. "By early morning he was dead. He didn't suffer at all."

I didn't see a tear. The fortitude of that family. We went

back to the dead-man. He was going to be cremated.

"In this expensive casket?" I exclaimed.

"No, this is only for the wake. People get buried or cremated in another one, something cheaper."

In a pine box, maybe, I wondered to myself.

We went to the funeral, but I refused to watch the cremation. She watched through a little glass window in the wall of the crematorium and was shocked. A big blast of fire, and Leopoldinho was a pile of ashes. *Quia pulvia es, et in pulvis reverteris*—excuse my Latin.

I didn't see much of them after that. One day the brother telephoned me.

"Mother and Dininha went to the Azores to visit relatives. Without family and friends, I feel very lonely. It's only home to work, work to home. I read books."

He was a handsome young man with dark, fine features; and he didn't even have a girlfriend. I invited him to lunch.

"They don't write. I'm worried. If this keeps up, I'm going to the Azores, too."

A few days later he told me.

"I sent them a telegram. No answer. I've decided to go; I've asked them at work to let me go. It must be something serious. Good-bye."

Weeks went by. Then one day another call. He was back, with Dininha.

"Imagine! The day I arrived in Ponta Delgada, I was on my way to the relatives' house when I met a big funeral procession, music, the whole town was there. I asked whose funeral it was, somebody important, no doubt. Someone told me. It was for a lady who came back from America with her daughter. She was a widow, her son had died, and yesterday her time came suddenly. It was Mother. I thought I'd go crazy. She'd died just as my ship was pulling in. I'd made it in time to say good-bye to her, poor thing. Now there's just the two of us."

I heard him sobbing. It was the last time we saw or spoke to each other. Isn't it strange? In America, friendships are made and unmade quickly. Perhaps tragedy separates people just as self-centered happiness does. I did hear that they gave away the dogs, sold the house, and went off to live with an uncle in New Jersey. I guess it's good to have aunts and uncles. I am the one who is alone in the world except for her.

*Translated by* Gregory McNab

# THE INAUGURATION

There's a lot of work going on in the new quarters, on the second floor, an industrial loft with windows on one wall overlooking the street. It's just the place for the club, for parties, dances, raffles, meetings, speeches, singing. Two hundred people can fit here easily. The men are all over, sawing, planing, nailing, fitting, putting up the gold framing for the damask silk panels on the walls.

"So, aren't we entitled to some luxury? in the workers' club?"

"Of course, why of course, you're absolutely right."

Others set up the kitchen and the bar, touch up paint work, redo the electrical setup. One of them, who knows more about such things, tests the microphone and the loudspeakers hung high up in the corners of the room. All of this is mixed in with arguments, differences of opinion and discussion, the way it always is with people who think for themselves.

"One man's opinion's just as good as another's," says Costa, and it must be true.

But is it really? They went against Rola's advice and set up the platform, just a couple of feet off the floor, close to the entrance, where it almost blocks the door, intead of in the back of the room by the windows, leaving the doorway free. Later they'll regret it and wind up changing it around. There's nothing like experience to convince people. And nobody wants to antagonize them.

The big jug of red wine passes from hand to hand, mouth to mouth. They'll have to work well into the night, and the wine helps. In the kitchen, Carrelhas' wife gets supper ready.

"Hold your tongue, boys."

Hovering all over the place is the mixed smell of shellfish, onions, fresh wood, and the healthy sweat of work.

"Come see, come over here and see. Now we've even got a decent bathroom, with a sink. It's too bad we can't have two, one for Women (or Ladies?) and one for Men (or Gentlemen?)."

Some people may not think so, but such things are important. They even had a meeting, a serious debate as to whether they should address themselves formally, as do cultured, educated people, or informally, like the workers they are. They approved the informal way, which is less stuffy and more in accordance with our tradition, so say the older ones who remember what unions in Portugal were like.

The fellow who suggested the formal approach, poor man, pressed the point, and then got embarrassed. They laughed at him, and he resigned. He won't be back. Such nonsense. He joined another, more respectable club. A group of conformists, where there's no difference of opinion, because there's no opinion. There's where the 'ladies' of the community, upright store keepers and women who like to hang around bars go.

One night, and this happened while we were still at the other place, in walked Lazeira, a short woman from the Minho, fresh and pretty with great big eyes, the widow of a Portuguese bootlegger, a hero who died at sea fighting the Feds. She was a lady of the night, on the make for customers. She speaks English well enough, but, oh my friends, if she comes out in Portuguese, it's enough to send people running. She never came back to our place; the other club fits her better. Anyway, that same night, in came one of those guys to see what was going on, or maybe somebody brought him in by mistgake. It must have been around one in the morning. The men were in the kitchen-bar when they heard a loud noise and all came running to see what happened. This guy had fallen asleep, bent over the chairs, and his pistol, a piece this big, had fallen out of his pocket. They made it clear that bums and hoods weren't welcome, just working people.

Well, things are getting there. The place'll be opened on Sunday, so there's no time to waste. The pamphlets are printed and ready. Leituga calls them 'imprinted.' All we have to do is mail them out. That's what we'll do tonight. A person's just got to think about everything, even after a whole day's work.

And what about Roque, he hasn't been in today? At this time, I don't think he'll come. Last night he was here, but he left before midnight. Maybe he's sick, he was complaining about a pain and coughing. Yes, he looked pale to me. Why doesn't he go see the club's doctor? What do we pay him for?

See a doctor? Come on now! A man like that, in the prime of life, healthy as a horse. That's what Lampas says. It's probably a little cold he caught when he was working here. Winter. And him without gloves, lugging around lumber and iron bars, like ice. Not many'd do that. But whiskey'll cure anything. I've even seen him with a flask in his pocket. The best kind, pure, the kind we make up in the Bronx. No medicine like it.

But there's no Roque yet, and Lampas glances around, his eyes oblique, small, upset, inquiring. They're friends, from the same place; they both come from the mountains. We're neighbors in Harlem.

"Well, does he live alone? Isn't he married, by God's law or man's?"

He's married, yes, but separated. And that Peruvian woman who came around looking for him, well! They lived together for a few years, but her jealousy made his life miserable. He got tired of putting up with her. Now he's got himself an Italian, a nice pretty girl who really loves him. And he loves her. Let's be honest. He's good-looking, hard-working and has a way about him. He's never without a woman. Okay, but they don't live together. That's life. Can you believe it? A married man.

Most of them were peasants from every part of the country: Beira, Minho, Algarve. Not many from the islands, just a couple from Madeira. Almost all were laborers and stevedores—more than a hundred of them on just the Clyde-Mallory Line's docks. Sonia, a Russian Jew who worked there, used to say they were good men. Above all, they worked in excavations, demolitions, bridge and road work, in restaurants and cafeterias, although they all preferred working outdoors. It was better for one's health.

Few of them had any real skills. There were gardeners, who were much sought out by well-to-do suburban American families, and there were some construction carpenters. Others had come from the factories. The Massachusetts textile crisis was sending the millworkers to New York and New Jersey. In general, they were unattached men, no wives, no family, no home, living in boarding houses, on the long dark streets of the Lower East Side, the West Side of the Village, near the docks, even in Harlem. And former sailors, one of them, Costa, from the Navy. He was lively, impulsive, gallant, a lover of wine and cards. He had served in Africa under Cerqueira's command and had gone back there later, exiled by Sidónio Pais.

Some were or appeared old, like Bexiga and Galeão, both from the Algarve.

Their strength was admirable. How could they all endure so much? Those who lived far away, in the suburbs, like Cosme, and even those who lived in town, would get up at four or five in morning and travel hours and miles, soaking wet in some old jalopy, to their work or to the club. They wouldn't miss a meeting. Hard lives.

One night, Lampa came in with his right hand bandaged.

"They jumped me, a whole gang. But I'm from the mountains, you know. I grabbed the knife of one of them and took it away. I cut my fingers, but he's in the hospital and won't be out in a hurry either."

And good old Fernandes: he was going into a poolroom on

110 St., and they jumped him, beat him up and took his whole week's pay. Because he got his trachea fractured, he's been going around without any voice. No one helped him, and the poolroom was full.

He was drawn to the side of those sincere men, who, even though sometimes violent, were basically good and generous. The surroundings aggravated their roughness without giving them anything new or better than bread and a certain amount of freedom. It wasn't insignificant. They helped him perhaps to have a personality or function in surroundings which were strange or even hostile and where he didn't belong, a nobody. It was as if he needed their company to feel complete, at one with his conscience and his fate. They strengthened him. Satisfying love was no longer enough for him. He was looking for resignation, sacrifice, identification with the others. And where would he find it if not with them?

She encouraged him, went with him when she could, worked with him. She saw that he was happy that way, and perhaps that was what made him stay with her. After a day of back-breaking work and a quick, meager dinner, he'd run off to his meetings, to the discussions where he'd see the tiny spark of understanding in those brains warmed by work, fatigue, liquor at times, anger always. His enthusiasm was endless. Coming back to the bare house late at night, he'd wake her up to tell her, bursting with enthusiasm, how well everything had gone, how they reacted. Everything seemed easy, the dogmas and the struggle, although victory was far off. He'd closed his eyes to the risk and to the consequences. Fragile, sensitive, nervous, he made himself heard and respected by them.

In the beginning, Roque had been suspicious of him because he wore ties and a white shirt. There was even one of the group who followed and kept an eye on him for a while. But Roque, too, had become his friend.

He was a good-looking man, medium complexion, deep-set, sullen eyes under a broad shining forehead. Almost everybody respected and liked him. He was trying to ransom himself, to redeem himself from the "intellectual" or "literary" sin.

"Intelligence is in action," he'd say and repeat. He was giving them the example of his devotion to the cause. No task was beneath him. Ever since he discovered them (someone had brought him a card with the name and address of the "Tuna-Club" in some drinking place downtown) he did a bit of everything. He wrote their bylaws, chaired their discussion, organized their work committees, talked to them about parliamentary procedure (Tony dug up the book somewhere), presided or served as secretary, took the minutes, made contacts. He composed manifestos, pamphlets, programs and menus, sold brochures and newspapers alongside them, made speeches, designed posters, helped with decorations and cleaning up, even sold beer at the bar.

One day he offered to help cook supper using his secret recipe for shellfish. Costa protested vehemently.

"What the hell, one man *can't* know everything."

He changed his mind. He'd gone too far. To do all that would be to take away from them the importance and satisfaction of their work, to downgrade them, to offend them. How practice makes perfect. How much one can learn in the company of men.

Enamoured or intoxicated with fraternity and action, ideas and doctrines, he spoke for two hours one Sunday to tell them the life and works of a great man of thought and action. They listened to him respectfully and when he was finished, gave him a warm round of applause. But no one asked questions; they were instinctively passive.

He had one ambition: he wanted his men to be recognized and respected. People were already beginning to talk about them. And he wanted people to consider him representative. But that's all he wanted, nothing more than membership in the basic group. Had he wanted to be something more, a leader? At the same time, he was completely humble and he loved those men with a father-and-son love, as if he came from them and wanted to go back to them.

It's around four, winter and almost dark. A friend arrives from Uptown and goes straight to Lampas.

"Bad news about Roque."

"And what is it?"

"This morning the landlady at his rooming-house wondered why he didn't come down. She went up with a cup of coffee for him, but there was no answer when she knocked. So she opened the door and found him in bed, breathing heavily and burning up with fever. He couldn't talk. He was almost unconscious. She called an ambulance right away. They took him to Welfare Island Hospital. Double pneumonia."

The man hesitates, wanting to say "lobar," but he can't get it out.

The group becomes sad, they decide to stop work and discuss the situation.

"Are we going to leave Roque there, all alone?"

"We can't stop work now," bellows Costa. "Name a committee to visit him—you, Lampas, Leituga and Cardão. That's enough. We need the rest of you here."

"But no visitors are allowed evenings."

"Well then, tomorrow morning, early. Dammit. At least we can ask how he is, send him a message, let him know we're with him. Make him understand. And doesn't he have his girlfriend? He's in good hands. Has anyone told her?"

The hammering begins again vigorously, the saws buzz, the drills hum, the nails squeak in the wood. Dinner-time comes. Mrs. Carrelhas' rice is lip-smacking good. They wash it down well. Later in the evening, the platform for the orquestra and speakers will be finished. Everything's going to be ready on time, don't worry. The inauguration'll be a big hit, the others'll be green with envy.

The night passes quickly. People are getting exhausted, their voices sound irritated. Lampas' eyes look tired and worried.

Friday afternoon, the weather lets up a bit. The damask panels are up. All that's left to do is finish the decorations: streamers, colored little paper flags, balloons around the lamps. The bar's ready, the paint's already dry, but the tub for the beer's still needed and the ice, too. How many barrels did they order? The purchasing committee is really busy. And the supper? Will it be kid-goat or suckling pig? Somebody suggests codfish. Costa's in favor of a monstrous pork-fry.

"Let's see if we can buy a quarter-section. I hope the market isn't closed yet."

His idea carries the day: fried pork, rice with clams, just like yesterday.

"Free? Well of course. You don't want to make the guests pay, at the inauguration party, do you? Let those people eat until they burst. Okay! Nobody sleeps tonight, fellas. Let's finish the job."

Leituga sticks his fat hand into his pants pocket, takes out a roll of bills and throws it on the table. Somebody has to set an example, help the cause. After all, what's money for? A week's pay.

With the chairs placed against the walls, all around, the place even looks like a ballroom at the Royal Palace. It was when they were still at the other place that they got the chairs. One night—it was past one—they went to an old abandoned shoe store on Sixth Avenue. There must have been eight or ten who went along, led by Jasmim, because it was his idea.

"I *know* where they are, all we have to do is get them."

Jasmim was no fool. Did he have the key or was the store open? There they were—in the half-light of the street, which was deserted at that time, the parade of men-ghosts, smiling, carrying the lines of armchairs with folding seats, like in a movie theater, used but still comfortable and in good condition, what luxury! They were laughing on the side.

The chairs go almost all the way around the room. And since there was no money in the treasury, no one had asked where they came from. "Sagesse oblige!"

Lampas approaches him.

"Friend, you speak good English. Let's see if there's anyone down in the candy-story so we can call the hospital. With all this work and no sleep, we almost forgot about him. See how he is and when we can go see him. His woman is probably there with him, but still... And don't worry, we'll all go together. And on Sunday, before the party—visits all afternoon."

The three of them—Lampas, Cardão, Rola—go with him.

They enter the dimly-lit candy-store, which smells of mold and cold tobacco, and go toward the telephone booths in the back. Out in the street, it's nighttime. He looks in the phone book and dials the hospital number. The others look in from outside the booth, as at a fish in an aquarium. He waits and listens to the far-away ringing. They're taking so long to answer.

"Hello?"

He asks for the information, the name's Roque, R-O-Q-U-E. The hurried, mechanical, professional voice of the woman on the other end seems to come from another world. She answers something he doesn't quite hear—there are a lot of voices in the background.

"There's no way I can understand those people."

He hangs up the receiver hesitantly and gestures to his friends outside to be patient. They look in anxiously, trying to guess what he says, perhaps what he heard. A few moments go by.

"Dammit, why did we wait so long. We should've gone yesterday."

He calls again, listens to the same far-off ringing. They take so long to answer. The same voice finally answers.

"Hello."

He repeats the question. "I'm sorry, I didn't get that," he says.

Crisp and casual, the voice hammers at him.

"I just told you that Tomé Roque died fifteen minutes ago."

She hangs up.

He feels himself go pale. He hangs up the receiver.

"How the devil am I going to... it's going to be a real blow. Could they suspect, have they already figured it out?"

He opens the door slowly.

"So?"

"Well, my friends, I'm very sorry, but... I even called a second time, thought I misunderstood. Now I see I understood the first time, but I refused to believe it. Our comrade passed away fifteen minutes ago. They're going to take him to the mortuary."

Cardão lowers his head without talking. Rola is quiet, too. Lampas' hands are at his chest, which pains him. He moans, bending over.

"Oh, my God."

His face is straight off Nuno Gonçalves' painting: tanned and dark, an acute triangle, now withdrawn like a boiled fig. Even his nose looks longer.

"How am I going to...?"

It's not just for his dead companion and friend that he weeps. It's for this long, solitary life, with its threats, its obscure death, its lack of greatness, of family and company in a hospital where they don't understand you. A sauce of symptoms and pus. It doesn't take long for a body to...

His throat is dry. How much it hurts him to see them suffer so, to suffer with them, to be one of them.

Back at the Club, the news spreads, work stops. Taken by surprise, the men cannot believe it. The death of a friend is like being orphaned unexpectedly. Costa is suddenly calm and serious.

"Maybe they made a mistake, that in the hospital they..."

Not so. Unfortunately the nurse at the hospital repeated the information. And now what do they do? Some of them are mumbling. They all feel a bit to blame, but nobody knows exactly what to do.

Rola raises his hand. A simple gesture, just in time, which seems to make them remember what they have to do and what the group means. Motionless and attentive all around, they are a gallery of figures carved in brownstone of old cathedrals: faces burned by sun and cold, furrowed by work, sleepless nights, efforts and amassed sorrows. Rola says:

"Everybody on the board of directors is here, right? Let's supose an emergency meeting has just been called. Tony, you take the minutes, o.k.? I want to make a motion."

They all wait silently.

"I move, first, that the inauguration party be put off until we can set a new date and that we send a cancellation notice immediately to all members and guests. Second, that the funeral of our friend Roque be held here on the same day, the day after

192

tomorrow, Sunday, at the Club's new quarters."

Tony, trembling with emotion, says, "I second Rola's motion."

There is the whispering sound of held-back sobs.

Serious, brusque, his chin trembling, Cardão moves up with his hand outstreched: "That motion, that proposal... will be etched here in my heart." He stops and cries openly.

A loud round of applause rings out like wood being hammered. "Approved by acclamation." Carrelhas, an openhearted Galician, watches them, his eyes watery to overflowing. Everybody likes the idea. Someone has found the way to express what was in those hearts strangled by frustration and suffering, sensitive under the hard crust of necessity.

The men split up. Some keep on working. Others, Tony in the lead because he knows about those things, go to the hospital to claim the body, and then to the undertaker to make arrangements for the funeral. Others will go from house to house, neighborhood to neighborhood, to the edge of town if they have to, to tell families, neighbors and friends. The death notice always gets around quickly. And suddenly, the building seems deserted.

It's Saturday, two in the afternoon and raining. Roque's two "widows," both present, are arguing about which one of them has the honor of being in the cortege and the right to the $150 or so in the dead man's account. It's a ticklish situation, one finally resolved by the good sense of a chunky, tongue-tied man with hands like wooden blocks.

Leituga, who was the dead man's brother (they say they're sons of the same father, but of different mothers), sets himself up as referee. He proposes that the Peruvian woman, who calls him "brother-in-law," keep the savings and that the Club and the Mutual Aid Society pay for the funeral. And the Italian, serious and composed, will be the one to attend the funeral as his widow.

His suggestion has a magical effect. The Peruvian, a short *mestiça*, leaves satisfied, giving her "brother-in-law" an almost-loving smile of thanks. And the Italian, from Sicily she was, sits down, serene and resigned. For her it was her man's love that mattered; a love that she didn't enjoy for long.

Meanwhile, the undertaker and his helpers arrive. They take certain steps, follow certain procedures, and get things ready for the ceremony.

"But no black draperies," bellows Costa. "The funeral is his party. He won't get another."

The body, already embalmed, will come here tonight, for the wake. The catafalque points toward the platform, the windows are covered by draperies. With the decorations, the damasks and gold trim, and the lighting, the large room really looks like a chapel, or in any case, a mourning chamber. The men are secretly proud of this luxury in death.

"And a priest?" asks the undertaker, who's Italian and a bit shy.

The widow demands it. She wants the body blessed, since it's too late for Roque to receive the last rites.

The men look at each other: "What would Roque say if...?"

"Well do what she wants," exclaims Costa, outwardly grouchy, but inside, his heart breaking with grief and love. He's quite a tough man. There's no one in the world to cry for him or take care of him when he goes.

It's Sunday, early afternoon: a neighborhood street, narrow and dark, sad beneath the rain. It doesn't seem big enough for so many cars. He had a lot of friends. The whole neighborhood looking out the windows, a *festa*.

With the crucifix in front of him and the lit candles crackling and dripping in the half-light of the room, Roque, in a new dark suit, looks pale, serene, almost smiling. No one could say what he suffered. His strong forehead shines like polished wax. His widow, in black and sitting by herself next to the coffin, looks at him in a long, silent, nostalgic goodbye, hoping for another, better life. In the heavy silence, there are whispers of grief, and comments. The place is unbelievably full. More than a hundred people are here, many of them women. One of them murmurs that this is bad luck for the Club. Piles of flowers. Death brings them together. Well-dressed, in their Sunday best, Roque's companions show a ceremonious dignity, one that is quite Portuguese.

Suddenly, there's a commotion at the door: talking, shouts, some men run over. The Peruvian insists on appearing. She tries to get in to see the dead man, to make her scene of Iber-Indo-American grief. They convince her to go home.

Followed by his acolyte and properly attired, the priest enters running. The widow kneels, face hidden in her hands. All around, the women do the same. The ceremony lasts only a few moments. When it's over, the priest adjusts his biretta and leaves running, as he came—a wake of incense and holy water behind him, as if he were running away from heathens.

The undertaker hurries forward to close the coffin.

"Wait a minute, please. Just a few words."

The widow sits down again and waits, dignified and impassive.

Rola steps forward, puts his hand on the edge of the coffin.

"What can I say?" he thinks. "Be brief, be brief. It's Sunday, these good people are in a hurry, they have places to go, the movies, a dance, a party at the other club."

He clears his throat, and says:

"Our friend and companion, Roque, was one of the founders of the Club. He worked here tirelessly at our side. Here he fell, we can say, at his post. Now that death has taken him from us, his presence becomes greater and more constant because we all miss him. Here with us he is not alone in death, as he was not in life. He had love, friendship and camaraderie. And today, at his funeral, we are gathered to show him how we feel, to say good-bye to him with affection, gratitude and sorrow. This day which sees him depart is a sad one. But it would have been a great day, one which he would have greeted with joy and confidence, the day of the opening of his and our Club, his and our home. It's only right that he be the one to inaugurate it, and that is the homage we do him today. Thank you, Tomé Roque, thank you and have a good trip."

The Italian may not have understood it all, but she stands up sobbing, kisses the dead man on the forehead, and puts a red winter carnation in his lapel. The men, some of them red-eyed from crying, come forward to shake Rola's hand. They lean over to touch the cold hand of their dead companion. The undertaker can finally close the coffin and, in a few moments, his assistants—correct, somber, efficient, dressed in black—remove all the signs and symbols of death and mourning. The crowd moves out, the cars wait in the rain. His closest friends grab the handles: his brother, Leituga, clean-shaven, bursting out of his Sunday suit; Tony, standing straight, pale; big Cosme; Costa, steady as in the procession; a few others; and Rola. On the steep, narrow stairs, the coffin creaks, followed by the wreath of immortelles given by the Club "to our dear member and loyal comrade."

All bent over, his face red, bathed with sweat and tears, Lampas holds his free hand over his heart and moans endlessly: "Oh, Lord! Dear God! I can't take it."

His voice echoes the mourners'.

The Club has been inaugurated.

*Translated by* Gregory McNab

## TENDRESSE

Three a.m. and she's still not back. And I, wide awake. Restless, thinking of her, of the future that awaits her, of the helpless love that she instills in me. Where is she, what is she do-ing, what new urge, caprice or passion is driving her, what new chain is holding her back? Impatient, I get up and go to the win-dow to gaze at the Monster-City that sleeps soundly under the scourging Northeast wind. The bright city lights, amber in col-or, turn the metropolis, now more vast, deserted and solitary, into the silence of a sleeping giant. Where is the daily hullabaloo? What fear forces me to withdraw again into the comforting warmth of the room? The blue night-light of sleepless nights (I haven't had them lately) casts a ghostly hue about the room; I put it out. All I really need is the golden glow that comes from the outside. I lie down and continue to think, more calmly now. Yet, the persistent stiletto of jealousy pierces my heart. But what can I do if such is the pact that binds our lives: Freedom. And what else can I expect, if she's only thirty, and I, though hale and hardy, am practically seventy? I don't have and never have had any illusions along these lines.

197

The wind continues to shake the windowpanes with rage. Through the narrow slit I somewhere left open to refresh the air in the house, a melancholic, musical wind, blowing up and down its chromatic scale passes through from time to time. Why do you go out and expose yourself like that to the hard winter?

I unwillingly evoke my past... Love. My first wife, whom I passionately loved, committed suicide, a victim of a one-track mind that neither my devoted affection nor psychiatry managed to set free. The second one, an adorable woman, died a few years later in a spectacular highway accident. I thus developed an aversion to marriage. Since then, oh the many women I have known. (Even a stripper, who never managed to corrupt me.) None of them, however, satisfied me. I could never fall in love until you came along—after thirty years of widowhood which, by the way, also happens to add up to your age.

One afternoon, I went into that boutique for the first time; I don't know if to buy a tie for myself, or a present for some "girlfriend." That's how I met you—diligent, solicitous and strong in your ostensible frailty. Tired of loneliness, of ephemeral and sterile adventures, I believe I loved you right away. The presence of a Woman was always indispensable to me, like a complement of my own self. So, I began to weave the dream. But so young—I kept repeating. I returned several times on the pretext of some bagatelle—a pair of gloves or cuff links. You waited on me, smiling and serene. An elderly, respectable, silver-gray customer, who despite his full head of hair, could be your father, or even your grandfather. But something in us inspired mutual trust. What did you see in me? Your last chance for a marriage? A kind of paternal protectiveness? Or a simple living arrangement without the threat of enslavement that makes a woman an object, used only when needed? Could you really be attracted to me?

One afternoon I was bold enough to invite you for tea. You cheerfully accepted. You even closed the shop early. Your company was vivacious, laughing, infectiously happy. It became a habit for me to invite you. We talked with increasing intimacy. Without courting you, without speaking of love, I soon after proposed that we have dinner together in a discreet restaurant they still existed then. We repeated the evening. Slowly you began to tell me about your life (and I, about mine). You were alone and free. You hardly knew the father you lost when you were three. Your mother, disconsolate and faithful to her husband's memory, was, as a result, mistrusting and possessive, and always kept you under her watchful eye. She gave you a strict schoolgirl education, persuaded you to work hard, and never allowed boyfriends. She had a millinery store at that time, just a modest hat shop. Her clientele was almost exclusively women. There you grew up without knowing anything about the Man who orphaned you so early and with whom you never experienced intimacy. Your natural curiosity never found an outlet. And this is how you were until eighteen.

Then an incident occurred. You had gone alone (unusual for you) to a movie-house where you first met each other. Ten years older than you, he followed you, accompanied you, and courted you persistently. Blindly in love, ardent, and sick of purity, protectiveness and Sunday masses, you ended up running away to escape from your mother's forbidding strictness. To reestablish relations with her and to appease her, he, a sensible fellow, asked her for your hand. He was an enterprising automobile salesman, gallant and experienced with women, a real smooth talker. Total disillusionment. The marriage was not what you had romantically imagined, but merely passive submission, a household life with the usual nightly obligations in bed. Withdrawn, you turned cold. Sensing your lack of responsiveness, he wasted no time in returning to his casual girlfriends, usually automobile customers, mature and worldly women, and also to those trips out of town on the pretext of some business. That lasted a few years. There were no children. He became sullen and rude, at times, even brutal. He even hit you. You were a lodger, an intruder in his life, one who insisted in occupying the bed where he expected varied and more cooperative company.

Uterine cancer, neglected out of modesty or prudishness, spread and took your mother's life. You then saw yourself, almost in a flash, the heiress of a shop whose location, near the center of town, had over the years become quite choice.

You then felt within you the taste for activity, a business sense, the love of independence (with its ensuing opportunities). You didn't feel lonely at that time. Filled with initiative and an innate sense of good taste, you modernized the establishment into a boutique—the latest fads, perfumes, cosmetics, costume jewelry, apparel. Relieved, he, without any difficulty, granted you a divorce by mutual consent. He also gave you some financial assistance, and even some good advice as well as the beginning of a chic clientele. You thought you were happy. But marriage had made you ignorant of that enigma called Man, and of his ways. The freedom you had with your new contacts revived your curiosity, one that had never before been fully satisfied. There you were, free and alone, overflowing with youth and eager for affections and pleasures you had never experienced nor barely dreamed of, but had known of by hearsay.

You expanded the business. Your clientele grew, multiplied itself. Many men would now come in, attracted by your presence, to buy ties, handkerchiefs, socks, gloves, and gifts for their girlfriends, fiancées and wives. All of that attention excited your imagination, particularly so when some of these men, the more daring ones, made proposals to you, underlined with tempting promises—jewels, a stole of otter or mink (imitation?), a necklace of pearls (cultured?). You had practically no girlfriends, only two or three high school chums whose advice you didn't dare ask. Astonished, as were the men in your life, by your own chastity or virtue, you became ashamed.

You held back as long as you could, but your youth and hot blood had demands which aggravated those of a heart deprived of tenderness. Who knows if a new marriage... You made concessions but always with the utmost discretion. You had somewhat fleeting affairs with gentlemen of a certain social position. Worldly, elegant, athletic, they were intellectuals, prosperous businessmen, and even influential politicians. You even chalked up an effeminate poet. From lover to friend, surprised and hurt, you started losing faith in your own self and in them. In the final analysis, all men were, or seemed to you to be, identical: thirsty for pleasures, hurried; at times, impotent, domineering (whenever they weren't little boys searching for a mother). And there were even some who surreptitiously tried to take over your business in order to turn it into a high-class brothel. Total possession was their overall goal, and bed was the destiny that they reserved for you, along with the expected submissiveness. Rebellious, you defended your integrity and your independence. They would come and go, and soon be forgotten. You were afraid that your promiscuity would turn you into a high-class prostitute, like so many others. Anything but that. On the other hand, you feared not being a woman—feminine, sensitive to male charms, and sexually fulfilled. In their eyes, you were "selfish." You read books, consulted studies, learned words such as "frigidity" and "nymphomania." But you felt like a lost soul, a wanton woman.

You sought solace in your work, in your business sense, your clientele, your good taste. All in vain. An exasperating devil pushed you periodically toward new experiences—toward a new hope—but always leaving you crushed. This is the way things were when we first met.

In love but apprehensive, I one day tentatively proposed to you what others had undoubtedly suggested but had no intention of fulfilling: "Why don't you come and stay with me?" I purposely avoided using the word "live" because of its suspicious and delicate connotation. You caught on and laughed: "Together? In the same house? I never tried anything like that since my marriage. Who knows?" What danger was there, what with my being almost forty years older than you? Would you see a trap in this? I still hadn't spoken to you of love. You thought it over but imposed one condition: "As friends, as brother and sister, but not as man and wife, nor as lovers." "But that's precisely what I'm offering you." You looked at me with that rare, serious-as-life gaze in your impenetrable black eyes: "We can try. But I keep all my freedom."

Such was our understanding. You hid your problems, your discontent. There would be a whole new way of being in which I wouldn't intervene. It hurt me to accept our pact since what I felt for you was pure love from the heart (and, for sure, desire too, though lessened by age). Resigned, I consented, suppressing my male pride. Old. I loved and admired you—feminine, active, enterprising, and of such robust and wholesome beauty. Who knows if, happy by my side, you wouldn't find the means to resolve the enigma, or to abolish that compulsive curiosity about Men that continually haunts you? With me, it would undoubtedly be just trust, not vertiginous nor tumultuous passion. My love, serene and tender, still undeclared, wouldn't that be enough for you? Oh, the many fantasies a wise and experienced man nurtures.

The apartment, large and comfortable, offered space for each of us to live in complete independence. I saved you a sizeable room at the right end of a corridor with its own sitting room and private bath. Your own apartment. Only the entrance was shared. All furnished tastefully but subject, of course, to whatever alterations you might want to make, to suit your own needs. For whatever reason, you kept your own apartment above the boutique. "Where no man has ever trod, I want you to know," you said, raising your eyebrows. You came to live with me and shared everything in my life, except my bed. Since I placed at your service the limited culinary talents of my bachelor-widower existence, we would almost always dine together at home. We would talk, read silently, listen to music—radio, records, cassettes, television. If you were in the mood, you would open up, confessing painful secrets, episodes that upset me without my letting you know. We would openly discuss the problems of love, sexual crimes, interracial relationships, the foibles of sex and age. We were like two good old friends, almost like an uninhibited father and his daughter but without disguised incestuous ploys. There wasn't the slightest carnal tie between us, not even from me, controlling as best I could my own desires and fantasies. You continued to see in me, or that's what I presumed, only a venerable and respectable man, a safe confidant, and even a counselor. I managed to see in that something strange and comforting. The truth, however, is that on occasion I have caught you looking steadily at me with the pensive and questioning expression of one who withholds a hidden thought.

Every once in a while, you, all of a sudden, become less

communicative, as if absent. You telephone me to say that you can't make it to dinner, or not to wait up for you at night, without any explanation, which, by the way, I never ask of you. Your voice sounds tense, quick, worried, distant. You get in late; you even spend a few days and nights away, without even the customary telephone call to let me know you're all right. Some unconfessable situation is bothering you that I try to figure out. I disguise, as much as possible, my anxiety, my jealousy, my trembling agony. Oh, I never imagined myself capable of loving so much, nor with such control. I imposed upon myself the monastic rule: I am deaf, dumb and blind.

I cannot, however, stop thinking. This good girl, who was faithful to her husband and saw herself mistreated and betrayed, continues to suffer from her unsatisfied, childish curiosity; thus, her promiscuity on the one hand, and her holding back on the other. I see you return home crushed and worn out. And since I have nothing that can alleviate your pain, this only increases my own suffering. My tolerance neither makes up for my love, nor ends my love, nor my jealousy. Pale, dark-skinned, thin, but vibrant as a steel spring, and spirited as a restless bird—everything makes you ripe for provoking the blindest passion. Why don't men understand you? Could I ever be able to understand you? Poor, honorable and talented woman, why won't you find someone who will eventually give you the satisfaction, affection, respect that you deserve? If you would only give me a chance to try.

In this way...

From the quiet street, I hear the screech of tires that stop near the building. (It's nearly four in the morning.) Soon after, the familiar and deafening drone of the ascending elevator. I lift my head to listen. Is it some neighbor getting in at this ungodly hour? The elevator stops on our floor, the gate opens and closes. A key turns almost inaudibly in the lock. It's you. My heart starts beating faster. You carefully close the door. I now imagine your moving along on the long velvety runner. But what's happening? You didn't turn down the corridor on the way to your room. You're coming here. Am I crazy? Now what do I do? You gently push my bedroom door open, the inlaid floor creaks under your weight, in spite of the carpet. What a decision for you to make. I pretend to be sleeping. My heart is a ringing bell. I'm scared that you'll hear it. Through the slit of my half-opened eyelids, I see clearly in the light coming from the outside. You have left your coat in the hall closet, and you tear off your dress and undergarments with the fury of one who is anxious to see herself snugly in bed. Naked, your body is luminescent. You carefully—in order not to wake me?—lift the bed-covers and discreetly slide in between the sheets. Perhaps you want to save the surprise for when I awaken. (The winter wind continues to shake the windows.) On my skin I feel the cold breath of your freezing body. Without moving, I have the impulse to hold you tightly in my arms, to warm you. But, little by little, as if a magnet within me were pulling you, you wrap yourself around me, and take shelter in my warmth. I feel you tremble, with cold, for sure—who knows, maybe even with emotion. Then I turn toward you as though sleeping and I envelop you. You don't resist. Oh, it's so good to feel you this way— everything within me strives to shelter and console you. I caress your tense neck, and I notice that you swallow with difficulty. My hands go down to your shoulders, cold as those of a statue exposed to the night air. I rub your breasts of hardened snow, I breathe warmly upon your cheeks. But what is this, tears? "You're crying," I say, as if I were speaking in a dream. (But isn't this all a dream?) I gently kiss your closed eyes. The salt of your tears is for me a soothing balm. There's a slight perspiration on your forehead. My hands run over your body, encircle your waist, vibrating and offering itself, and then clasp your buttocks that are like two pieces of fruit under the morning dew. Our arms and legs are already entwined, and our stomachs press against each other. Icy cold, your hand searches for and cools the fever of my awakened virility. Your lips, just a moment ago, dry and cracked, are now wet and soft from the anticipated intimacy. Our mouths cling in an anxious and unbelievable kiss. You sob without holding back. I breathe your sighs in; deeply they give me a second wind.

You free and emancipated woman, what was it that brought you to me? The distant and secret love of the child for its father, never to be known? Are you looking for the sheltering bosom where you find refuge from so much and such brutal disillusionment?

This is how our love began, undeclared until now—tranquil, deep, peaceful. Your groans and cries are, at the same time, of discovery and fulfillment, of relief and pleasure, of trust and peace—a tepid spring breeze, after a hard winter. At last, you understand that tenderness—even in an incestuous guise—is the essence of pure and lasting love.

*Translated by* Nelson H. Vieira

# Afterword: Miguéis—Witness and Wanderer

"Mere teller of true stories and in-
vented experiences that I am..."
*O espelho poliédrico*, 1972*

I

José Claudino Rodrigues Miguéis, who preferred to be
known as José R. Miguéis, once he had acquired American
citizenship, spent about half of his long life (1901-1980) in
Manhattan. He knew English well, as he knew French and
Spanish; but he wrote in Portuguese, his mother tongue. For
that reason, few in this country are aware of his works,
although they belong to the best and clearest prose written in
our time and deal with the lives ordinary people led during the
first thirty years of our century. In such lives he searched for
keys to the complex, contradictory enigma of human nature.

---

* The English translations of all quotations from Miguéis's
writings are my own.

At last, a collection of Miguéis's stories has been made accessible to a wider public through English translation. Who was this author that sought refuge in the anonymity a big city like New York can offer?

Miguéis was born at the beginning of the century in Lisbon, the beautiful old port and capital of Portugal, into a middle-class family of humble origins. As he was growing up, the country underwent great turmoil following the murder of its king and its crown prince, the proclamation of a republic, and a series of military coups which finally replaced it with a fascistic dictatorship. Having been active in moderate socialist movements, such as *Seara Nova* ("New Crop"), while studying law, he embarked simultaneously on two further careers, becoming an illustrator for a short time and a writer for life. As a writer, he contributed countless narratives and prose sketches to Portuguese periodicals from 1923 on. In 1932 his first book appeared, *Páscoa feliz* ("Happy Easter"), a novella with a paranoid schizophrenic as the protagonist, telling his own story. The work caught the eye of influential critics in Portugal so that Miguéis became well known although he was abroad at the time, studying the education of abnormal children in Belgium. That two-year stay was to have a lasting effect, furnishing him many ideas for future stories, such as *Léah*. It brought him in touch with many expatriates, particularly those of the White Russian colony in Brussels.

Political activity merely led to disputes within the organizations and to lasting disillusionment. Furthermore, his writing annoyed the censors working for Dr. Oliveira Salazar's regime so much that they forbade him to publish anything under his name. At that point Miguéis decided to exile himself. In 1935 he came to the United States as a visitor. He quickly took up permanent residence and within seven years became an American citizen, soon after the entry of our country into the Second World War. From 1942 until 1951, he worked as an editor and translator for the Portuguese edition of the *Reader's Digest*, a period that included a stint in Brazil of almost one year. Already another book of his, the second, had been published in Rio de Janeiro: *Onde a noite se acaba* ("Where Night Comes to an

End,'' 1946)—a collection of short stories including the one from which the first tale in the present anthology is taken. In the same year of 1946, he returned to Portugal to be with his family while convalescing from several severe illnesses. From then on he was to wander restlessly back and forth between New York and Lisbon, longing for the one soon after arrival in the other. Thus he went back to Lisbon six times, in 1946, 1952, 1957-59, 1963-64, 1966 and 1967. He had been anxious to reintegrate himself in the only country where he could count on faithful readers. His dream seemed close to fulfilment when he reached the pinnacle of local celebrity as the winner of a newly created literary prize, not awarded by the government like most, but by the publishers and the writers. He won it for the collection *Léah e outras histórias* ("Léah and Other Stories,'' 1959). But he seemed to arouse more envy and jealousy than admiration among Portuguese intellectuals, who resented the success of an "outsider.'' He found life in Portugal too upsetting and re-returned to America. The third visit to his homeland also began auspiciously, but when the censors abruptly halted the publication of his new serial novel *Idealista no mundo real* ("An Idealist in the Real World''), he realized that he required freedom. Frail health prevented him from any transatlantic crossings after 1967.

During the last years of his life he concentrated entirely on his writing and even gave up traveling and making public appearances within the United States. He practically stopped corresponding with friends. On October 27, 1980, a sudden massive heart attack put an end to his life in New York City. His widow Camila took his ashes to Lisbon, to be buried among thousands of Lisbonese on the Alto de São João, the largest cemetery of the city, near their old apartment.

To date, all of Miguéis's books except one and almost all of his articles have appeared in Portugal, his spiritual home to the end, in spite of his affection for his adopted country. Writing in Portuguese, he was not in the fortunate position of, say, American authors who are able to reach readers in the many other English-speaking lands.

In this age of refugees by the millions, the expatriate writer shares their fate. Although Miguéis's exile was willed by himself and he could return to Europe when and if he chose to, life in Portugal amounted to joining another, "inner" emigration. Hundreds of liberal and leftist intellectuals could not speak or write freely for almost half a century, until the collapse of the dictatorship in 1974. Among them were his best friends, such as the fellow writer and educator Irene Lisboa, who tried to dissuade him in 1938 from returning to the spiritual prison that was Portugal: "You long for Portugal? Forget it. And don't return." Yet, hardly any Portuguese writer had accompanied the thousands of poor, illiterate sailors, peasants and laborers who had sought a better life in America. Miguéis remained the only major exception. Feeling isolated for most of the years he spent in this country, he identified with them and liked to write about them.

All too briefly, Miguéis was to enjoy the company of a notable Portuguese Angolan writer in 1961, the novelist Fernando Castro Soromenho. Soromenho did not linger long in New York City and returned to exile in France after some months of lecturing. Miguéis was joined by another extraordinary Portuguese intellectual, the teacher and writer Jorge de Sena, when Sena turned his back on Brazil, his first choice for exile, and moved to Wisconsin in 1965 and then to California. Their friendship had to be epistolary, and unlike Sena, Miguéis did not write letters easily. Thus he lacked the constant stimulation which one receives in his own tongue from friends and strangers alike. The expatriate's solitude had two advantages nevertheless. It allowed for his complete immersion in the earlier experience of a lifetime and it provided perspective in that it enabled him to see his people and country from a distance. That distance only increased his love for them—a critical love, out of care for their happiness—or at least for making them as aware of reality as *he* tried to be.

## II

Miguéis's reputation as an author will rest, I venture to predict, on the more than a hundred tales he wrote—*narrativas, histórias* and *noveletas*. One "novelette" with a Dostoevskyan touch, *Páscoa feliz*, brought recognition, no doubt because it responded to the interest in a new social science, psychology. Other tales appealed to his Portuguese readers for other reasons—sentimentality seasoned with humor in the long *Saudades para a Dona Genciana* ("Yearning for Dona Genciana," 1956) or the vicarious excitement of a struggle between two jealous males in *Regresso à cúpola da Pena* ("Return to the Cupola" or, more literally, "My Return to the Cupola of Pena Castle," 1948). Both stories evoked life in Lisbon, such as it had been in the author's youth and—a further attraction—the youth of many readers, before the outbreak of the First World War. Miguéis rendered characteristic details that only a very observant and subtle writer would capture. To do it, he had to know Lisbon as intimately as Balzac had known the Paris of his time or Dickens his London. Miguéis completed the portrait of Lisbonese life during the transition from monarchy to republic in a largely autobiographical novel, *A escola do paraíso* ("Apprenticeship in Paradise," 1960), consisting of stories in chronological sequence.

In other tales that became favorites he catered to the thirst for adventure and travel in other lands; his fictitious Portuguese narrators told of meeting certain simple but big-hearted folk in foreign settings, such as Cosme, among the construction workers in New York City, or Léah, the Flemish chambermaid, in Brussels.

Although he tried his hand at poetry and drama, Miguéis devoted most of his energy to works in a couple of other prose genres, the *crónica* (prose sketch) and the novel. He excelled in both. Because of their large number, his commentaries on persons and places in the form of *crónicas* deserve special mention. He did not dash them off but composed them with the same scrupulous attention as his fiction, to find just the right phrasing. Moreover, they reveal his personal experiences, feelings and opinions without any fictional disguise. While he did not try to revolutionize the technique of novel writing, he varied his approach from novel to novel. One, the detective story *Uma aventura inquietante* ("A Disturbing Adventure," published as a serial in 1934-35), was written purely to entertain. Another dealt with a regional theme that has tempted many Portuguese essayists and novelists; in *O pão não cai do céu* ("Bread Does Not Drop Out of a Blue Sky," first written, about 1937, in the form of a drama, then posthumously published in 1981), narrated the struggle of the landless peasants of homesteads in the Alentejo province, Portugal's breadbasket. No other Portuguese writer equaled its epic style. But more than anything else he wanted to fill a gap by writing *the* fictional chronicle of Portuguese life during the first quarter of the twentieth century. To give a faithful account of republican Portugal could not be tolerated by the propagandists of the dictatorial régime that had destroyed the Republic in 1926. *A escola do paraíso* had only been a first, subtle approach to the prelude of the crucial period. When Miguéis became more outspoken in its sequel, *Idealista no mundo real* ("An Idealist in the Real World"), the censors intervened promptly, to the author's despair. "Though their action simplifies my work," he wrote with grim humor, "it worsens my fears: what should I—or what can I write?" A planned second novel went further. Its central episode gave a fictional but rationally plausible interpretation of the miraculous apparitions of the Virgin Mary in Fátima. The protagonist Salomé, a good girl forced into prostitution, ironically happens to be taken for the Virgin when she appears to three dazzled children on a heath, in the poorest region of Portugal. The novel could not be published. "My novel *The Miracle* (unpublishable)," he wrote to me, "is my chief work, the *only one* that so far matters to me. Imagine the dramatic situation of an author who knows that he cannot publish what he is writing! And I have written other novels like that..." After the overthrow of the dictatorship, the novel did appear, in 1975, but it failed to interest the critics or the readers, perhaps because the revolutionary ferment of the mid-seventies was not the right atmosphere for reading fiction dealing with a painful past unpolitically, without any anticlerical pamphleteering.

    *O Milagre* fitted to a T the definition given earlier by one critic. It was "ethical realism," if by "ethical" one means sympathy for humble protagonists, faithfulness to observed events, sincerity that unmasks hypocrisy and destroys delusions, and a constructive use of the imagination. The author gave his own definition in a note appended to the work: *O Milagre* was to be Salomé's novel and that of the political disasters; it was to be the novel of himself, his people, and his time. This was no mere *divertissement* or *entertainment*, he added, but a serious work, the symbolic representation of the epoch, the atmosphere, the collective state of mind, that had led to the coup of the 26th of May, 1926, and its aftermath.

Miguéis's fiction usually elaborates experiences, many of them his own, with a newspaperman's investigative curiosity, a lawyer's concern for truthful testimony, and an educator's zeal to dispense knowledge. Most of all, having written for newspapers throughout his life, he wanted to report. At his best, he observed the flaws in human beings, including himself, with wit and humor, among them the amazing ability we possess of deluding ourselves, as well as others. To make the point, he chose two historical phenomena that he had followed closely, the fantastic hopes raised by false pretenders among the White Russian exiles and the messianic excitement caused since 1917 by the apparitions at Fátima among millions of Catholics.

In the stories Miguéis typically begins with objective reality, placed in a recent past and at some distance, uses it as a springboard for developing a wishful dream or an oppressive nightmare, and ends up by a return to reality. Thus *Léah* begins with the minute evocation of the lodgers in a Brussels rooming house, its proprietress and her maid Léah, with the words: "I perfectly remember the quiet afternoon when..." Then the time is put into perspective: "Only today, at a distance of so many years..." Léah irresistibly attracts the lonely stranger who narrates the experience. She becomes the ideal lover: "How natural she was, how exuberant and how healthy!" She is always available to him. But when she proposes that they run off together to Paris, he shrinks back—and regrets his pusillanimity. Returning to the same places many years later, he finds the rooming house gone and Léah with a husband and a child.

The figure of the young woman who offers love or utmost kindness to an unhappy man returned again and again to the stories. Thus it appeared twice as a young nurse in the autobiographical account of a paralysis that almost killed him in the Bellevue Hospital of New York, *Um homem sorri à morte—com meia cara* ("A Man Smiles at Death—With Half a Face," 1959) and once in the deeply moving novella *A múmia* ("The Mummy," 1971). "What makes women so goodhearted, so sensitive to our pain?" he wonders in the former work. "A kind of vague motherliness perhaps? Or are women perhaps better able to feel the pain of others because they suffer more? How grateful we must be to them, and how much we have to expect from them! How much we have yet to repent, to atone for and to understand!"

For good personal reasons, the exiled writer was preoccupied as well with the problem of relating the past to the present. He experienced many times the impossibility of picking up the threads that had been torn, seeing himself searching for "the lost or imaginary worlds that had ceased to exist in space and time" (*Comércio com o inimigo e outros contos*, "Trading With the Enemy and Other Tales," 1973). Imaginatively, he dealt with the irretrievable past in *A múmia*, a title that is a metaphor for man's predicament: "The past is a corpse we carry with us, the mummy in its glass case, apparently intàct, yet really hollow."

The same tale, *A múmia*, raised a second problem that troubled the writer, as it troubles many in this paranoid age—the problem of man's identity. The male protagonist of the tale is driven to the realization of how greatly he has changed with age and exile. He finds himself divided between two personalities: the protective hard shell of the pragmatist ready for any new turn of fate, and within it the repressed core of the intransigent, ingenuous idealist he had been as a young man.

Reflections abound in Miguéis's works. Many concern the task of the writer. Many more, such as the two just mentioned, have to do with problems of the human mind. He liked to contrast the notion of authenticity, rigid like a crystal, with the continuous growth and the slow sedimentation of the many layers composing a personality. "We behold the individual as we behold a crystal, as facets and edges, but never in the slow process of its growth," he observed in *O espelho poliédrico* ("The

Polyhedric Mirror"). The difficulty of grasping the variable, many-sided, contradictory nature of people made him very humble when facing his task. "There are times," he mused in another sketch of the same book, "when I feel like a man who is forever painting a chaotic panorama on a moving, parabolic wall. Stubbornly, he reaches out to experience the reality of his presence in a world that he can know to the extent—and only to the extent—that he can paint it."

Miguéis endeavored to be objective and to be lucid, fighting off fits of nostalgic sentimentality of the kind cherished by the Portuguese under the name of *saudades*. He protested once, when I discovered *saudades* in the beautiful evocations of the old Lisbon of his childhood which he incorporated in *A escola do paraíso*. "But," he wrote to me in 1962, "(with your leave,) my goal is not nostalgia. It is not to 'recall,' but to reconstruct a personality by seeing how time and environment have shaped it. Nostalgia may color what I am doing, but so does bitterness." Endowed with an excellent memory, he was obsessed by the past. But faithful to the spirit of the *Seara Nova* group, he wished to destroy the dead weight of the myths that obfuscated the recent past.

### III

What this Portuguese author has to offer the American reader may be put under three headings: a well-informed outsider's view of America, particularly New York City; a better understanding of the ordinary Portuguese immigrants in this country; and some profound insights into the Portuguese frame of mind.

American settings are basic to a dozen of Miguéis's stories, among them five of the eleven contained in this collection: "Proud Beauty," "Cosme," "Dr. Crosby's Christmas," "A Portuguese Home," and "The Inauguration." Other American settings occur in many more of his newspaper columns, as do accounts of experiences in America with officials, workers, "bums," artists, doctors, etc., and with streets, taverns, bridges—within the city and in the countryside. We witness the changes, for example, in the appearance of Manhattan or, for

215

another, in racial attitudes over the forty-five years' period after the Portuguese author landed in 1935. His approach is affectionate. He cannot but be grateful for the calm, the anonymity, and the relative comfort that allowed him to follow his calling as a writer, even while he and his wife Camila had to work hard to make a living. Not everyone with whom they had to rub shoulders was pleasant, and the writer does not pass over disagreeable episodes; but the total picture he presents is that of a society more open on the whole, more egalitarian, more considerate, and, in moments of crisis, more disciplined than the peoples Miguéis had known elsewhere. In one *crónica* he contrasts the chaos he imagines as imminent with the actual orderliness he witnessed one night in New York City when a power failure brought on a blackout lasting into the wee morning hours. His description ends on a note of mischievous humor: the birthrate rose because of that night and so, strangely enough, did the divorce rate. Was it perhaps because people, floors and bedrooms were mixed up in the dark? (*A noite em que o pânico falhou*, "The Night of the Panic Failure").

Miguéis provides intimate insights into the character, exertions, pleasures and plights of the humble Portuguese who, like the stowaway in "The Stowaway's Christmas," often entered this country illegally, under duress. He knew them well, having assisted them with their organizations during his early years in America. Although he reaped ingratitude for his pains, he evoked his countrymen without bitterness, understanding the hardships they, like other poor immigrants, had to undergo.

Sketched rapidly in stories, the Portuguese psyche is revealed in the behavior of the immigrants and in their utterings. It shows more fully in the novellas, where we see a panorama of the different classes in Portuguese society. "Return to the Cupola" and "Yearning for Dona Genciana" offer good examples of this. But the best are to be found in the three Lisbonese novels published so far. There we observe the Portuguese as they manage their lives in the small, overcrowded and class-ridden country, always mindful of past history, a frustrating existence for any ambitious young man or woman. "All of this irritates me," says the narrator in *Saudades para a*

*Dona Genciana*, "this mediocrity, this monotony, these amoeba floating in stagnant waters. I am fed up!"

Miguéis was much more than a "poor Portuguese story teller," as he once called himself with mock-modesty. He was more than a columnist mass-producing human interest stories. Above all, he was a novelist who took contemporary society as his subject matter. Although he remained attached to the old and small country whence he came, there was nothing provincial or narrow-minded about him His writing spans continents. Having also lived in Belgium, the United States and Brazil, he found it easy to write about the Portuguese who went to live in many parts of the world, as well as about other "Latins," or Belgians, Russians and Americans.

His mind was a bundle of contradictions and nervous tensions. A wanderer between two cities, Lisbon and New York, he was also torn between the desire for a quiet, anonymous life and a need for public recognition (given him now and then by his countrymen and even by their government at the very end of his life), between the duty to live responsibly and consciously in the present and wrestling with the vivid memories of the past.

Translations of works by Miguéis exist in German, Polish, Italian and Esperanto, but in English there are versions of only two or three short stories. Someone did translate the novella *Páscoa feliz* in England, but the translation went unpublished.* Sooner or later, these works of pensive, ironic humanism will come into their own on this side of the Atlantic.

---

* Ann Stevens translated *Léah* into English in Great Britain, but two English periodicals rejected it, as Miguéis informed me on July 27, 1962. In the same letter, he told of two French translations and a German one of *Páscoa feliz* that failed to find a publisher. This work was translated and published in Poland, however, either in 1979 or 1980, according to Mrs. Camila Miguéis. Its English translation is being prepared by William B. Edgerton.

No other contemporary Portuguese prose writer deserves it more. Of good poets, Portugal has always had aplenty. Her prose writers are, as a rule, too wrapped up in the provinciality in custom and speech, to bear translation into other languages. Only one novelist, Eça de Queiroz, had universal human appeal—sometimes. Perhaps it took that long exile to give Miguéis perspective and depth.

## IV

Try as I may, I cannot be coolly objective about Miguéis for we knew each other for over thirty years. A couple of months before he died I saw him once more in New York City, after a long interval. In spite of his age (he was seventy-nine), his weak heart, and his increasing deafness, he spoke enthusiastically of the several manuscripts he had just readied for publication, among them another novel, *O pão não cai do céu*. He was now engaged in new projects, he said, such as making a selection from his *twelve thousand* prose sketches that had appeared in a Lisbonese daily, the *Diário Popular*. For some time he had refused invitations to lecture. Besides, when he did prepare a talk, he would write enough for thirty lectures, he complained, only to find it impossible to decide what to use and what shape to give it. No, what he really longed for was to sit in the shade of a tree in the green countryside, to meditate, and to write. Then, after a hearty luncheon in one of Manhattan's Brazilian restaurants, the Cabana Carioca, we shook hands to say goodbye—forever.

Gerald M. Moser

# Bibliographical Note

*A few aids exist for readers who would like to have further information on the personality, life, and works of José Rodrigues Miguéis, but who are unfamiliar with the Portuguese language:*
1. *A short but substantial biographical article by Jorge de Sena is contained in the* Columbia Dictionary of Modern European Literature, *second ed. J.-A. Bédé and W. B. Edgerton (New York: Columbia University Press, 1980).*
2. *An excellent guide to the works and the essential facts of his life is John Austin Kerr, Jr.'s* Miguéis—To the Seventh Decade *(University, Mississippi: Romance Monographs, 1977).*
3. *William B. Edgerton has examined Miguéis's debt to Dostoevsky in "Spanish and Portuguese Responses to Dostoevskij,"* Revue de Littérature Comparée, *55 (July-December 1981), 419-38.*
4. *The influence of the* Seara Nova *doctrines on Miguéis during his formative years is traced by G. Moser in "The Campaign of* Seara Nova *and Its Impact on Portuguese literature, 1921-61,"* Luso-Brazilian Review, *2 (Summer 1965), 15-42.*
5. *Those who know Portuguese will be interested in Miguéis's final opinions on his task as a writer and his reflections on the many years he spent in the United States as voiced in an interview conducted by Carolina Matos. For this, perhaps the last of many interviews he granted during his life, see* Gávea-Brown, *1 (Jan.-June 1980), 42-48.*

*G. M. M.*

# LAST WORD: MIGUÉIS ON MIGUÉIS

*Portuguese critics, often oriented by ideology, doctrines, or the simple routine of school, style, etc., have variously called me an "ethical realist," a "critical realist," a "poetic realist," and even a "neo-realist" or a "proletarian" writer. Whether I am or am not a "realist" has little or no influence on the enigmas and tragedies of the "real." For some of them I am a disciple of the Russian naturalists of the nineteenth century, for others an adept of "psychologism" and even of "passadism." One critic, a brilliant poet and my dear friend, reproached me for my occasional excursions into the "fantastic" as if, at least since the time of Homer, such deviations had not inspired innumerable literary masterpieces.*

*Perhaps, ambitious as I am, I do wish to deserve all of that: a sign of wealth! Unfortunately, it only succeeds in making me feel like a plant or an animal, pigeonholed into orders, classes, genres and varieties. I would not mind it so much if at least they attempted (there are exceptions) to penetrate into the meaning of my stories. The writer, in my opinion, should be judged by what he writes and not by what the others think he should write.*

221

*What moves me is the compulsive need to evoke or reconstruct an ambiance, mood, or climate—a cultural character be it individual or collective. A subjacent tendency of which I only later became aware is to imagine myself, through my characters, in a situation of danger, crisis, disaster, or imminent death, and find out how I would face up to it, resolve it, or free myself from it. For instance, I once discovered to my surprise that out of fourteen stories in one of my books, eleven deal with the question of death. But is not death the overriding problem of human life? As for style, I am totally indifferent to it. I tell a story because I like to tell it. For me the style is the subject itself. It is the subject which sets the style, as the substance of a given mineral predetermines the shape into which it must crystallize. On the other hand, the clearness of my writing may pose greater problems than the contrived obscurity and structural complexity of certain authors who thirst for novelty and have little to say.*

# NOTES ON CONTRIBUTORS

CAROL DOW, who holds the Ph.D. in Portuguese from the University of Wisconsin, has taught at Brown University and the University of Pittsburgh. Besides Brazilian literature, she is interested in that country's carnival, cinema, music, and popular religion.

MARIA ANGELINA DUARTE, the author of a doctoral dissertation on "Social Political Undercurrents in Four Works by José Rodrigues Miguéis," holds the Ph.D. from the University of Minnesota. She has taught at U.C.L.A., the University of Minnesota, and, since August 1982, the University of Iowa.

ALEXIS LEVITIN has taught extensively at universities in the United States, Brazil, and Portugal. His translations have appeared in over fifty literary magazines and several anthologies. He is now at SUNY/ Plattsburgh, teaching English and completing work on a book of stories by Clarice Lispector.

CAROLINA MATOS holds the A.B. and A.M. from Brown University. Her Portuguese translations of Emily Dickinson's poetry have appeared in Brazil and the United States, most recently in the *Journal of the American Portuguese Society*.

GREGORY MCNAB, Associate Professor at the University of Rhode Island, has contributed to the *Grande Dicionário de Literatura Portuguesa e de Teoria Literária*, to *Colóquio/Letras* and to *África*. He is currently translating Dias de Melo's novel *Pedras Negras* and working on a critical study of that Azorean writer's literary works.

CAMILA CAMPANELLA MIGUÉIS taught at the New School for Social Research in New York City. As José Rodrigues Miguéis' widow and his literary executor, she is overseeing the publication of Miguéis' complete works now issuing in Lisbon under the Estampa imprint.

GEORGE MONTEIRO, Professor of English at Brown University, has translated *In Crete With the Minotaur*, poems by Jorge de Sena (1980), edited *The Man Who Never Was: Essays on Fernando Pessoa* (1982), and published a book of poems, *The Coffee Exchange* (1982).

GERALD M. MOSER, Professor Emeritus of Spanish and Portuguese, Pennsylvania State University, has in recent years edited Artur Azevedo's *Teatro a Vapor* (1977) and José da Silva Maia Ferreira's *Espontaneidades da Minha Alma* (1980). He has also contributed articles and book reviews to *Luso-Brazilian Review, Research in African Literatures, Africa, Colóquio/Letras* and *Hispania*.

RAYMOND SAYERS, Professor Emeritus of Romance Languages, Queens College, C.U.N.Y., is the author of *The Negro in Brazilian Literature* (1956), the editor of *Portugal and Brazil in Transition* (1968), and the translator (with Henry Keith) of *Poems in Translation by Cecília Meireles* (1977).

NELSON H. VIEIRA, Associate Professor of Portuguese and Director of the Center for Portuguese and Brazilian Studies at Brown University, has translated works of Portuguese literature, most notably *A Promessa* by Bernardo Santareno, and has published several studies in modern Brazilian prose fiction.